U0133140

CET-4

大学英语四级

710分

新题型特训

编 著⊙黎锦荣

华东理工大学出版社
EAST CHINA UNIVERSITY OF SCIENCE AND TECHNOLOGY PRESS

图书在版编目(CIP)数据

大学英语四级 710 分新题型特训 / 黎锦荣编著. —上海：华东理工大学出版社，2008.7
ISBN 978 - 7 - 5628 - 2358 - 2

Ⅰ.大... Ⅱ.黎... Ⅲ.英语-高等学校-水平考试-习题 Ⅳ.H319.6

中国版本图书馆 CIP 数据核字(2008)第 101214 号

大学英语四级 710 分新题型特训

编　　著 / 黎锦荣
策　　划 / 陈　勤
责任编辑 / 何　蕊
封面设计 / 戚亮轩
责任校对 / 张　波
出版发行 / 华东理工大学出版社
　　　　　　社　址：上海市梅陇路 130 号,200237
　　　　　　电　话：(021)64250306(营销部)
　　　　　　　　　　(021)64252717(编辑室)
　　　　　　传　真：(021)64252707
　　　　　　网　址：www. hdlgpress. com. cn
印　　刷 / 常熟华顺印刷有限公司
开　　本 / 787mm×1092mm　1/16
印　　张 / 10
字　　数 / 269 千字
版　　次 / 2008 年 7 月第 1 版
印　　次 / 2008 年 7 月第 1 次
印　　数 / 1—7050 册
书　　号 / ISBN 978 - 7 - 5628 - 2358 - 2/H · 754
定　　价 / 19.80 元

(本书如有印装质量问题,请到出版社营销部调换。)

前　言

作为大学英语四、六级考试改革的"重头戏"以及所占分值比例最大的题型之一,阅读理解题向来为广大考生所重视。根据全国大学英语四、六级考试委员会颁布的《大学英语四级考试大纲(2006 年修订版)》,四级阅读理解测试内容、题型、分值详情如下:

分类	快速阅读(Skimming and Scanning)	仔细阅读(Reading in Depth)
题型	是非判断 + 句子填空或其他	多项选择
		选词填空或简答题
长度	总长度约 1000 词	多项选择:300—350 词/篇
		选词填空:200—250 词/篇
		简答:300—350 词/篇
比例	10%	25%
	35%	

虽然大纲已给出了较明确的指引,然而,不少考生在解题时仍显得底气不足,如 2007 年 12 月的四级考试中快速阅读题型的一次调整就曾令许多考生措手不及。这其中固然有教与学方面的深层次原因,而更直接的原因是未能吃透新大纲、重视不足或备考不当。本书的编写宗旨,正是针对这种状况,力求为广大考生提供准确、全面、高效的备考指导。

本书具有以下特色:

一、紧扣大纲,题型全面。本书严格遵循教育部于 2007 年 7 月颁布的《大学英语课程教学大纲》及大学英语四、六级考试委员会最新颁布的《大学英语四级考试大纲(2006 年修订版)》进行编写。全书囊括了考试大纲所述的所有题型,从宏观的体系编排到微观的试题设置,无不贯彻上述纲领性文件的核心思想。

二、点拨精当,举一反三。本书对历年真题、模拟题的点拨均以准确、实用、简明为宗旨,简单知识点要言不烦,点到即止,重点难点则不惜笔墨,深入浅出。既注重技巧的点拨和解题应试能力的提高,又充分考虑培养考生良好的阅读习惯,真正提高各位考生从英文资料获取信息的能力。

三、选材严格,设题科学。本书不仅涵盖四级考试历年具有代表性的真题,同时还有一定数量的强化训练题。这些模拟题的语料均选自英文原版材料,无论是题材、体裁、难度,还是命题方式均契合真题,相信能够帮助各位考生深入理解新的考试大纲,熟悉新四级阅读的各类题型,使各位考生在考前成竹在胸,考场上游刃有余。

在本书的成书过程中,编者曾征询多位专家的意见,也用心听取了各位考生的心声,然囿于编者学识水平,错讹之处,在所难免,敬请读者批评指正。

编　者

2008 年 5 月

目　录

第一章　快速阅读

第一节　快速阅读应试技巧

一、快速阅读题型简介

根据《大学英语课程教学要求(试行)》(2004 年),大学阶段英语教学要求分为三个层次,即一般要求、较高要求和更高要求。三个层次对阅读理解能力要求分别如下:

一般要求:能基本读懂一般性题材的英文文章,阅读速度达到每分钟 70 个词;在快速阅读篇幅较长、难度略低的材料时,阅读速度达到每分钟 100 个词;能基本读懂国内英文报刊,掌握中心意思,理解主要事实和有关细节;能读懂工作、生活中常见的应用文体的材料;能在阅读中使用有效的阅读方法。

较高要求:能基本读懂英语国家大众性报纸杂志的一般性题材的文章,阅读速度为每分钟 80 词,在快速阅读篇幅较长的材料时,阅读速度达到每分钟 120 词,能就阅读材料进行略读或寻读。能够基本读懂自己专业方面的综述性文献,并能正确理解中心大意,抓住主要事实和有关细节。

更高要求:能读懂有一定难度的文章,理解其意义,借助词典能阅读英语原版书籍和英语国家报纸杂志上的文章。能比较顺利地阅读与自己专业有关的综述性文献。

大学英语四级考试阅读理解部分要求考生达到《教学要求》中的一般要求。根据最新修订的《大学英语四级考试大纲》,四级阅读理解部分包括仔细阅读(Reading in Depth)和快速阅读(Skimming and Scanning),主要测试学生通过阅读获取书面信息的能力;所占分值比例为 35%,其中仔细阅读部分 25%,快速阅读部分 10%,考试时间 40 分钟。

快速阅读部分采用 1—2 篇较长篇幅的文章或多篇短文,总长度约为 1 000 词。要求考生运用略读和寻读的技能从篇章中获取信息。略读考核学生通过快速阅读获取文章主旨大意或中心思想的能力,阅读速度约每分钟 100 词。寻读考核学生利用各种提示,如数字、大写单词、段首或句首词等,快速查找特定信息的能力。样题中快速阅读部分采用的题型有是非判断、句子填空、完成句子等。考生要在限定的 15 分钟内完成。文章后有 10 道题,其中前 7 道是判断正误题,后 3 道是填空题。判断正误题除了提供 Yes 和 No 两个备选项之外,还有第三个选择 Not Given。值得注意的是,在 2007 年 12 月的快速阅读题中,原来判断 Y、N 或 NG 的部分改成了与仔细阅读类似的选择题。虽然出题形式有变化,但无论是从出题风格还是总体难度水平来看起伏都不大。对考生来说,关键还是要从词汇、阅读速度等方面扎扎实实地提高自己的快速阅读技能,并通过做题、总结掌握必要的应试技巧。

快速阅读理解的引入是十分必要的。在当今的信息时代,各类文献浩如烟海,要仔细阅读每一本书或每一篇文章是不可能的,也没有这个必要。因此,要快速、准确地从大量资料中筛选出我们所需的信息,就必须提高阅读的效率,而快速阅读理解试题考查的正是把握文章的总体逻辑走向和信息要点的能力。这种能力依赖于多方面的因素,如阅读习惯、知识结构和语言能力等。

阅读能力的培养有一个循序渐进的过程。但是,只要在日常学习中有意识地克服障碍,掌握方法,进行大量的快速阅读训练,并持之以恒,就一定能较快地提高阅读水平。

二、快速阅读技能培养

1. 改变不良的阅读习惯

阅读能力弱的考生往往有许多不良的阅读习惯,其中最常见的就是阅读过程中身体的某些部位做多余的活动。例如,有些考生为了在阅读时集中注意力,常常用手指、钢笔等指着文章一个词一个词地读,或者是头跟着摆动,以使眼睛对准正在读的每个单词上。阅读过程中这些动作对阅读速度和理解率的提高没有帮助,因为眼部的肌肉完全有能力使眼睛从一个词移到另一个词上,根本不需要其他部分的肌肉运动。况且阅读时脑力活动也是相当紧张的,多余的动作通常会降低阅读速度。另外一种阅读中常见的毛病就是复视。复视指的是读完一个句子或段落后回过头去重复阅读。习惯性的复视对阅读速度的提高是极为不利的。还有一种不良的阅读习惯就是边读边译。部分考生习惯于在阅读过程中逐字逐句地在脑海中进行翻译,平时进行阅读练习译不通时还要查字典或仔细推敲一番,似乎这样才算是真正读懂了。殊不知这种方法不但费时费力,还往往会由于缺乏上下文的融会贯通而造成理解错误。要克服以上这些毛病,关键是要在平时的阅读训练中总结出有效的阅读方法和培养良好的习惯。

2. 快速阅读方法点拨

1) 扩大视幅和按照意群(sense group)阅读

一个人的阅读速度不仅取决于视线在阅读材料上的移动速度,同时还取决于视幅,即视线所及的范围的大小。因此,如果我们进行阅读时,能以意群或句子为单位,而不是逐个单词地进行阅读,阅读速度就可大幅度提高。所谓意群,指的是那些有意义的语法结构或词组。下面我们用"/"来划分一段文章的意群:

Country life, / on the other hand, / differs from / this kind of / isolated existence / in that / a sense of community / generally binds / the inhabitants of small villages / together. / People have the advantage of / knowing that / there is always someone to turn to / when they need help. / But country life / has disadvantages too. / While it is true that / you may be among friends / in a village, / it is also true that / you are cut off from / the exciting and important events / that take place in cities. / There's little possibility of / going to a new show / or the latest movie. / Shopping becomes a major problem, / and for anything / slightly out of the ordinary / you have to go on an expedition / to the nearest large town. / The city-dweller / who leaves for the country / is often oppressed by / a sense of unbearable stillness and quiet.

阅读时对句子进行意群划分,不仅可以大大提高阅读速度,同时也能加深对文章的理解。

2) 略读(skimming)

略读(skimming)又称跳读(reading and skipping)或浏览(glancing),是一种非常实用的快速阅读技能。所谓略读,是指快速阅读文章,掌握其大意及几个能说明问题的关键细节。换句话说,略读是要求读者有选择地进行阅读,可跳过某些细节,以求抓住文章的大概,从而加快阅读速度。据统计,训练有素的读者的阅读速度可以达到每分钟3 000到4 000个词。略读有下列四个特点:

(1)快速阅读大量材料,寻找事实细节信息和相关的阐述信息;

（2）可以跳过某个部分或某些部分不读；

（3）理解水平可以稍低一些,但也不能太低；

（4）根据文章的难易程度和阅读目的,灵活地调整阅读速度。

由此可以看出,略读这种技巧要求的是对整篇文章的快速阅读,阅读目的是获取文章的主要大意和能说明问题的一些重要细节。

3）寻读（scanning）

寻读（scanning）是一种从大量的资料中迅速查找某一项具体事实或某一项特定信息,如人物、事件、时间、地点、数字等,而对其他无关部分略去不读的快速阅读方法。运用这种方法,读者就能在最短的时间内掠过尽可能多的印刷材料,找到所需要的信息。例如,在车站寻找某次列车或汽车的运行时刻,在机场寻找某次班机的飞行时刻,在图书馆查找书刊的目录,在文献中查找某一日期、名字、数字或号码等,都可能用到这种方法。作为一种快速寻找信息的阅读技巧,寻读既要求速度,又要求有较高的准确性。具体地说,寻读带有明确的目的性,有针对性地选择问题的答案。因此在寻读时不必字字句句过目。视线在印刷材料上掠过时,一旦发现有关的内容,就要稍作停留,将它记住或摘录下来,这样既保证了寻读的速度,也能提高定位的准确性。

三、快速阅读解题技巧

→利用细节,如文章的标题、副标题、小标题等,对文章进行预测略读。预测略读的目的是了解作者的思路、文章大意、有关的细节及其相互关系。

→以一般阅读速度阅读文章开头的第一、第二段,力求抓住文章大意、背景情况、作者的文章风格、叙述口吻或语气等。

→抓住关键词句。关键词句是连接上下文的纽带,快速阅读时如果能准确地把握关键词,其他问题便可迎刃而解。而抓住关键句子也就是找出主题句。主题句是文章中用来概括大意的句子,主题句往往是每个段落的第一个句子,有时也可能是最后一个句子,在特殊情况下还可能出现在段落当中。通过识别主题句,可以快速、准确地抓住文章中各个段落的主要意思,如果能把每一段落的大意抓住了,那么全篇文章的中心思想也就把握住了。

→标记细节信息。对一些关键的名词,如人名、术语等,必须予以重视。同时应留意数字和符号,因为年代、百分比等数据很有可能成为考点。如样题中的第9题：9. To dispose of a ton of trash in a landfill, customers have to pay a tipping fee of _____. 答题依据就在原文的：Customers are charged tipping fees for using the site. The tipping fees vary from $10 to $40 per ton.

→准确表达。快速阅读的最后三道题是填空题。和简答题一样,回答要做到内容正确,用词简练,符合语法,拼写无误。答题时应尽量以原文中出现过的词句为基础,不要作任意的修改。

第二节 快速阅读真题详解

★**2007 年 12 月考题**

Part Ⅱ Reading Comprehension（Skimming and Scanning）（15 minutes）

Directions：In this part, you will have 15 minutes to go over the passage quickly and answer the questions on **Answer Sheet 1.**

For questions 1—7, choose the best answer from the four choices marked A), B), C) and D).

For questions 8—10, complete the sentences with the information given in the passage.

Universities Branch Out

As never before in their long history, universities have become instruments of national competition as well as instruments of peace. They are the place of the scientific discoveries that move economies forward, and the primary means of educating the talent required to obtain and maintain competitive advantage. But at the same time, the opening of national borders to the flow of goods, services, information and especially people has made universities a powerful force for global integration, mutual understanding and geopolitical stability.

In response to the same forces that have driven the world economy, universities have become more self-consciously global: seeking students from around the world who represent the entire range of cultures and values, sending their own students abroad to prepare them for global careers, offering courses of study that address the challenges of an interconnected world and collaborative (合作的) research programs to advance science for the benefit of all humanity.

Of the forces shaping higher education none is more sweeping than the movement across borders. Over the past three decades the number of students leaving home each year to study abroad has grown at an annual rate of 3. 9 percent, from 800,000 in 1975 to 2. 5 million in 2004. Most travel from one developed nation to another, but the flow from developing to developed countries is growing rapidly. The reverse flow, from developed to developing countries, is on the rise, too. Today foreign students earn 30 percent of the doctoral degrees awarded in the United States and 38 percent of those in the United Kingdom. And the number crossing borders for undergraduate study is growing as well, to 8 percent of the undergraduates at America's best institutions and 10 percent of all undergraduates in the U. K. In the United States, 20 percent of the newly hired professors in science and engineering are foreign-born, and in China many newly hired faculty members at the top research universities received their graduate education abroad.

Universities are also encouraging students to spend some of their undergraduate years in another country. In Europe, more than 140,000 students participate in the Erasmus program each year, taking courses for credit in one of 2,200 participating institutions across the continent. And in the United States, institutions are helping place students in the summer internships (实习) abroad to prepare them for global careers. Yale and Harvard have led the way, offering every undergraduate at least one international study or internship opportunity— and providing the financial resources to make it possible.

Globalization is also reshaping the way research is done. One new trend involves sourcing portions of a research program to another country. Yale professor and Howard Hughes Medical Institute investigator Tian Xu directs a research center focused on the genetics of human disease at Shanghai's Fudan University, in collaboration with faculty colleagues from both schools. The

Shanghai center has 95 employees and graduate students working in a 4,300-square-meter laboratory facility. Yale faculty, postdoctors and graduate students visit regularly and attend videoconference seminars with scientists from both campuses. The arrangement benefits both countries; Xu's Yale lab is more productive, thanks to the lower costs of conducting research in China, and Chinese graduate students, postdoctors and faculty get on-the-job training from a world-class scientist and his U.S. team.

As a result of its strength in science, the United States has consistently led the world in the commercialization of major new technologies, from the mainframe computer and the integrated circuit of the 1960s to the Internet infrastructure (基础设施) and applications software of the 1990s. The link between university-based science and industrial application is often indirect but sometimes highly visible: Silicon Valley was intentionally created by Stanford University, and Route 128 outside Boston has long housed companies spun off from MIT and Harvard. Around the world, governments have encouraged copying of this model, perhaps most successfully in Cambridge, England, where Microsoft and scores of other leading software and biotechnology companies have set up shop around the university.

For all its success, the United States remains deeply hesitant about sustaining the research-university model. Most politicians recognize the link between investment in science and national economic strength, but support for research funding has been unsteady. The budget of the National Institutes of Health doubled between 1998 and 2003, but has risen more slowly than inflation since then. Support for the physical sciences and engineering barely kept pace with inflation during that same period. The attempt to make up lost ground is welcome, but the nation would be better served by steady, predictable increases in science funding at the rate of long-term GDP growth, which is on the order of inflation plus 3 percent per year.

American politicians have great difficulty recognizing that admitting more foreign students can greatly promote the national interest by increasing international understanding. Adjusted for inflation, public funding for international exchanges and foreign-language study is well below the levels of 40 years ago. In the wake of September 11, changes in the visa process caused a dramatic decline in the number of foreign students seeking admission to U.S. universities, and a corresponding surge in enrollments in Australia, Singapore and the U.K. Objections from American university and business leaders led to improvements in the process and a reversal of the decline, but the United States is still seen by many as unwelcoming to international students.

Most Americans recognize that universities contribute to the nation's well-being through their scientific research, but many fear that foreign students threaten American competitiveness by taking their knowledge and skills back home. They fail to grasp that welcoming foreign students to the United States has two important positive effects: first, the very best of them stay in the States and—like immigrants throughout history—strengthen the nation; and second, foreign students who study in the United States become ambassadors for many of its most cherished (珍视) values when they return home. Or at least they understand them better. In America as elsewhere, few instruments of foreign policy are as effective in promoting peace and stability as welcoming international university students.

1. From the first paragraph we know that present-day universities have become _____.
   A) more popularized than ever before
   B) in-service training organizations
   C) a powerful force for global integration
   D) more and more research-oriented

2. Over the past three decades, the enrollment of overseas students has increased _____.
   A) at an annual rate of 8 percent
   B) at an annual rate of 3.9 percent
   C) by 800,000
   D) by 2.5 million

3. In the United States, how many of the newly hired professors in science and engineering are foreign-born?
   A) 38%.
   B) 10%.
   C) 30%.
   D) 20%.

4. How do Yale and Harvard prepare their undergraduates for global careers?
   A) They give them chances for international study or internship.
   B) They arrange for them to participate in the Erasmus program.
   C) They offer them various courses in international politics.
   D) They organize a series of seminars on world economy.

5. An example illustrating the general trend of universities' globalization is _____.
   A) Yale's establishing branch campuses throughout the world
   B) Yale's student exchange program with European institutions
   C) Yale's helping Chinese universities to launch research projects
   D) Yale's collaboration with Fudan University on genetic research

6. What do we learn about Silicon Valley from the passage?
   A) It is known to be the birthplace of Microsoft Company.
   B) It was intentionally created by Stanford University.
   C) It is where the Internet infrastructure was built up.
   D) It houses many companies spun off from MIT and Harvard.

7. What is said about the U.S. federal funding for research?
   A) It has increased by 3 percent.
   B) It doubled between 1998 and 2003.
   C) It has been unsteady for years.

D) It has been more than sufficient.

8. The dramatic decline in the enrollment of foreign students in the U. S. after September 11 was caused by _____.

9. Many Americans fear that American competitiveness may be threatened by foreign students who will _____.

10. The policy of welcoming foreign students can benefit the U. S. in that the very best of them will stay and _____.

【答案及解析】

1. C 2. B 3. D 4. A 5. D 6. B 7. C

8. changes in the visa process

9. take their knowledge and skills back home

10. strengthen the nation

1. [C] 文章第一段为主旨段。该段提到大学在提升国家竞争力、促进和平和经济发展等方面的作用,但其重点在后半部分:大学已成为促进全球一体化、相互理解和地缘政治稳定的重要力量。因此本题选 C。

2. [B] 本题考查对文章细节的理解。根据文章第三段第二句可直接选出正确答案 B。

3. [D] 本题同样为细节理解题。题干中的关键词为"foreign-born",根据文章第三段最后一句可知,在美国,在科学和工程领域最新聘请的教授中,有 20% 是在国外出生的。

4. [A] 第四段末句提到,耶鲁大学和哈佛大学为每位本科生提供至少一次在海外进修或实习的机会。备选项中只有 A 提到"international study"和"internship",故为正确选项。

5. [D] 从备选项看,该例子与耶鲁大学有关。原文第五段开头提到,全球化改变了科研的方式,接下来便以美国大学和中国大学之间的一个科研项目合作为例加以说明。因此本题选 D。

6. [B] 根据题干关键词"Silicon Valley"可定位至第六段。解答本题可根据选项的关键词进行排除。第六段最后一句提到"Microsoft"的诞生地是"Cambridge"而非"Silicon Valley",故不选 A;选项 C 中的 "Internet infrastructure" 在该段首句,从该句我们知道 "Internet infrastructure"是科技商业应用的一个例子,文中也没有提到其与硅谷的关系,故不选;又据原文"Route 128 outside Boston has long housed companies spun off from MIT and Harvard"可排除 D。

7. [C] 本题考查对文章细节的理解。根据题干中的关键词"funding"可定位至文章第七段。根据该段第二句可知本题正确选项为 C。

8. changes in the visa process。原文表述是:"In the wake of September 11, changes in the visa process caused a dramatic decline in the number of foreign students seeking admission to U. S. universities...". "in the wake of"意思是"在……之后"。

9. take their knowledge and skills back home。答题依据在第九段:"... but many fear that foreign students threaten American competitiveness by taking their knowledge and skills back

home"。

10. strengthen the nation。见文章最后一段："the very best of them stay in the States and-like immigrants throughout history—strengthen the nation"。细读该句不难得出句中插入语后面的部分即为答案。

★2007 年 6 月考题

Directions：In this part, you will have 15 minutes to go over the passage quickly and answer the questions on **Answer sheet 1.**

For questions 1－7, mark

Y (for YES) if the statement agrees with the information given in the passage;

N (for NO) if statement contradicts the information given in the passage;

NG (for NOT GIVEN) if the information is not given in the passage.

For question 8－10, complete the sentences with the information given in the passage.

Protect Your Privacy When Job-hunting Online

Identity theft and identity fraud are terms used to refer to all types of crime in which someone wrongfully obtains and uses another person's personal data in some way that involves fraud or deception, typically for economic gain.

The numbers associated with identity theft are beginning to add up fast these days. A recent General Accounting Office report estimates that as many as 750,000 Americans are victims of identity theft every year. And that number may be low, as many people choose not to report the crime even if they know they have been victimized.

Identity theft is "an absolute epidemic," states Robert Ellis Smith, a respected author and advocate of privacy. "It's certainly picked up in the last four or five years. It's worldwide. It affects everybody, and there's very little you can do to prevent it and, worst of all, you can't detect it until it's probably too late."

Unlike your fingerprints, which are unique to you and cannot be given to someone else for their use, your personal data, especially your social security number, your bank account or credit card number, your telephone calling card number, and other valuable identifying data, can be used, if they fall into the wrong hands, to personally profit at your expense. In the United States and Canada, for example, many people have reported that unauthorized persons have taken funds out of their bank or financial accounts, or, in the worst cases, taken over their identities altogether, running up vast debts and committing crimes while using the victims' names. In many cases, a victim's losses may include not only out-of-pocket financial losses, but substantial additional financial costs associated with trying to restore his reputation in the community and correcting erroneous information for which the criminal is responsible.

According to the FBI, identity theft is the number one fraud committed on the Internet. So how do job seekers protect themselves while continuing to circulate their resumes online? The key to a successful online job search is learning to manage the risks. Here are some tips for staying safe while conducting a job search on the Internet.

1. Check for a privacy policy.

If you are considering posting your resume online, make sure the job search site you are considering has a privacy policy, like CareerBuilder. com. The policy should spell out how your information will be used, stored and whether or not it will be shared. You may want to think twice about posting your resume on a site that automatically shares your information with others. You could be opening yourself up to unwanted calls from solicitors (推销员).

When reviewing the site's privacy policy, you'll be able to delete your resume just as easily as you posted it. You won't necessarily want your resume to remain out there on the Internet once you land a job. Remember, the longer your resume remains posted on a job board, the more exposure, both positive and not-so-positive, it will receive.

2. Take advantage of site features.

Lawful job search sites offer levels of privacy protection. Before posting your resume, carefully consider your job search objectives and the level of risk you are willing to assume.

CareerBuilder. com, for example, offers three levels of privacy from which job seekers can choose. The first is standard posting. This option gives job seekers who post their resumes the most visibility to the broadest employer audience possible.

The second is anonymous (匿名的) posting. This allows job seekers the same visibility as those in the standard posting category without any of their contact information being displayed. Job seekers who wish to remain anonymous but want to share some other information may choose which pieces of contact information to display.

The third is private posting. This option allows a job seeker to post a resume without having it searched by employers. Private posting allows job seekers to quickly and easily apply for jobs that appear on CareerBuilder. com without retyping their information.

3. Safeguard your identity.

Career experts say that one of the ways job seekers can stay safe while using the Internet to search out jobs is to conceal their identities. Replace your name on your resume with a generic (泛指的) identifier, such as "Intranet Developer Candidate," or "Experienced Marketing Representative."

You should also consider eliminating the name and location of your current employer. Depending on your title, it may not be all that difficult to determine who you are once the name of your company is provided. Use a general description of the company such as "Major auto manufacturer." or "International packaged goods supplier."

If your job title is unique, consider using the generic equivalent instead of the exact title assigned by your employer.

4. Establish an email address for your search.

Another way to protect your privacy while seeking employment online is to open up an email account specifically for your online job search. This will safeguard your existing email box in the event someone you don't know gets hold of your email address and shares it with others.

Using an email address specifically for your job search also eliminates the possibility that you will receive unwelcome emails in your primary mailbox. When naming your new email address, be sure that it doesn't contain references to your name or other information that will give away your identity. The best solution is an email address that is relevant to the job you are seeking such as Salesmgr2004@provider.com.

5. Protect your references.

If your resume contains a section with the names and contact information of your references, take it out. There's no sense in safeguarding your information while sharing private contact information of your references.

6. Keep confidential(机密的) information confidential.

Do not, under any circumstances, share your social security, driver's license, and bank account numbers or other personal information, such as race or eye color. Honest employers do not need this information with an initial application. Don't provide this even if they say they need it in order to conduct a background check. This is one of the oldest tricks in the book — don't fall for it.

1. Robert Ellis Smith believes identity theft is difficult to detect and one can hardly do anything to prevent it.
2. In many cases, identity theft not only causes the victims' immediate financial losses but costs them a lot to restore their reputation.
3. Identity theft is a minor offence and its harm has been somewhat overestimated.
4. It is important that your resume not stay online longer than is necessary.
5. Of the three options offered by CareerBuilder. com in Suggestion 2, the third one is apparently most strongly recommended.
6. Employers require applicants to submit very personal information on background checks.
7. Applicants are advised to use generic names for themselves and their current employers when seeking employment online.
8. Using a special email address in the job search can help prevent you from receiving _____.
9. To protect your references, you should not post online their _____.
10. According to the passage, identity theft is committed typically for _____.

【答案及解析】

1. Y　2. Y　3. N　4. Y　5. NG　6. N　7. Y

8. unwelcome emails

9. names and contact information

10. economic gains

1. 根据题干中的人名 Robert Ellis Smith 可迅速定位至文章第三段。根据 Robert Ellis Smith 所说的内容,盗用他人身份的行为影响很广且难于预防。可见题干说法正确。

2. 据原文第四段最后一句可知题干说法正确。

3. 根据文章前四段可知,盗用身份的行为涉及面广、危害大。题干的说法明显与文意不符。

4. 由文章第一个小标题第二段: You won't necessarily want your resume to remain out there on the Internet once you land a job. 可知题干说法正确。

5. 文章第二个小标题中提到 CareerBuilder. com 提出的三点建议,但至于哪一条建议是最重要的,文中并没有给出相关信息。故本题答案为 NG。

6. 根据题干中的 personal information 及 background check 等关键词可定位至文章第六个小标题。由文章的叙述可知,雇主一般不会要求求职者提供这类信息。因此题干的说法是错误的。

7. 文中第三个小标题提到,保护自己的真实身份信息的一个有效手段是用泛指的称谓来代替真实的身份信息。因此题干说法正确。

8. 根据题干中的 using a special email address 可定位至文章的第四个小标题。原文的表述是: Using an email address specifically for your job search also eliminates the possibility that you will receive unwelcome emails in your primary mailbox. 因此本题应填 unwelcome emails。

9. 根据题干中的 reference 不难定位到第五个小标题。从该段的表述看,本题完整答案应是: names and contact information。

10. 据文章首段易知本题应填 economic gains。

★2006 年 12 月考题

Directions: In this part, you will have 15 minutes to go over the passage quickly and answer the questions on **Answer sheet 1.**

For questions 1—7, mark

Y (for YES) if the statement agrees with the information given in the passage;

N (for NO) if statement contradicts the information given in the passage;

NG (for NOT GIVEN) if the information is not given in the passage.

For question 8—10, complete the sentences with the information given in the passage.

Six Secrets of High-Energy People

There's an energy crisis in America, and it has nothing to do with fossil fuels. Millions of us get up each morning already weary over the day holds. "I just can't get started." People say. But it's not physical energy that most of us lack. Sure, we could all use extra sleep and a better diet. But in truth, people are healthier today than at any time in history. I can almost guarantee that if you long for more energy, the problem is not with your body.

What you're seeking is not physical energy. It's emotional energy. Yet, sad to say life sometimes seems designed to exhaust our supply. We work too hard. We have family obligations. We encounter emergencies and personal crises. No wonder so many of us suffer from emotional fatigue, a kind of utter exhaustion of the spirit.

And yet we all know people who are filled with joy, despite the unpleasant circumstances of their lives. Even as a child I observed people who were poor or disabled or ill, but who nonetheless faced life with optimism and vigor. Consider Laura Hillenbrand, who despite an extremely weak body wrote the best-seller *Seabiscuit* . Hillenbrand barely had enough physical energy to drag herself out of bed to write. But she was fueled by having a story she wanted to share. It was emotional energy that helped her succeed.

Unlike physical energy, which is finite and diminishes with age, emotional energy is unlimited and has nothing to do with genes or upbringing. So how do you get it? You can't simply tell yourself to be positive. You must take action. Here are six practical strategies that work.

1. Do something new.

Very little that's new occurs in our lives. The impact of this sameness on our emotional energy is gradual, but huge: It's like a tire with a slow leak. You don't notice it at first, but eventually you'll get a flat. It's up to you to plug the leak — even though there are always a dozen reasons to stay stuck in your dull routines of life. That's where Maura, 36, a waitress, found herself a year ago.

Fortunately, Maura had a lifeline — a group of women friends who meet regularly to discuss their lives. Their lively discussions spurred Maura to make small but nevertheless life altering changes. She joined a gym in the next town. She changed her look with a short haircut and new black T-shirts. Eventually, Maura gathered the courage to quit her job and start her own business.

Here's a challenge: If it's something you wouldn't ordinarily do, do it. Try a dish you've never eaten. Listen to music you'd ordinarily tune out. You'll discover these small things add to your emotional energy.

2. Reclaim life's meaning.

So many of my patients tell me that their lives used to have meaning, but that somewhere along the line things went stale.

The first step in solving this meaning shortage is to figure out what you really care about, and then do something about it. A case in point is Ivy, 57, a pioneer in investment banking. "I mistakenly believed that all the money I made would mean something." she says. "But I feel lost, like a 22-year-old wondering what to do with her life." Ivy's solution? She started a program that shows Wall Streeters how to donate time and money to poor children. In the process, Ivy filled her life with meaning.

3. Put yourself in the fun zone.

Most of us grown-ups are seriously fun-deprived. High-energy people have the same day-to-day work as the rest of us, but they manage to find something enjoyable in every situation. A real estate broker I know keeps herself amused on the job by mentally redecorating the houses she shows to clients. "I love imagining what even the most run-down house could look like with a little tender loving care," she says. "It's a challenge—and the least desirable properties are usually the most fun. "

We all define fun differently, of course, but I can guarantee this: If you put just a bit of it into your day, your energy will increase quickly.

4. Bid farewell to guilt and regret.

Everyone's past is filled with regrets that still cause pain. But from an emotional energy point of view, they are dead weights that keep us from moving forward. While they can't merely be willed away, I do recommend you remind yourself that whatever happened is in the past, and nothing can change that. Holding on to the memory only allows the damage to continue into the present.

5. Make up your mind.

Say you've been thinking about cutting your hair short. Will it look stylish—or too extreme?

You endlessly think it over. Having the decision hanging over your head is a huge energy drain.

Every time you can't decide, you burden yourself with alternatives. Quit thinking that you have to make the right decision; instead, make a choice and don't look back.

6. Give to get.

Emotional energy has a kind of magical quality; the more you give, the more you get back. This is the difference between emotional and physical energy. With the latter, you have to get it to be able to give it. With the former, however, you get it by giving it.

Start by asking everyone you meet, "How are you?" as if you really want to know, then listen to the reply. Be the one who hears. Most of us also need to smile more often. If you don't smile at the person you love first thing in the morning, you're sucking energy out of your relationship. Finally, help another person—and make the help real, concrete. Give a massage (按摩) to someone you love, or cook her dinner. Then, expand the circle to work. Try asking yourself what you'd do if your goal were to be helpful rather than efficient.

After all, if it's true that what goes around comes around, why not make sure that what's circulating around you is the good stuff?

1. The energy crisis in America discussed here mainly refers to a shortage of fossil fuels.
2. People these days tend to lack physical energy.
3. Laura Hillenbrand is an example cited to show how emotional energy can contribute to one's success in life.
4. The author believes emotional energy is inherited and genetically determined.
5. Even small changes people make in their lives can help increase their emotional energy.
6. Ivy filled her life with meaning by launching a program to help poor children.
7. The real-estate broker the author knows is talented in home redecoration.
8. People holding on to sad memories of the past will find it difficult to _____.
9. When it comes to decision-making, one should make a quick choice without _____.
10. Emotional energy is in a way different from physical energy in that the more you give, _____.

【答案及解析】

1. N 2. N 3. Y 4. N 5. Y 6. Y 7. NG

8. move forward

9. looking back

10. the more you get back

1. 见文章首句：There's an energy crisis in America, and it has nothing to do with fossil fuels. 可见题干说法错误。

2. 解题依据同样在文章第一段：But it's not physical energy that most of us lack.

3. 题干的关键词显然是"Laura Hillenbrand"。关于其事迹的描写在文章第三段。该段末有一个总结性的句子：It was emotional energy that helped her succeed. 因此题干的说法是正确的。

4. 本题考查对作者的观点、态度的理解，事实上还是考查对定位细节的能力。文章第四段开头有这样一句话：Unlike physical energy, which is finite and diminishes with age, emotional energy is unlimited and has nothing to do with genes or upbringing. 由此可知，在作者看来，emotional energy 并不是由遗传因素决定的。故题干说法错误。

5. 由于题干涉及"生活中的变化"，浏览全文可发现第一点建议所论述的内容与其相符。在该节作者指出：You'll discover these small things add to your emotional energy. 可见题干说法正确。

6. 根据题干的关键词"Ivy"可定位至作者给出的第二点建议"Reclaim life's meaning"。从该段我们知道 Ivy 的做法是：... started a program that shows Wall Streeters how to donate time and money to poor children.

7. 原文提到该房地产经纪人 ... keeps herself amused on the job by mentally redecorating the houses she shows to clients. 但是文中并没有提及她是否在家居装饰方面的才能。故本题答案为 NG。

8. 根据题干中提到的"不愉快的记忆"浏览各个小标题，最为接近的内容在第四点建议"告别内疚与悔恨"。作者在该段提出了自己的观点：But from an emotional energy point of view, they are dead weights that keep us from moving forward. 由于问题是 find it difficult to，答题时必须对表述作相应调整。

9. 见第五点建议的最后一句：Quit thinking that you have to make the right decision; instead, make a choice and don't look back. 注意 without 后面应用动名词形式。

10. 见文章倒数第三段首句：Emotional energy has a kind of magical quality; the more you give, the more you get back.

★2006 年 6 月考题

Directions: In this part, you will have 15 minutes to go over the passage quickly and answer the questions on **Answer sheet 1.**

For questions 1—7, mark

Y (for YES) if the statement agrees with the information given in the passage;

N (for NO) if statement contradicts the information given in the passage;

NG (for NOT GIVEN) if the information is not given in the passage.

For question 8—10, complete the sentences with the information given in the passage.

Highways

Early in the 20th century, most of the streets and roads in the United States were made of dirt, brick, and cedar wood blocks. Built for horse, carriage, and foot traffic, they were usually poorly cared for and too narrow to accommodate automobiles.

With the increase in auto production, private turnpike companies under local authorities began to spring up, and by 1921 there were 387,000 miles of paved roads. Many were built by using specifications of 19th century Scottish engineer Thomas Telford and John Macadam (for whom the macadam surface is named), whose specifications stressed the importance of adequate drainage. Beyond that, there were no national standards for size, weight restrictions, or commercial signs. During World War Ⅰ, roads throughout the country were nearly destroyed by the weight of trucks. When General Eisenhower returned from German in 1919, after serving in the U.S. Army's first transcontinental motor convoy, he noted: "The old convoy had started me thinking about good, two-lane highways, but Germany's Autobahn or motorway had made me see the wisdom of broader ribbons across the land."

It would take another war before the federal government would act on a national highway system. During World War Ⅱ, a tremendous increase in trucks and new roads were required. The war demonstrated how critical highways were to the defense effort. Thirteen percent of defense plants received all their supplies by truck, and almost all other plans shipped more than half of their products by vehicle. The war also revealed that local control of highways had led to a confusing variety of design standards. Even federal and state highways did not follow basic standards. Some states allowed trucks up to 36,000 pounds, while others restricted anything over 7,000 pounds.

A government study recommended a national highway system of 33,920 miles, and Congress passed the Federal-Aid Highway Act of 1944, which called for strict, centrally controlled design criteria.

The interstate highway system was finally launched in 1956 and has been hailed as one of the greatest public works projects of the century. To build its 44,000-mile web of highways, bridge and tunnels, hundreds of unique engineering designs and solutions had to be worked out. Consider the many geographic features of the country: mountains, steep grades, wetlands, rivers, deserts and plains. Variables included the slope of the land, the ability of the pavement to support the load. Innovative designs of roadways, tunnels, bridges, overpasses, and interchanges that could run through or bypass urban areas soon began to weave their way across the country, forever altering the face of America.

Long-span, segmented-concrete, cable-stayed bridges such as Hale Boggs in Louisiana and the Sunshine Skyway in Florida, and remarkable tunnels like Fort Mchenry in Maryland and Mt. Baker in Washington, met many of the nation's physical challenges. Traffic control systems and methods of construction developed under the interstate program soon influenced highway construction around the world, and were invaluable in improving the condition of urban streets and traffic patterns.

Today, the interstate system links every major city in the United States, and the United States with Canada and Mexico. Built with safety in mind, the highways have wide lanes and shoulders, dividing medians or barriers, long entry and exit lanes. Curves engineered for safe turns, and limited access. The death rate on highways is half that of all other U.S. roads (0.86 deaths per 100 million passenger miles compared to 1.99 deaths per 100 million on all other roads).

By opening the North American continent, highways have enabled consumer goods and services to reach people in remote and rural areas of the country, spurred the growth of suburbs, and provided people with greater options in terms of job, access to cultural programs, health care, and other benefits. Above all, the interstate system provides individuals with what they cherish most: personal freedom of mobility.

The interstate system has been an essential element of the nation's economic growth in terms of shipping and job creation: more than 75 percent of the nation's freight deliveries arrive by truck; and most products that arrive by rail or air use interstates for the last leg of the journey by vehicle. Not only has the highway system affected the American economy by providing shipping routes, it has led to the growth of spin-off industries like service stations, motels, restaurants, and shopping centers. It has allowed the relocation of manufacturing plants and other industries from urban areas to rural ones.

By the end of the century there was an immense network of paved roads, residential streets, expressways, and freeways built to support millions of vehicles. The highway system was officially renamed for Eisenhower to honor his vision and leadership. The year construction began he said: "Together, the united forces of our communication and transportation systems are dynamic elements in the very name we bear—the United States. Without them, we would be a mere alliance of many separate parts."

1. National standards for paved roads were in place by 1921.
2. General Eisenhower felt that the broad German motorways made more sense than the two-lane highways of America.
3. It was in the 1950s the U.S. government finally took action to build a national highway system.
4. Many of the problems presented by the country's geographical features found solutions in innovative engineering projects.
5. In spite of safety considerations, the death rate on interstate highways is still higher than that of other American roads.
6. The interstate highway system provides access between major military installations in America.
7. Service stations, motels and restaurants promoted the development of the interstate highway system.
8. The greatest benefit brought about by the interstate system was _____.
9. Trucks using the interstate highways deliver more than _____.
10. The interstate system was renamed after Eisenhower in recognition of _____.

【答案及解析】

1. N 2. Y 3. Y 4. Y 5. N 6. NG 7. N

8. personal freedom of mobility

9. 75 percent

10. his vision and leadership

1. 由于问题与年代有关,可迅速定位到文中涉及"national standards"及"1921"年的部分。不难发现,这个部分在原文第二段:With the increase in auto production, private turnpike companies under local authorities began to spring up, and by 1921 there were 387,000 miles of paved roads. ... Beyond that, there were no national standards for size, weight restrictions, or commercial signs. 从上文可知,题干说法错误。

2. 阅读题干找出关键词"General Eisenhower"、"German"、"motorways"等,从而可定位到文章第二段。第二段末句提到了Eisenhower将军的观点:The old convoy had started me thinking about good, two-lane highways, but Germany's Autobahn or motorway had made me see the wisdom of broader ribbons across the land. 由此可知,题干说法是正确的。

3. 见文章第五段首句:The interstate highway system was finally launched in 1956 and has been hailed as one of the greatest public works projects of the century.

4. 见文章第五段:To build its 44,000-mile web of highways, bridge and tunnels, hundreds of unique engineering designs and solutions had to be worked out.

5. 本题考查根据文中所给信息进行推断的能力。依据见原文倒数第四段末句的表述:The death rate on highways is half that of all other U.S. roads (0.86 deaths per 100 million passenger miles compared to 1.99 deaths per 100 million on all other roads). 可见高速公路上的交通事故死亡率比其他道路上的要低。

6. 从题干来看,其关键词是"military installations",而文中并没有相关的叙述。因此本题应填NG。

7. 文章倒数第二、三段提到了州际高速公路带来的种种好处。从文章倒数第二段不难发现关于"service stations, motels and restaurants"的叙述:Not only has the highway system affected the American economy by providing shipping routes, it has led to the growth of spin-off industries like service stations, motels, restaurants, and shopping centers. 可见题干说法犯了因果关系倒置的错误。故本题应填N。

8. 见文章倒数第三段末句:Above all, the interstate system provides individuals with what they cherish most: personal freedom of mobility.

9. 见文章倒数第二段首句。

10. 见文章最后一段:The highway system was officially renamed for Eisenhower to honor his vision and leadership.

第三节 快速阅读强化训练

◎ **Passage 1**

Global English

"English is a global language." A headline of this kind must have appeared in a thousand newspapers and magazines in recent years. It is the kind of statement which seems so obvious that most people would give it hardly a second thought. English is now emerging as a medium of communication in growth areas which would gradually shape the character of twentieth-century domestic and professional life.

International Relations

English plays an official or working role in the proceedings of most major international political gatherings, in all parts of the world. Examples include the Association of South-East Asian Nations, the Commonwealth, the Council of Europe, the European Union and the North Atlantic Treaty Organization. English is the only official language of the Organization of Petroleum Exporting Countries, for example, and the only working language of the European Free Trade Association.

The extent to which English is used in this way is often not appreciated. In 1995—1996, according to the Union of International Associations' *Yearbook*, there were about 12,500 international organizations in the world. About a third list the languages they use in an official or working capacity. A sample of 500 of these (taken from the beginning of the alphabet) showed that 85 percent (424) made official use of English—far more than any other language. French was the only other language to show up strongly, with 49 percent (245) using it officially. Thirty other languages also attracted occasional official status, but only Arabic, Spanish, and German achieved over 10 percent recognition.

Of particular significance is the number of organizations in this sample which use only English to carry on their affairs: 169—a third. This reliance is especially noticeable in Asia and the Pacific, where about 90 percent of international bodies carry on their proceedings entirely in English. Many scientific organizations (such as the African Association of Science Editors, the Cairo Demographic Centre and Baltic Marine Biologists) are also English-only. By contrast, only a small number of international bodies (13 percent) make no official use of English at all: most of these are French organizations.

Broadcasting

Within twenty-five years of Marconi's first transmission, public broadcasting became a reality. The first commercial radio station was KDKA in Pittsburgh, Pennsylvania, which broadcast its first presidential election results. By 1922, in the USA, over 500 broadcasting stations had been licensed; and by 1995, the total was around 5,000. Advertising revenue eventually became the chief means of support, as it later did for television.

In Britain, experimental broadcasts were being made as early as 1919, and the British

Broadcasting Company (later, Corporation) was established in 1922. It was a monopoly: no other broadcasting company was allowed until the creation of the Independent Television Authority in 1954. In contrast with the USA, BBC revenue came not from advertising, but from royalties on broadcasting equipment and a public license system (eventually the only revenue). The first director-general of the BBC, John Reith, developed a concept of public-service broadcasting—to inform, educate, and entertain—which proved to be highly influential abroad.

The World Service of the BBC, launched (as the Empire Service) in 1932, though much cut back in recent years, in early 1996 was still broadcasting over 1,000 hours per week to a worldwide audience of 140 million in over forty countries—nearly a third in English.

Although later to develop, the USA rapidly overtook Britain, becoming the leading provider of English-language services abroad. The Voice of America, the external broadcasting services of the US Information Agency, was not founded until 1942, but it came into its own during the Cold War years. By the 1980s, it was broadcasting from the USA worldwide in English and forty-five other languages.

Most other countries showed sharp increases in external broadcasting during the post-War years. No comparative data are available about how many people listen to each of the languages provided by these services. However, if we list the languages in which these countries broadcast, it is noticeable that only one of these languages has a place on each of the lists: English.

International Travel

If there is a contemporary movement towards world English use, we would expect it to be particularly noticeable in the tourist industry. For example, worldwide international arrivals passed 500 million in 1993. the leading tourism earner and spender is the USA. In 1992, according to the World Tourism Organization, the USA earned over $50,000 million from tourism—twice as much as its nearest rival, France; it also spent nearly $40,000 million on tourism—ahead of Germany and Japan. Money talks very loudly in tourism—if only because the tourist has extra money to spend while on holiday. In the tourist spots of the world, accordingly, the signs in the shop windows are most commonly in English. Credit card facilities, such as American Express and MasterCard, are most noticeably in English.

International Safety

A special aspect of safety is the way that the language has come to be used as a means of controlling international transport operations, especially on water and in the air. As world travel has grown, more people and goods are being transported more quickly and simultaneously to more places than ever before. The communicative demands placed on air and sea personnel, given the variety of language background involved, have thus grown correspondingly.

English has long been recognized as the international language of the sea, and in recent years there have been attempts to refine its use to make it as efficient as possible. In 1980, a project was set up to produce Essential English for International Maritime Use—often referred to as "Seaspeak". The recommendations related mainly to communication by VHF radio, and included procedures for initiating, maintaining, and terminating conversations, as well as a recommended grammar, vocabulary and structure for messages on a wide range of maritime subjects. Though it is far more restricted than everyday language, Seaspeak has considerable expressive power.

Progress has also been made in recent years in devising systems of unambiguous communication between organizations which are involved in handling emergencies on the ground—notably, the fire service, the ambulance service and the police. Research has been ongoing into a way of standardizing communication between the UK and the Continent of Europe since 1994: it is called "Emergencyspeak".

A great deal of the motivation for these restricted languages has come from the language of air traffic control, which presents international safety with its greatest challenge. The official use of English as the language of international aircraft control did not emerge until after the Second World War.

The arguments in favor of a single language of air traffic control are obvious. It is safer if all pilots understand all conversations. However, the issue is not simply to do with choosing one language; it is far more to do with molding that language so that it is suitable for its purpose. Great efforts have been made to develop such a system for English, widely called "Airspeak".

Education

Nowadays the dominant view is certainly that a person is more likely to be in touch with the latest thinking and research in a subject by learning English than by learning any other language.

It is important to appreciate that the use of English does vary, in this respect. A 1981 study of the use of English in scientific periodicals showed that 85 percent of papers in biology and physics were being written in English at that time, whereas medical papers were some way behind (73 percent), and papers in mathematics and chemistry further behind still (69 percent and 67 percent respectively). However, all these areas had shown a significant increase in their use of English during the preceding fifteen years—over 30 percent, in the case of chemistry, and over 40 percent, in the case of medicine—and the figures fifteen years further on would certainly be much higher. This can be seen even in a language-sensitive subject such as linguistics, where in 1995 nearly 90 percent of the 1,500 papers listed in the journal *Linguistics Abstracts* were in English. In computer science, the proportion is even higher.

Since the 1960s, English has become the normal medium, of instruction in higher education for many countries—including where the language has no official status. Advanced courses in Netherlands, for example, are widely taught in English.

1. Which of the following statements is NOT true?
   A) Two thirds of the 12,500 international organizations made official language use of English.
   B) Only a small number of scientific organizations are English-only.
   C) 90 percent of the international bodies in Asia carry on their proceedings in English.
   D) English is the only working language of the European Free Trade Association.

2. Compared with the broadcasting companies in the USA, BBC was characterized by
_____.
   A) its only purpose was to educate and entertain the public
   B) its revenue came from the royalties on broadcasting equipment and a public license system
   C) it was the leading provider of English-language services abroad
   D) its growth was restricted by taxation at the beginning

3. According to the passage, the Voice of America _____.
   A) was founded in 1932
   B) offers news service to 1,000 radio stations worldwide
   C) was broadcasting in English and forty-five other languages by the 1980s
   D) produced programs aiming specifically at audiences abroad

4. We can learn from the passage that the World Service of the BBC _____.
   A) was much cut back in recent years
   B) was not founded until 1942
   C) broadcast through a network of local stations all over the world
   D) was the external broadcasting service of the US Information Agency

5. According to the World Tourism Organization, in 1992 _____.
   A) worldwide international arrivals passed 500 million
   B) the German government spent nearly $40,000 million on tourism
   C) English road signs had become commonplace in Japan
   D) the USA earned twice as much as France

6. Which of the following statement concerning "Airspeak" is true?
   A) It can be used in handling emergencies on the ground.
   B) It was developed to avoid ambiguity in air traffic control.
   C) It is very similar to everyday language.
   D) It emerged during the Second World War.

7. The study of the use of English in scientific periodicals showed that _____.
   A) about a half of the papers in mathematics are written in English
   B) there's a slight decrease in the use of English in some areas
   C) 67 percent of the papers in chemistry were written in English
   D) the number of papers in computer science had increased by 30 percent

8. English is the only _____ of the Organization of Petroleum Exporting Countries.

9. A special aspect of safety is the way the language has come to be used as a means of
controlling _____.

10. In many countries, English has become the normal medium of instruction in _____ since the 1960s.

◎ **Passage 2**

Attending to Attendance

If we grade attendance the same way we do academic tests, the nation's high schools would receive an A. In 1997, the average daily attendance rate for U.S. high schools stood at 92.7 percent. Seems impressive, doesn't it? That's the problem.

Reform efforts will not amount to much if students aren't in school; attendance and achievement are closely linked.

With all the attention being paid these days to school accountability for students' performance assessments, it's easy to overlook an indictor like attendance, especially when the data don't set off alarm bells. But consider this: In the typical 180-day school year, an average daily attendance rate of 93 percent means students are missing more than 13 days of school. There isn't an employer anywhere who wouldn't be concerned about such a record.

What's worse, many urban schools don't come close to that national average. In the Los Angeles Unified School District, which alone accounts for nearly 1.5 percent of all public school students in the country, seven senior high schools ranging in size from 1,300 to 4,400 students had attendance rates of 85 percent or less in 1999-2000. Students in those schools missed an average of 24 days or more during the school year. Attendance rates were less than 90 percent (18 days missed) in another 29 of the district's high schools.

In 1999, Baltimore city high schools had an average daily attendance rate of 77.3 percent (more than 41 days missed). School report cards from other cities like California, Chicago, New York, and San Francisco show that attendance rates there are less than 88 percent.

Moreover, these figures probably understate the true problem by a large margin. In most states, attendance, not enrollment, drives state funding of schools. That's a powerful incentive for schools to define and measure attendance literally. As long as absent students have an acceptable excuse, school in many states may count these students are present for funding purposes, even they are nowhere near a classroom. Excused absence may include those related to legitimate school functions such as field trips or sporting events, illness, and often almost anything else that will produce a written note from a parent.

As important as it is to stress student achievement and to focus educators and the public on raising academic standards, strengthening curriculum, and improving test scores, the simple fact is that these efforts will not account to much if students aren't in school. One of the stronger findings from education research is that attendance and achievement are closely linked. School must combat a pervasive attitude on the part of both students and parents that attendance is a matter of choice.

Some schools understand how important to push for higher attendance rates. One example is Paul M. Hodgson Vocational-Technical School in Deleware, which made attendance a priority when it launched a school wide plan in 1990.

Hodgson gradually raised its attendance rate from 89 percent in 1990 to 96.1 percent in 1999. This achievement exceeds both the district's standard of excellence and even the school's own original goal.

The first seeds of progress were sown in a committee that met monthly to brainstorm incentives that might get more students to school. The teachers, administrators, and counselors on the committee had to combat a pervasive attitude on the part of both students and parents that attendance was a matter of choice. Missing entire school days for activities like routine doctor appointments and hunting trips had been acceptable practice for both students and parents.

Part of this lackadaisical (懒散的) attitude might have been traced to Hodgson's former status as a shared-time vocational center that attracted many low-achieving students. In the 1980s, however, the school converted to a full-time, comprehensive vocational-technical high school. The emphases placed on attendance and high learning standards were first key steps to become a quality school.

The effort began modestly with rewards for perfect attendance, such as free breakfasts, announcements over intercom system, certificates of recognition, and letters of praise sent home to parents. These friendly competitions among homerooms and grade levels yielded an increase of about 3.5 percent between 1990 and 1996. At the start of the 1996-97 school year, Hodgson established an attendance-review board to deal with issues of chronic absenteeism. Students who had missed more than 12 days of schools were scheduled for meetings with their parents, the principal, guidance counselors, and selected teachers. As it turned out, this intervention helped somewhat, but it didn't make a large enough dent in the absentee problem.

In September 1998, Hodgson adopted what it calls the No Credit Status Plan, which allows students to miss no more than five days of school in a semester regardless of the reason. If they do, they cannot earn course credit unless they make up the time through the school's extra-help program. They can do this in one of the three ways:

They may attend special one-to-two-hour sessions after school with selected teachers (who are paid overtime).

They may complete an independent-study project with teacher or administrator approval.

They may work directly with their teachers on a prearranged schedule.

There are generally no exceptions to this no-credit-status rule, other than students with chronic medical conditions. But the policy is not intended to be draconian (严厉的). Students who are designated as "NC" may appeal the decision, and others, who do not have attendance problems, may take advantage of the extra-help sessions for tutoring or general enrichment.

After one year, the school's new policy produced a jump of a full percentage point in the attendance rate, its most impressive result to date. Since 1992, Hodgson has reduced annual absences by 9.26 days per student. Multiply that by the school's population of 950 students and the total equals more than 9,000 instructional days saved during the year.

An upward trend on a line chart isn't the only cause for celebration at Hodgson. Although the school hasn't done controlled studies to link attendance to achievement, there is a palpable attitude change among students, who often go to great lengths to schedule appointments or handle family obligations at times that won't interfere with class. During the same period that attendance rose at the school, disciplinary problems diminished, and the school wide range increased 2.51 percent.

At a time when some states are debating whether to increase the length of the school year to help raise student achievement, this school's relatively low-cost alternative keeping more students in class during the regular school year should get special notice. So should the efforts of other schools and districts. For example, Kentucky's Jefferson County school, which encompasses the city of Louisville and surrounding towns, has a large team of assessment counselors who intervene in cases of chronic absenteeism. Their job is to find out why students aren't in school and try to help them get past the obstacles. This service and others have helped Jefferson County increase its attendance rate from 92.1 percent in 1996 to 93.1 in 2000.

Keeping more students in class during the regular school year should get special notice. Some state departments of education also recognize the link between time in class and achievement. For example, Kentucky made attendance a priority in its statewide reform act of 1990, and Pennsylvania offers incentive grants to schools that improve attendance rates. Still, attendance is often missing from the indicators published in statewide school report cards. The Web sites of many state education departments do not offer information on statewide or even district attendance averages, although they are chock full of data on student test scores.

This absence is ironic, since attendance is one piece of information that virtually every school in the country has been collecting for many years. Unfortunately, most school administrators believe the data serve only one purpose: securing state funding. Hodgson is just one of the schools that has discovered how valuable attendance numbers can be in the effort to gauge progress on overall improvement.

Getting students to spend more time in school will not automatically produce higher achievement gains. Schools also must take many other steps to strengthen instruction and other practices. But paying more attention to attendance is a sound, practical strategy that every school can pursue.

1. According to the author, _____ is usually neglected by the public
   A) academic assessments
   B) attendance
   C) attitude toward study
   D) attitude toward the teachers

2. Which of the following statements is the main reason for most schools to be not very strict when measuring attendance?
   A) The principals are very kind.
   B) The students are very docile.
   C) Attendance rate is closely related to the education funds they may get from the governments.
   D) The schools think that attendance is not very important.

3. Hodgson Vocational-Technical School used to be _____.

    A) a college for graduates from high school

    B) shared-time vocational center

    C) a full-time, comprehensive vocational-technical high school

    D) an elementary school

4. When a student can't earn course credit because of breaking the No Credit Status Plan, which of the following is not a remedy for making up the mistake?

    A) Complete an independent-study project with teacher or administrator approval.

    B) Work directly with their teachers on a prearranged schedule.

    C) Attend special sessions after school with selected teachers.

    D) Try to pretend that the reason for breaking the rule is chronic medical conditions.

5. Which of the following statements is true according to the passage?

    A) The students can't get higher achievements only by spending more time at school.

    B) The only cause for celebration at Hodgson is the increasing trend of attendance rate.

    C) According to the author, the best way to raise student achievement is to increase the length of school year.

    D) The attendance-review board plays a decisive role in solving the attendance problem.

6. What is the main reason for the lackadaisical attitude once existed at Hodgson?

    A) Missing entire school days had been acceptable practice for students and teachers.

    B) There were too many extracurricular activities in the school.

    C) It had attracted many low-achieving students.

    D) The principal did not understand how important it is to push for higher attendance rates.

7. Which of the following statements is NOT true?

    A) In many urban schools, the attendance rate is lower than the national average.

    B) Generally speaking, the real attendance rate is lower than the data most schools give to the government.

    C) Under the rule of the No Credit Status Plan, the students who are designated as "NC" still have some chances to make it up.

    D) The author thinks that the attendance is not important compared with academic tests.

8. The average daily attendance rate for US high school in 1997 is _____.

9. Hodgson's effort to raise attendance rate began with rewards for _____.

10. To improve attendance rates, Pennsylvania offers _____ to schools.

◎ **Passage 3**

The Emerging Luxury Markets

European New Luxury Market

As in the United States, the consumer markets in Western Europe and Japan are being restructured by emerging buyers of "New Luxury"—items, products and services that deliver higher levels of quality, taste, and aspiration than conventional ones—according to a new report from The Boston Consulting Group (BCG).

The market for the U.S. "new luxury" products and services was $440 billion in 2003 in the U.S. , and an additional $400 billion outside the U.S. , primarily in Japan, UK and other Western European countries, according to BCG estimates. In 'Trading Up: Trends, Brands, And Practices—2004 Research Update', BCG examines the socioeconomic factors driving European and Asian middle-market consumers to "trade up" to high-quality, costlier goods and describes how and why some overseas New Luxury brands have met with great success in their home markets.

The report also explores how demographics and tastes put different faces on New Luxury in the United Kingdom, France, Germany, Italy and Japan.

Shifting Demographics In Europe Help Usher In New Luxury

Many of the socioeconomic and demographic forces driving the New Luxury phenomenon in the U.S. are also transforming European consumer economies, including those in the U.K., France, Germany and Italy. For example:

• European household income has increased steadily over the past 30 years.

• Household wealth in Europe has also increased, buoyed by a steady rise in property values.

• A proliferation of mass retailers and deep-discounters has freed up significant flows of consumer capital, which is being redirected to more discretionary spending.

• Today there is far more consumer credit extended and used by European consumers. (Outstanding consumer credit in the U.K. grew almost 13% from 1993 to 2002.)

• European women, who are significant drivers of New Luxury spending, are working more, earning more and playing a more influential role in purchase decisions.

• The number of singles, who spend much more on discretionary items, is increasing dramatically across Europe, though still less than in the United States.

• Europeans are marrying later, having fewer children and divorcing more frequently.

• European consumers have a higher level of education than ever before, and are traveling more internationally, imbuing them with more diverse material appetites.

Income Distribution in Europe

Over the last few decades in Europe, income growth has been more evenly distributed than in the U.S. In France, Italy and Germany, growth of family incomes has been more pronounced among the middle- and lower-income brackets, unlike in the U.S. , where more has been distributed among the top 40 percent of households. This means that there are now many more middle-market European households, with greater access to consumer credit, who are "rocketing"—trading up in a limited number of consumer categories, while also trading down in others. Rocketing is one of the key behaviors driving New Luxury.

Seniors' Role In European New Luxury

As a percentage of the population, there are many more seniors in Europe than in the United States. People age 60 and older make up nearly a quarter of the European population, compared with 16% in the U.S. And European seniors wield considerable economic influence and have a propensity to spend more on New Luxury goods.

For example, in France, individuals age 50 and over account for a third of the population; earn 45% of net domestic income, hold 50% of the population's net financial assets, and represent a market for goods and services estimated at 150 billion euros. And French seniors are noted "rocketers," according to the report. Among the most popular categories in which French seniors splurge are premium hotels, custom kitchens, mineral water and high-end cars.

Luxury Market Trends In Europe and Japan

Europeans Obsess About Style, Authenticity

The emotional dimension of how and why Europeans trade up is a bit different than it is for Americans. While all New Luxury buyers are concerned with quality and emotional payback, European consumers tend to be much more focused on conveying a personalized and individual sense of style in their clothing and accessory choices. Also, Europeans tend to be more concerned about a product's "genuineness." They care greatly about an item's "provenance," where its ingredients came from, how it was made. As a result, successful New Luxury players in Europe tend to trumpet their authenticity.

Immigrant Influx Expands European Appetites and Tastes

All across Europe, waves of immigration have diversified the ethnic make-up of local populations.

This is especially true in the United Kingdom, where immigrants from India, Pakistan, Asia and the Caribbean have helped shape the national culture and identity and whose influences have affected the styles, tastes and product preferences of the entire country. This backdrop creates a fertile breeding ground for New Luxury brands to emerge. For example, many New Luxury goods thrive because they deliver a sense of the exotic into the consumer's ho-hum life, such as a premium tea with special ingredients from a far-flung locale.

Japan's Spa-Loving Seniors and "Parasite Singles" Define New Luxury

In Japan, socio-demographic shifts are also helping fuel New Luxury appetites. About 40% of the Japanese population, or 50 million people, are over the age of 50, and they control much of its wealth. These predominately post-War Boomers are spending more freely now that housing loans are paid off and children are grown-up and working. For example, there has been a remarkable rise in spa membership in Japan among those people over 50. In 2003, this cohort represented 26% of all spa memberships, up from just 15% in 2002.

Another group, known locally as "parasite singles," is also emerging as a major force in the consumer economy. These five million young, single working women who still live at home are the single largest spending segment in Japan, using up to 10% of their annual salary on fashion items, and playing an influential role in their parent's buying decisions.

Japanese New Luxury Helped By Rise of Deep Discounters

Although older Boomers and their parasite single children have access to substantial discretionary wealth, average household income in Japan has been on the decline for some time, as has consumer spending. This has made Japanese consumers exceptionally discerning in their purchase decisions. It has also meant that consumers "trade down" more frequently, and in more categories, in order to be able to "trade up" in others. In fact, deep-discount outlets have become quite popular in Japan, such as Tsurukame, a supermarket whose goods retail for about 20% less than those at rival Daiei stores.

The Japanese have also taken to New Luxury offerings in a range of categories, including food, personal care products, cars and home appliances, especially tankless, automatic-open toilets. But the biggest growth has been in traditionally low-ticket categories and staples, such as soy sauce. Like premium olive oil in the U. S. , super-quality soy sauces in Japan, which demand a 200% premium over conventional brands, have become an iconic New Luxury item.

According to Michael J. Silverstein, BCG partner and co-author of "Trading Up", "The New Luxury phenomenon is increasingly a global story. It's apparent and growing throughout Western Europe, Japan and Australia, and will certainly emerge among the rising middle class in mega markets like China. We believe the global and local players who can design, build and deliver superior offerings in these markets will outperform their competitors in growth, market share, profitability and total shareholder return."

1. The overseas market for the U. S. "new luxury" products and service in 2003 amounted to

_____.
   A) $ 440 billion
   B) $ 400 billion
   C) $ 840 billion
   D) $ 150 billion

2. During the last few decades, in Europe, _____.
   A) most of the income growth has been distributed among the top 40 percent of households
   B) individuals age 50 and over account for a third of the population
   C) household income has decreased sharply
   D) income distribution has been more equal than that in the U. S.

3. In Europe, how many of the population age 60 and older?
   A) 25%.

B) 16%.

C) 45%.

D) 50%.

4. Which of the following statements about the "parasite singles" in Japan is NOT true?

A) They spend nearly 10% of their annual salary on fashion items.

B) They are the single largest spending segment in Japan.

C) They control much of the nation's wealth.

D) They play an important role in their parents' buying decisions.

5. We can see from the passage that in 2003, of all spa memberships in Japan, _____.

A) 26% are over 50

B) most are single working women

C) 15% are under 18

D) half are post-War Boomers

6. One of the characteristics of the European consumer is that _____.

A) they are more concerned with product quality and emotional payback

B) they usually spend a lot on discount goods

C) they tend to be more concerned about whether the product is genuine

D) they are exceptionally interested in clothes and accessories

7. What is said about the European families in this passage?

A) The number of singles is on the decline.

B) The women are working shorter hours.

C) Children are playing a more influential role in buying decision.

D) The divorce rate is increasing.

8. According to the BCG, the market for the U. S. "new luxury" products and services are mainly in Japan, UK and other _____.

9. In France, individuals age 50 and over represent a market for goods and services estimated at _____.

10. The increase in household wealth in Europe is buoyed by a steady rise in _____.

◎ **Passage 4**

Binoculars(双筒望远镜)

How binoculars work?

　　Essentially, all binoculars and scopes are derived from classical telescopes(望远镜), which consist, in their most basic fashion, of two lenses. The lens nearest whatever is under scrutiny (objective lens)（目镜）provides an image, which can then be enlarged by the lens nearest the viewer's eye (eyepiece lens), by moving it closer or further away from the objective lens.

A pair of binoculars can be seen as two such telescopes, side by side, which together produce an image which has the depth of field that we are used to, rather than just a large flat image.

Since the light has been refracted (bent) as it has been directed through the lenses, by the time the viewer sees the image it is back to front, and upside-down. To correct this, two prisms (棱镜) are placed inside the binoculars, between the objective and the eyepiece.

All binoculars are not created equal.

Just as a high-quality camera takes better pictures than a "disposable" camera from the drugstore, a pair of high-quality binoculars does a better job of magnifying distant scenes than a cheap, no-name pair. Plus, some models are equipped with specialized features that make them particularly good for certain sports or activities. We've offered the tips below to help identify some important things to look for when you start shopping.

Understanding the numbers

If you're new to binoculars, some of the terms and numbers can be a little confusing. But once they're explained, you'll find it fairly simple to understand exactly what they mean.

Binoculars are generally described by two numbers. The first number tells you the magnification(放大率), or how many times larger a distant object will appear with binoculars compared to the unaided eye. Sometimes people call this "power" instead of magnification. The second number describes the objective lens diameter, or the size of the front lenses, in millimeters. Since larger lenses collect more light, the greater this second number, the brighter images will appear (other factors being equal). That's useful for improved low-light viewing.

Let's look at an example. If you're researching a pair of binoculars described as "8 × 32", you know that they'll let you see distant objects as eight times larger than you would without the binoculars. You also know that the objective lens diameter is 32mm. Using that number, you can predict that you'll be able to view far-off objects more closely than with a pair described as "6 × 32".

How much magnification do you really need?

That depends. Increased magnification reduces the brightness of an image and decreases your field of view. You'll also find that the higher the magnification, the more tiny hand movements can contribute to a jumpy, shaky image. Therefore, you should stick to 7X or 8X power unless you have a very specific need for long-distance viewing. And if you do need higher power, be sure your binoculars have a large objective lens diameter so you get the most brightness possible even at extended magnifications.

Field of view

Field of view is another important consideration when you're checking binocular specs. Simply put, this measurement indicates the width of the area you see through your binoculars.

The advantage of a wide field of view is that it's easier to spot things without moving your binoculars around. That's particularly useful for watching birds, or tracking the movement of an athlete on a playing field.

Field of view can be affected by lens design, as well as the binoculars' objective lens diameter in relation to the magnification.

Easy on the eyes

Most high-quality binoculars list a measurement called eye relief. Eye relief is the maximum distance you can have between your eye and the eyepiece lens before the field of view is reduced. Basically, as you move binoculars farther away from you, you see a smaller and smaller portion of the image, like looking through a tunnel. If you wear glasses, you're going to have to hold the binoculars a little farther away than someone who doesn't. With good eye relief, say 14mm or more, you don't miss out on the full image, even while holding the binoculars' eyepiece against your glasses.

For additional viewing comfort and flexibility, many binoculars offer rubber eyecups which can be folded down to reduce your distance from the eyepiece lens. Some even have a turn-and-slide mechanism which extends or retracts the eyecups smoothly.

Other attractive features

There's more to consider than just numbers when choosing a pair of binoculars. Here are a few other handy features you may be in search of—or not even know are available.

Compact size. Many people prefer binoculars which offer relatively light weight and compact size. Fortunately, it's getting easier to find powerful, high-quality binoculars that hover in the 1—1.5-pound range.

Water-resistant or waterproof design. So many activities which include the use of binoculars, such as hunting, bird watching, and marine use, involve damp, foggy, or humid conditions. Water-resistant and waterproof binoculars eliminate concerns about fogged-over inner optics and other kinds of moisture-related damage.

Coated(镀膜)lenses. Often, a primary difference between lower-end binoculars and better models is in lens quality. Well-made binoculars have multi-coated lenses that improve image contrast and clarity, for the most accurate, detailed viewing possible.

Warranty. Good-quality binoculars are usually made to last. When you're binocular shopping, look for a lengthy warranty for traditional binoculars, and at least a 3-year warranty for high-tech models with moving internal parts.

Which binoculars are right for you?

In an ideal world, we would all get the best binoculars available, with every bell and whistle we could desire. But realistically, we often don't need the top-of-the-line binoculars if they're going to be used for a very specific purpose. Here, we've looked at some popular activities, and developed some very general recommendations for what you should look for.

Of course, sometimes you may give up one thing in order to gain another advantage. For instance, you may not need as wide a field of view if you're choosing binoculars with image stabilizer technology which make it easier to scan your surroundings. So please take these suggestions as guidelines, not rules.

1. The brightness of the images is determined partly by the objective lens diameter.
2. The observer will find it more difficult to hold the binoculars steadily as the magnification getting higher.
3. A pair of binoculars described as "8 × 32" indicates that the width of the area is 32 meters.
4. You will get a wider field of view through the binoculars with coated lens.
5. Glasses wearers usually need better eye relief in order to make the observation more comfortable.
6. Most of the high-quality binoculars weigh over two pounds.
7. You can see more objects in the darkness with a pair binoculars described as "8 × 32" than a pair described as "6 × 32".
8. Two _____ are placed inside the binoculars to correct the images.
9. The term "magnification" means how many times larger a distant object will appear with binoculars compared to the _____.
10. The field of view indicates the _____ of the area you see through your binoculars.

◎ **Passage 5**

Outer-space Profits

Here's a tag you don't see much, but should: "Made in Outer Space." Thanks to the commercial minds inside NASA, many of Earth's consumer goods have distant origins in the U.S. space program. There's Zen perfume from Shiseido, derived from a 1998 shuttle experiment that found that a rose's scent changes outside the atmosphere. There are shock-resistant shoes—made by Modellista—that use a special foam of NASA origin. And Berlei's Shock Absorber sports bra claimed (accurately) in an ad featuring tennis bombshell Anna Kournikova that it was made with NASA technology.

A Pleasant Outlook

Although we planted an American flag on the moon, we cannot lay claim to space. We have to treat it as we did our own earthly frontiers, investing ourselves, risking our fortunes and our dreams for a better life, conquering them and making them fruitful. Here is an opportunity for the Government to encourage private risk:

• **Space Hotels**

The utmost in getting away from it all, orbital(轨道的)hotel suites would offer rooms with a view at prices starting at about $ 25,000 a night.

• **Space Tourism**

For thrill seekers, this would be the ultimate ride: suborbital (and eventually orbital) adventures on spacecraft like SpaceShip Two, starting at $ 200,000 a flight.

• **Mars**

There are many nations and possible competitors to think about in the effort to make Mars viable, and, like with any business venture, if the competition gets there first, they can easily corner the market. ESA, China, Russia, and other nations intend on making it to Mars in the next few decades. Businesses would be wise to consider this in respect to Mars as well. The U.S. government is mounting an effort to land humans on Mars by 2030.

- **Orbital Labs**

With the exception of the lunar surface, the space environment offers zero gravity, which creates many options not available on Earth. Zero-gravity manufacturing facilities would open up new possibilities for the chip fabrication and biotech industries.

- **Solar Power Satellites**

The solar energy collected by solar power satellites would be converted into electricity, then into microwaves. The microwaves would be beamed to the Earth's surface, where they would be received and converted back into electricity by a large array of devices known as a rectifying antenna, theoretically providing enough juice to meet all the planet's electricity needs.

Asteroid(小行星)Mining

Asteroids may be a much better place to get the supplies. Early evidence suggests that there are trillions of dollars' worth of minerals and metals buried in asteroids that come close to the Earth. Cobalt, gold, iron, magnesium, nickel, platinum, silver: All these metals, increasingly rare on Earth, can be found in raw form—and multitrillion-dollar quantities—in the 3,000-plus near-Earth asteroids, or NEAs, tracked by NASA. In theory, only one expedition would be required for a space-mining company to break even.

Itch to Try

The lining up of American companies for boosts into space aboard France's Ariane rockets suggests that the race for space is becoming increasingly international. NASA has identified 250 customers for the launching of communications satellites over the next 10 years. The White House's decision to open space to commercially sponsored(赞助)launches means there are more American ways of getting American firms into business in space. Increasing attention is being given to the joint endeavor of McDonnell-Douglas, Ortho Pharmaceutical and NASA in a separation process for the manufacture of drugs in the low-gravity environment of space. Experiments continuing during the recent space shuttle mission demonstrate that this process can achieve far greater levels of purity and 700 times greater production of biological materials from batches of cells in space than on earth. A multibillion dollar global market is anticipated. If the endeavor meets the sponsors' high expectations, many other private space ventures will follow.

Mission Critical

To promote American leadership in the commercial uses of space, NASA needs to take the following steps:

It should declare a major commitment to the commercialization of space technology. It ought to establish relationships with industry that will provide opportunities for profitable new processes and a fair return on investment of risk capital.

It should give reasonable access to NASA facilities and services to encourage industry to design promising experiments that would be too expensive for a private corporation to underwrite in full and to build the facilities.

It should continue carrying out its responsibility for conducting further innovative research to provide a source of long-range opportunities for future commercial exploitation(开发).

And it should maintain a presence in the marketplace. Problems that might impede commercial ventures in space call for Government institutions that can act in the interest of the investor, corporations interested in exploiting commercial opportunities in space and the public at large.

1. NASA is planning to produce consumer goods in the outer space.
2. Many rare metals have been found on Mars.
3. It has been proved that drugs made in outer space are much purer than those made on earth.
4. The commercialization of outer space was affected by the space shuttle accident.
5. NASA has had 250 customers for the launching of communications satellites over the past decade.
6. The orbital labs can supply the earth with enough electricity.
7. The Government should ask the banks to offer interest-rate loans to the companies which invest in outer-space business.
8. The lowest price for orbital hotel suites is about _____ a night.
9. The U. S. government is planning to land humans on Mars by _____.
10. Early evidence suggests that there are trillions of dollars' worth of minerals and metals buried in asteroids that _____.

◎ **Passage 6**

Stopping That Rebound in Weight

Ask U.S. adults if they're trying to lose weight, and three out of four say "yes," polls show. Weight loss is a major industry, from support programs to diet books to special foods. Yet more than 60 percent of Americans are overweight, and the numbers are getting higher.

With all this dieting, why are so many people still unsuccessful at controlling their weight? One reason is that although many people manage to lose weight, they usually don't keep it off.

Even in medically supervised weight-loss programs, people often regain, says Eva Obarzanek, a nutritionist for the U. S. government's National Heart, Lung, and Blood Institute. "In a period after weight loss, usually about six months, the weight starts going back up," she says. Even in the best medically supervised programs, nearly two-thirds of participants are back where they started within three years and 80 to 90 percent within five years, says Gary Foster, Ph. D. , clinical director of the Weight and Eating Disorders Program at the University of Pennsylvania. For people who lose weight on their own, the relapse rate may be even higher.

Why Weight Bounces Back

Why is it so difficult to avoid putting those pounds back on? Biology, environment and the pressures of everyday life all play a role.

Biology—The body's metabolism(新陈代谢), programmed for survival in times of food shortage, works against dieters. "Your metabolism slows down because it's trying to conserve energy," Obarzanek says. "So you get hungry, your body doesn't expend as many calories as before doing the same things, and you have to reduce calories even more."

Environment—"It's tougher to lose weight and keep weight off now than it was 20 years ago because there are so many incentives to eat more and move less," Foster says. "The cheapest foods are often the unhealthiest." Activity is reduced by labor-saving devices, sit-down entertainment such as television, and the growing number of people in desk jobs.

Life pressures—"Weight control takes a lot of work, hard work," Foster says. "If life gets in the way—a spouse gets ill, your child is going through behavioral problems—the disposable energy that you have for any project, including weight control, gets diverted." So you go back to old habits, and you regain weight.

You Can Succeed

Is it possible to lose weight and keep it off for a long time? Plenty of highly motivated people have succeeded. Now, research is starting to provide a clearer picture of how they do it.

Some of the most detailed information comes from a national long-term study. The National Weight Control Registry contains information on 3,000 people who have lost 30 to 100 pounds (average, 60 pounds) and then kept their weight stable for at least one year (average, five years).

They lost weight using many different diets or programs, says James Hill, Ph. D., co-director of the study along with Rena Wing, Ph. D., of Brown University. But those who keep it off have several things in common, he says.

Diets

Some studies suggest that replacing foods high in fats with low-fat complex carbohydrates (碳水化合物)(fruits, vegetables, and whole grains) may be more effective than calorie counting, particularly in maintaining weight loss. This dietary approach requires counting only grams of fat with the goal of achieving 30% or fewer calories from fat. Simply switching to low-fat or skimmed diary products may be sufficient for some people.

Many Americans follow popular diets, such as the Atkins, Zone, Protein Power, Sugar Busters and Stillman diets. Most of these diets aren't balanced in terms of the essential nutrients our bodies need. Some are high protein and emphasize foods like meat, eggs and cheese, which are rich in protein and saturated fat. Some restrict important carbohydrates such as cereals, grains, fruits, vegetables and low-fat dairy products. If followed for a long time, they can result in potential health problems. And while they may result in quick weight loss, more research is needed on their effectiveness for long-term weight loss.

Exercise

People in the weight-control registry, on average, burn up about 2,700 calories a week in physical activity. That's equal to about one hour of moderately intense activity every day—for example, five miles of walking. It's not clear if people who lose smaller amounts of weight need to exercise this much. Still, a large body of research agrees that exercise is essential in counteracting the body's tendency to regain weight. "Without exercise, the other efforts are simply temporary," says Harold Solomon, M. D., director of the Weight Loss and Lifestyle Enhancement program at Beth Israel Deaconess Medical Center in Boston. "There are very few people who can lose weight and keep it off without changing the amount of energy they expend."

Guidelines from the National Heart, Lung, and Blood Institute make the following recommendations about exercise to prevent weight gain:

Schedule your physical activity a week in advance, budget the time to do it, and use a diary to record the amount of time you spend exercising. Record the type of activity as well as the intensity.

Changing Sedentary(久坐) Habits. Making even small changes in physical activity can expend energy. For example, simply getting up to turn on and off the TV instead of using the remote and standing while talking on the phone may drop up to five pounds a year. Other suggestions include walking to as many places as possible, using stairs instead of escalators or elevators, and gardening. Even fidgeting may be helpful in keeping pounds off, and, in one study, chewing gum increased energy expenditure. No one should rely on such mild activities, however, for serious weight loss. Only high levels of physical activity—not just using up energy—help prevent rebound in weight.

The Role of Support

It's difficult to keep weight off, but research indicates that it helps to have some outside support. "The form of support you need may depend on your personality," Foster says. "My sense is that in an attempt to find out what works we generalize too much. Some people are solo dieters and some like buddies. The most consistent data show that consistent contact with a professional improves the long-term outcome."

"But ultimately what matters is individual vigilance(警惕)," he says. "Maintenance is a very active process. If you go with the tide, you will gain weight."

1. According to the polls, the number of Americans who are overweight is decreasing.
2. The medically supervised weight-loss programs are very successful in helping people prevent rebound in weight.
3. Jogging is the best type of exercise for weight loss.
4. According to the passage, some of the popular diets may cause potential health problems.
5. Taking regular exercise will result in lasting weight loss.
6. Weight control entirely depends on one's strength of will to carry out one's decisions.
7. Regular mild to moderate exercise can help minimize loss of muscle in a weight loss program.

8. It is generally believed that that exercise is essential in counteracting the body's tendency to _____.

9. More research is needed on the role the popular diets play in _____.

10. The body's metabolism works against dieters by slowing down to _____.

◎ **Passage 7**

Children and Pets

The childcare setting, whether home or center-based, as well as many preschool and extended daycare programs, may have pets or other animals on the premises. Pets and animals that children may encounter may range from fish in a bowl, rabbits in a cage, or a cat or dog to which the children have free access. In home childcare settings, a neighbor may have a dog with only a fence separating the animal from the childcare playground. In more wooded areas, wild creatures such as chipmunks(花栗鼠), squirrels, toads, and lizards or wild birds may make their home on or near play areas.

In some settings, and for some children, having a pet on the premises offers a wonderful addition to a child's learning experience. While some children are afraid of animals, most children have a natural curiosity and will want to touch an animal. For this and other reasons, children and animals must be closely monitored, and in some cases, pets and animals should not be in the childcare setting. This article discusses some general considerations involving children and pets.

Pets as Non-demanding Companions

Pets offer children the one luxury they often don't receive, the opportunity to be part of a non-demanding relationship. During a preschooler's developmental years, there are pressures to behave in socially acceptable ways, pressures to learn fundamental skills, and pressures to learn how to relate to adult caregivers and to other children. But the pet is constant, offering love and physical closeness—asking for nothing and demanding nothing in return—no matter how stressful the day. Pets become a good friend that youngsters can count on, can tell their troubles to, share their joys, or invite into their imaginations.

Pets as Good Teachers

In some situations, having an appropriate pet in the childcare setting can help children learn about caring for others and the importance of responsibility. Domestic animals such as dogs or cats can show unconditional love to a child when taken care of properly. A relationship with a pet can help nurture children's love for themselves and for others. Caring for the animal, including providing the right kind of diet, observing steps necessary for cleanliness such as brushing a dog's fur, and discussing regular veterinary care, can help children learn about their own health promotion. Observing and practicing respect for animals can reinforce children's respect for themselves and others.

Pets may also teach our children about death. The passing of a pet is often a child's first experience with death and it may help prepare the child for the loss of family members. Parents who take seriously the death of a pet take advantage of an invaluable experience in preparing the young child for the realities of the adult world.

Caregivers must remember, however, that not all animals are appropriate in a childcare setting. Ferrets, turtles, psittacine birds (birds of the parrot family), or any wild or dangerous animals should not be kept in a childcare facility. These and other animals can transmit diseases. Also, ferrets can be dangerous to children because they are attracted to the smell of milk. Animals may openly exhibit behaviors such as breeding, biting, and harmless play fighting which, while normal animal behaviors, may not be desirable or appropriate for children to observe. Caregivers should use discretion in allowing children to observe animals.

Health and Safety Concerns

When children and animals interact, safety and health are important, first for the child, but also for the animal. It is often difficult for a child (or adult) to understand an animal's actions and reactions to attention or playfulness.

Whatever the situation, the caregiver must be aware of potential dangers. An animal may play, be aggressive, bite and scratch, or lick in friendship. For example, a cat may seem to enjoy petting and even roll over for you to rub its stomach, and then suddenly begin to scratch and bite the hand that is rubbing. A neighbor's dog may appear friendly from a distance, but could become aggressive if a child placed their hand on or through the fence.

Children's allergies(过敏性反应)to animal fur, dander, or mites can be a serious health concern. A child may develop a rash(皮疹)or hives(麻疹)after crawling on a carpet which contains dog or cat dander. Having reptiles such as lizards, turtles, or frogs in the classroom can add to the learning experience, but create the potential for exposure to harmful bacteria if careful hand washing procedures are not followed.

Most dogs and cats acquire some type of intestinal parasite(肠道寄生虫)during their lifetime, and these worms can not only be annoying, but can cause medical problems, especially in young animals. It is important to remove these parasites for the sake of your pet, and also because humans can become infected.

Health and Safety Tips

Children should not be allowed to approach or touch an unknown animal, even if the animal's owner believes the animal to be friendly.

A responsible adult should always be within "touching distance" when a child is interacting with an animal. A child may unknowingly become too rough with the animal, resulting in an injury to either the child or the animal.

Help children to wash their hands thoroughly after touching any animal or product used with animals, such as fish food.

Remember that children may be seriously injured by an animal more quickly than an adult because of their size and their proximity to the animal. A child is more likely to be at face level to a cat or dog, and facial injuries can be serious. Likewise, a pinch by a bird's beak may cause only minor discomfort to an adult, but could cause a laceration on a child's small finger. Teach children how to stay safe around animals. Animals may react aggressively to teasing or having their food removed.

To prevent problems with intestinal parasites for your pet and for you, consult your local veterinarian on deworming and parasite control.

Your veterinarian can diagnose roundworms, hookworms, and whipworms by doing a fecal examination in which the eggs of the worm are identified. The worms can easily be removed by the administration of a dewormer prescribed by your veterinarian.

It's natural. Youngsters love pets and pets love youngsters. On the surface the reason appears simple enough: young children enjoy a living, breathing playmate of their own—one that's just about their size and always ready to play.

1. Most children have a natural fear of animals.
2. Pets such as dogs may ask something in return for amusing the children.
3. Some animals are not appropriate in a childcare setting.
4. A very common problem is that pets often respond only to adults, while taking advantage of smaller children.
5. If a child unintentionally annoys an animal, he may hurt the animal as well as himself.
6. Children should not be allowed to approach or touch an unknown animal whether the animal's owner permits them to do or not.
7. There are many alternatives to owning a cat or dog.
8. Pets may help children learn about caring for others and _____.
9. Parents who take seriously the death of a pet take advantage of an invaluable experience in preparing the young child for _____.
10. Parents must be aware of potential _____ involved in the interaction between children and pets.

◎ **Passage 8**

The Challenge of School Violence

School violence is in the headlines again, this time after the tragic shootings at Virginia Tech University. After hearing the news, it's natural for students—no matter how old they are or where they go to school—to worry about whether this type of incident may someday happen to them.

Every year, 3 million young people in the United States fall victim to crimes at school. Almost 2 million of these incidents involve violence. Although most school violence takes the form of minor assaults, some episodes are far more serious. Some end in tragedy. For example, in two recent academic years, a total of 85 young people died violently in U. S. schools. Seventy-five percent of these incidents involved firearms.

The threat of attacks in schools can create fear and disorder among students and teachers. According to a study conducted in 1995, 34 percent of middle school students and 20 percent of high school students admitted that they feared becoming victims of school violence. Eight percent of teachers say they are threatened with violence at school on an average of once a month. Two percent report being physically attacked each year. In a single school year in New York City, 3,984 teachers reported violent crimes against them.

What Can Be Done?

Educators and school boards across the nation are trying various measures to improve school safety. Although the goal of each school board is the same, the problem varies from district to district and even from school to school. Some school districts are relatively safe and seek to remain so. Others are plagued with problems of violence and need to restore order. So a number of different strategies are being tried in schools across the United States.

Stricter Codes

Seeing a need for discipline, many schools are enacting discipline codes. The U. S. Department of Education suggests that schools set guidelines for behavior that are clear and easily understood. Students, teachers, and parents should discuss the school's discipline policies and talk about how school rules support the rights of students to get a good education. Students should know how to respond clearly to other young people who are intoxicated, abusive, aggressive, or hostile. Students, parents, and teachers can meet and develop an honor code that will contribute to a positive learning environment.

Many school districts have adopted a zero-tolerance policy for guns. In Los Angeles Unified School District, any student found with a gun is expelled. The policy seems to be weeding out students who are carrying guns. In its first year, about 500 students were recommended for expulsion(开除). The following year the number increased to almost 600 students.

School Uniforms

Another policy rising in popularity is school uniforms. A recent study by the U. S. Department of Education suggests that school uniforms can help reduce theft, violence, and the negative effects of peer pressure caused when some students come to school wearing designer clothing and expensive sneakers. A uniform code also prevents gang members from wearing colors and insignia(徽章) that could cause trouble and helps school officials recognize intruders who do not belong on campus.

Across the country, the adoption of school uniforms is so new that it's impossible to tell whether it will have a long-term impact on school violence. Critics have doubts. And some parents, students, and educators find uniforms coercive and demeaning. Some students complain that uniforms turn schools into prisons.

Increased Security Measures

Whenever a violent incident occurs on a campus, there usually are calls to institute stricter security. Many school districts are turning to security measures such as metal detectors, surveillance cameras, X-ray machines, high fences, uniformed security guards, and increased locker searches. Machines similar to those that line airports now stand in many school entrances. Video cameras common to convenience stores now monitor hallways of some schools.

These security measures definitely deter some violence, but they also have drawbacks. Take metal detectors as an example. First of all, they are expensive. Second, it takes a long time to scan every student. Third, metal detectors cannot deter anyone determined to carry a weapon.

Conflict Mediation(调解)and Other Education Programs

A number of schools have developed programs that focus on building students' self-esteem and developing social skills to improve student communication. And thousands of schools at all grade levels are teaching methods of conflict resolution and peer mediation to students, parents, and school staff. In some schools, teachers and students are required to get to know each other in discussion sessions where everyone describes their personal strengths and weaknesses, their likes and dislikes, what makes them laugh, and what makes them angry.

Other schools are adopting innovative curricular programs. Law-related education helps students understand the legal system and social issues through interactive classroom activities. Service learning links classroom learning to activities in the community. Character education teaches basic values.

Joining With the Community

Numerous schools have had success in reducing school violence by developing contacts with police, gang intervention workers, mental health workers and the business community. Community groups and businesses can work with schools to create "safe zones," for students on their way to and from school. Stores and offices can also identify themselves as "safe spaces," where young people can find protection if they are being threatened. Enlisting the aid of the community to deal with school violence raises awareness of the problem and helps educators put their money where it belongs. Still other school districts have set up outreach programs with local employers, so that students with good academic records or special vocational training can be placed in jobs.

1. About 2 million young people in the United States fall victim to crimes at school each year.
2. According to the study conducted in 1995, middle school students are more likely to fear becoming victims of school violence.
3. Not all people believe that the adoption of school uniforms will have a long-term impact on school violence.
4. Life skills programs usually offer methods to resolve conflict and develop friendships with peers and adults.
5. School uniforms help school officials recognize people who do not belong on campus.
6. Joining with the community helps students understand the legal system and social issues.
7. Police stands can protect those young people who are being threatened.
8. The threat of attacks in schools can create _____ among students and teachers.
9. According to the passage, in Los Angeles Unified School District, any student found with a gun is _____.
10. Some school districts have set up _____ with local employers, so that excellent students

can be placed in jobs.

◎ **Passage 1**

1. D 2. B 3. C 4. A 5. D 6. B 7. C

8. official language

9. international transport operations

10. higher education

◎ **Passage 2**

1. B 2. C 3. B 4. D 5. A 6. C 7. D

8. 92.7 percent

9. perfect attendance

10. incentive grants

◎ **Passage 3**

1. B 2. D 3. A 4. C 5. A 6. C 7. D

8. Western European countries

9. 150 billion euros

10. property values

◎ **Passage 4**

1. Y 2. Y 3. N 4. NG 5. Y 6. N 7. NG

8. prisms

9. unaided eye

10. width

◎ **Passage 5**

1. Y 2. NG 3. Y 4. NG 5. N 6. N 7. NG

8. $ 25,000 / 25,000 dollars

9. 2030

10. come close to the Earth

◎ **Passage 6**

1. N 2. N 3. NG 4. Y 5. Y 6. N 7. NG

8. regain weight

9. long-term weight loss

10. conserve energy

◎ **Passage 7**

1. N 2. N 3. Y 4. NG 5. Y 6. Y 7. NG

8. the importance of responsibility

9. the realities of the adult world

10. dangers

◎ **Passage 8**

1. N 2. Y 3. Y 4. NG 5. Y 6. N 7. N

8. fear and disorder

9. expelled

10. outreach programs

第二章 选词填空

第一节 选词填空应试技巧

一、选词填空题概述

根据最新的大学英语四、六级考试改革方案,阅读理解部分除了增加快速阅读这一新题型外,还在仔细阅读(Reading in Depth)部分增加了选词填空这种全新的题型。其考查方式为:从一篇与篇章阅读短文字数相当的文章中,留出 10 个单词的空格,要求考生从给出的 15 个备选单词中,选出 10 个正确的单词填入相应的空格,以使文章意思通顺、表达正确。备选单词不可重复使用。

二、选词填空解题技巧

1. 浏览全文,抓住文章的主题

一篇两三百字的短文的主题通常较为明确,而正确理解主题对理解文中的语句以及准确地选择词汇起着关键作用。因此,在做题时考生应首先通读全文,力争尽快把握文章及脉络,抓住短文大意。

2. 阅读备选词

快速浏览短文以后,接着就要阅读备选的单词。阅读时要仔细对备选词进行分析。可将它们按照词性进行分类,如名词、动词、形容词、副词、介词、连词等,看看各有几个备选项。当然也可能有的词既可以用作名词也可以用作动词,而有的词既可以是动词的过去式或过去分词,同时也可作形容词。这时候要特别小心。如果备选项中出现一对或一组同义词或反义词,则往往有一个或几个是干扰项。这时,考生应根据上下文仔细选择,要考虑整个语境,也要考虑文章细节。

3. 初步填词

阅读备选词之后,下一步就要仔细阅读短文,并在阅读的同时初步填词。按照选词填空题的一般命题规律,短文的第一句不留空,这样做是为了向考生传递足够的信息以帮助其理解下文。而第一句往往又是主题句或引入主题的句子,因此必须予以重视。此外,做题时不必拘泥于题目顺序,要先填自己有把握的空,并将其从备选单词中去掉,以减小其他空格的难度。

4. 复读全文,检查答案

在基本确定答案之后,需要做的工作就是再一次通读全文,检查所填入的答案是否正确。检查的重点应放在句子结构及上下文逻辑关系等方面。此外,还应从整篇文章的结构入手,保证填入的词能使文章意思完整。如发现与文意不符者,要大胆进行修改。

第二节 选词填空真题详解

As war spreads to many corners of the globe, children sadly have been drawn into the center of conflicts. In Afghanistan, Bosnia, and Colombia, however, groups of children have been taking part in peace education __47__. The children, after learning to resolve conflicts, took on the __48__ of peacemakers. The Children's Movement for Peace in Colombia was even nominated（提名）for the Nobel Peace Prize in 1998. Groups of children __49__ as peacemakers studied human rights and poverty issues in Colombia, eventually forming a group with five other schools in Bogota known as The Schools of Peace.

The classroom __50__ opportunities for children to replace angry, violent behaviors with __51__, peaceful ones. It is in the classroom that caring and respect for each person empowers children to take a step __52__ toward becoming peacemakers. Fortunately, educators have access to many online resources that are __53__ useful when helping children along the path to peace. The Young Peacemakers Club, started in 1992, provides a Website with resources for teachers and __54__ on starting a Kindness Campaign. The World Centers of Compassion for Children International call attention to children's rights and how to help the __55__ of war. Starting a Peacemakers' Club is a praiseworthy venture for a class and one that could spread to other classrooms and ideally affect the culture of the __56__ school.

A) acting	I) information
B) assuming	J) offers
C) comprehensive	K) projects
D) cooperative	L) respectively
E) entire	M) role
F) especially	N) technology
G) forward	O) victims
H) images	

【答案及解析】

47. [K] 根据句法可判断空白处应填入名词。据下文我们知道这篇短文讲的是和平教育项目，因此填入"projects"最为合适。

48. [M] "take on"有"呈现，承担"等意义，后跟名词。"take on the role of..."意思是"担任……角色"。常见的搭配还有"take on the responsibility of...",即"承担……职责"。

49. [A] 仔细分析该句可知谓语为"studied"，因此空白处应填入一个现在分词修饰"groups of children"。"assume"后不能跟"as"，故可排除。因此本题选 A。

50. [J] 很明显本句缺谓语动词。备选选项中时态相符的动词仅有 J 一项。

51. [D] 从该句结构看，空白处应填入一形容词，且该形容词词义应能与"angry"、"violent"等词相对应。故本题正确答案为"cooperative"(合作的、同心协力的)。

52. [G] "take a step forward"为常见搭配,意为"向前迈进一步"。

53. [F] 据句法可知该空白可填入一形容词或副词。用排除法对备选选项进行筛选可得知答案为F。

54. [I] 分析该句可知空白处应填入一个能与介词"on"搭配的名词。再从全句来看,这个部分应能与"resources for teachers"相对应,同为网站所提供的资源。因此正确答案是I。

55. [O] 根据句法知识可判断空白处应填入一名词。据上文不难得知,该组织的帮助对象之一是"战争的受害者",故本题选O。

56. [E] 此处可填入一个形容词或名词。据句中的"spread to other classrooms"可推断该处填入"entire"最为合适。

★2007 年 6 月考题

Years ago, doctors often said that pain was a normal part of life. In particular, when older patients ___47___ of pain, they were told it was a natural part of aging and they would have to learn to live with it.

Times have changed. Today, we take pain ___48___. Indeed, pain is now considered the fifth vital, as important as blood pressure, temperature, breathing rate and pulse in ___49___ a person's well-being. We know that chronic (慢性的) pain can disrupt (扰乱的) a person's life, causing problems that ___50___ from missed work to depression.

That's why a growing number of hospitals now depend upon physicians who ___51___ in pain medicine. Not only do we evaluate the cause of the pain, which can help us treat the pain better, but we also help provide comprehensive therapy for depression and other psychological and social ___52___ related to chronic pain. Such comprehensive therapy often ___53___ the work of social workers, psychiatrists (心理医生) and psychologists, as well as specialists in pain medicine.

This modern ___54___ for pain management has led to a wealth of innovative treatments which are more effective and with fewer side effects than ever before. Decades ago, there were only a ___55___ number of drugs available, and many of them caused ___56___ side effects in older people, including dizziness and fatigue. This created a double-edged sword: the medications helped relieve the pain but caused other problems that could be worse than the pain itself.

A) result	I) determining
B) involves	J) limited
C) significant	K) gravely
D) range	L) complained
E) relieved	M) respect
F) issues	N) prompting
G) seriously	O) specialize
H) magnificent	

【答案及解析】

47. [L] 根据上下文，此处应填入一个谓语动词，且该动词应能与 of 搭配。从文意及备选单词来看，该空格应选 L) complained。

48. [G] 本题考查固定搭配。take sth seriously 的意思是"认真对待……"。

49. [I] 空格前 in 是介词，后接 v-ing 形式。而前面所提到的血压、体温、呼吸频率及脉搏等都可作为判断一个人健康状况的依据。因此本题正确答案是 I) determining。

50. [D] 文中的从句缺少谓语，因此该空格应填入一个谓语动词，且该动词应能与 from 搭配。下文的 missed work 及 depression 表示疼痛所引起的各种可能的后果。由上述分析不难得出本题正确答案为 D) range。"range from... to..."的意思是"从……到……"。

51. [O] 与上题相似，该从句缺少一个能与介词 in 搭配的谓语动词。根据句中的 physicians 一词及上下文可知，有越来越多的医生开始专门从事止痛药的研究。即本题选 O) specialize。

52. [F] 根据句法此处应填入一个名词。选项中的 issue 有"问题，争端，论点"的意思，符合文意。

53. [B] 根据上下文，该句要表达的意思是这种综合的疗法涉及社会工作者、精神病学家、心理学者及从事止痛药研究的专家等各个领域的人的工作。因此本题答案是 B) involves。involve 一词有"包含，包括，牵涉，使卷入"等意思。

54. [M] 空白处要填一个可与介词 for 相搭配的名词。据上下文意思可知各种 innovative treatments 的出现正是得益于人们对这个问题的重视。故该空格应填 M) respect。

55. [J] 由上下文可知，数十年前能有效治疗疼痛的药物并不多，即其数量是有限的。故本题选 J) limited。

56. [C] 文章最后一段谈的是止痛药研究的进展。由该段首句中的"fewer side effects"可推知以前的止痛药副作用是十分明显的。因此本题选 C) significant。选项 H) magnificent 的意思是"宏伟的，豪华的，庄严的"。

★2006 年 12 月考题

The flood of women into the job market boosted economic growth and changed U. S. society in many ways. Many in-home jobs that used to be done   47   by women—ranging from family shopping to preparing meals to doing   48   work—still need to be done by someone. Husbands and children now do some of these jobs, a   49   that has changed the target market for many products. Or a working woman may face a crushing "poverty of time" and look for help elsewhere, creating opportunities for producers of frozen meals, child care centers, dry cleaners, financial services, and the like.

Although there is still a big wage   50   between men and women, the income working women   51   gives them new independence and buying power. For example, women now   52   about half of all cars. Not long ago, many car dealers   53   women shoppers by ignoring them or suggesting that they come back with their husbands. Now car companies have realized that women are   54   customers. It's interesting that some leading Japanese car dealers were the first to   55   pay attention to women customers. In Japan, fewer women have jobs or buy cars—the Japanese society is still very much male-oriented. Perhaps it was the

_____56_____ contrast with Japanese society that prompted American firms to pay more attention to women buyers.

A) scale	I) potential
B) retailed	J) gap
C) generate	K) voluntary
D) extreme	L) excessive
E) technically	M) insulted
F) affordable	N) purchase
G) situation	O) primarily
H) really	

【答案及解析】

47.［O］由上下文可以判断要填的应该是一个副词。在备选的三个副词中,只有 O) primarily (主要地)符合文意。

48.［K］家庭妇女在家中要做的除了家务外,还要承担一些社区义务工作。故此处应填 voluntary。

49.［G］这里要用一个词来指代上文中的 husbands and children now do some of these jobs。备选名词中,只有 G) situation 能对其作出概括。

50.［J］从整句话可知,尽管工资水平还比不上男性,职场女性所获得的工资已能让她们更加独立,购买力更强。因此该空格处填 gap(差距)。

51.［C］generate 的意思是"产生,创造"。

52.［N］该空格应填入一个动词。首先可从时态上缩小选择范围。其次,从文意上判断,此处用 purchase(购买)最为合适。

53.［M］从原文可知,过去的汽车经销商不重视女性顾客,而 insult 有"傲慢、无礼地对待"的含义,故本题正确答案为 M) insulted。

54.［I］由于现在有更多的女性进入职场,她们的购买力也在不断增强,因此汽车公司也一改过去的态度,开始把她们看成潜在的顾客。因此该空格处填 potential。

55.［H］该句子意思为:有趣的是,首先_____关注女性顾客的是日本的一些主要的汽车经销商。根据语法,此处应填入一个能修饰 pay attention to 的副词。由于 pay attention to 的主语是 Japanese car dealers,因此若填入 technically(技术上)是说不通的。因此本题最佳选项为 H) really。

56.［D］此处要求填入一个修饰 contrast(差异,对比)的形容词。从作者的语气和后半句来看,这种差异应该是很大的。在备选的词汇中,能表示该含义的只有 D) extreme。

★2006 年 6 月考题

EI Nino is a name given to the mysterious and often unpredictable change in the climate of the world. This strange _____47_____ happens every five to eight years. It starts in the Pacific Ocean and is thought to be caused by a failure in the trade winds(信风),which affects the ocean

currents driven by these winds. As the trade winds lessen in ___48___, the ocean temperatures rise causing the Peru current flowing in from the east to warm up by as much as 5℃.

The warming of the ocean has far-reaching effects. The hot, humid(潮湿的)air over the ocean causes severe ___49___ thunderstorms. The rainfall is increased across South American ___50___ floods to Peru. In the West pacific, there are droughts affecting Australia and Indonesia. So while some parts of the world prepare for heavy rains and floods, other parts face drought, poor crops and ___51___.

EI Nino usually lasts for about 18 months. The 1982-83 EI Nino brought the most ___52___ weather in modern history. Its effect was worldwide and it left more than 2,000 people dead and caused over eight billion pounds ___53___ of damage. The 1990 El Nino lasted until June 1995. Scientists ___54___ this to be the longest El Nino for 2,000 years.

Nowadays, weather experts are able to forecast when an El Nino will ___55___, but they are still not ___56___ sure what leads to it or what affects how strong it will be.

A) estimate	I) completely
B) strength	J) destructive
C) deliberately	K) starvation
D) notify	L) bringing
E) tropical	M) exhaustion
F) phenomenon	N) worth
G) stable	O) strike
H) attraction	

【答案及解析】

47. [F] 该空格要求填入一个名词来指代上句的厄尔尼诺(El Nino)。文章首句已对厄尔尼诺这个名词作了解释:它是指一种神秘而不可预测的全球气候变化。因此,该空格填"现象"(phenomenon)最为合适。

48. [B] 这个句子的意思是:随着信风的____减弱,海水温度上升,进而导致秘鲁洋流从东部流入,使其温度上升约五摄氏度。根据文意推断,减弱的应是信风的强度,故本题选 B) strength。

49. [E] 此处要填入一个形容词作定语,修饰名词 thunderstorms(雷暴)。从词性上看,在所给的词中,J) destructive 和 E) tropical(热带的)都可与其搭配。但从词义上看,同时用 severe 和 destructive 修饰 thunderstorm 是不妥的。再根据所叙述的地理位置来考虑,本题最佳答案是 E) tropical。

50. [L] 根据上下文,此处应填入一个动词。通过分析句子结构可以发现,空格前并没有 and 把这两个部分相连接,因此该动词必须为分词形式。故本题答案为 L) bringing。

51. [K] 该句子意思是:这就使得世界上一部分地区面临暴雨和洪水的威胁,而另一些地区则面临旱灾、庄稼歉收和_____。据此不难看出该空格应填入的词为 K) starvation(饥荒)。

52. [J] 由上一段及下文所述可知,厄尔尼诺(El Nino)的破坏力十分巨大。故此处应填 destructive。

53. [N] 根据上下文,此处应填入一个名词。而由上文的 over eight billion pounds 可知该名词应能衡量经济损失的程度。故最佳答案为 worth。

54. [A] 根据语法,这里应填入一个动词。符合时态要求的备选动词共有三个:estimate(估计);notify(通报);strike(打击,袭击)。从句意来看,后半句讲的是科学家的猜测,可见该空格应填 A)estimate。

55. [O] 分析该句结构可知,要填入的动词的主语为 El Nino。因此用 O)strike(袭击)最为恰当。

56. [I] 分析句子可知,该句结构基本完整,因此该空格应填一个副词来修饰 sure,而且该副词还应能表示程度,故本题正确答案为 I) completely。

第三节　选词填空强化训练

◎ **Passage 1**

Many theories concerning the causes of juvenile delinquency (crimes committed by young people) focus either on the individual or on society as the major contributing influence. Theories ___1___ on the individual suggest that children engage in criminal behavior because they were not sufficiently penalized for ___2___ misdeeds or that they have learned criminal behavior through interactions with others. Theories focusing on the role of society suggest that children commit crimes in ___3___ to their failure to rise above their socioeconomic(社会经济学的)status or as a ___4___ of middle-class values.

Most theories of juvenile delinquency have focused on children from disadvantaged families, ignoring the fact that children from ___5___ homes also commit crimes. The latter may commit crimes for lack of adequate parental control. All theories, however, are tentative and are subject to criticism.

Changes in the ___6___ structure may indirectly affect juvenile crime rates. For example, changes in the economy that lead to fewer job opportunities for youth and ___7___ unemployment in general make gainful employment increasingly difficult to obtain. The resulting discontent may in turn lead more youths into criminal behavior.

Families have also experienced changes these years. More families consist of one parent households or two working parents; ___8___, children are likely to have less supervision at home which was common in the traditional family structure. This lack of parental supervision is thought to be an ___9___ on juvenile crime rates. Other identifiable causes of offensive acts include frustration or failure in school, the increased availability of drugs and alcohol, and the growing incidence of child abuse and child neglect. All these conditions tend to increase the probability of a child committing a criminal act, ___10___ a direct causal(因果关系的)relationship has not yet been established.

A)	social	I)	way
B)	rejection	J)	building
C)	previous	K)	wealthy
D)	rising	L)	middle
E)	influence	M)	ideally
F)	consequently	N)	centering
G)	after	O)	although
H)	response		

◎ Passage 2

In some large American city schools, as many as 20—40% of the students are absent each day. There are two __1__ reasons for such absences: one is sickness, and the other is truancy (逃避). That is staying away from school without __2__. Since school __3__ can't do much about the illness, they are concentrating on reducing the number of truancy. One of the most __4__ schemes has been tried in Florida. The pupils there with good attendance have been given free hamburgers, toys and T-shirts. Classes are told if they show __5__ rates of attendance, they can win additional gifts. At the same time, teachers are encouraged to __6__ their students to come to school regularly. When those teachers are successful, they are also rewarded. "We've been punishing truancy for years, but that hasn't brought them back to school," One school principal said. "Now we are trying the __7__ approach. Not only do you learn by showing up every day, but you earn." In San Francisco, the board of education has had a somewhat similar idea. Schools that show a __8__ in deliberate destruction of property can receive the amount of money that would be spent on repairs and replacements. For example, 12,000 dollars had been set aside for a school's property damages every year. Since repair expenses of damaged property __9__ only 4,000 dollars, the remaining 8,000 dollars was turned over to the student activity fund. "Our democracy operates on hope and encouragement," said the school board member. "Why not provide some positive goals for students and teachers to __10__ at?"

A)	regret	I)	aim
B)	trend	J)	improved
C)	permission	K)	officials
D)	inspire	L)	works
E)	required	M)	major
F)	decrease	N)	dismay
G)	promising	O)	timely
H)	positive		

◎ Passage 3

Central banks are operator for the public welfare and not for the maximum profit. The modern central bank has had a long evolution, ___1___ back to the establishment of the Bank of England in 1694. In the process, central banks have become ___2___ in authority, autonomy, functions, and instruments of action. Virtually everywhere, however, there has been a vast and explicit broadening of central-bank responsibility for promoting domestic economic stability and ___3___ and for defending the international value of the currency. There also has been ___4___ emphasis on the interdependence of monetary and other national economic policies, ___5___ fiscal(财政的) and debt-management policies. Equally, there has evolved a ___6___ recognition of the need for international monetary cooperation, and central banks have played a ___7___ role in developing the institutional arrangements.

The broadened responsibilities of central banks in the second half of the 20th century were ___8___ by greater government interest in their policies. In a number of countries, there occurred institutional changes, in a variety of forms, designed to ___9___ the traditional independence of the central bank from the government. Central-bank independence, however, really rests much more on the degree of public ___10___ in the wisdom of the central bank's actions and the objectivity of the bank's leadership than on any legal provisions declaring to give it autonomy or to limit its freedom of action.

A) widespread	I) largely
B) major	J) comfort
C) varied	K) growth
D) interest	L) accompanied
E) especially	M) increased
F) beat	N) going
G) limit	O) dating
H) confidence	

◎ Passage 4

It is difficult to imagine what life would be like without memory. The meanings of thousands of everyday perceptions, the bases for the ___1___ we make, and the roots of our habits and skills are to be found in our past experiences, which are brought into the ___2___ by memory.

Memory can be defined as the capacity to keep information available for ___3___ use. It includes not only "remembering" things like arithmetic(算术) or historical facts, but also any change in the way an animal typically ___4___. Memory is involved when a rat gives up eating grain because he has sniffed something suspicious in the grain pile. Memory is also involved when a six-year-old child learns to swing a baseball bat.

Memory ___5___ not only in humans and animals but also in some physical objects and machines. Computers, for example, contain devices for ___6___ data for later use. It is

interesting to ___7___ the memory-storage capacity of a computer with that of a human being. The instant-access memory of a large computer may hold up to 100,000 "words" ready for instant use. An average American teenager ___8___ recognizes the meaning of about 100,000 words of English. However, this is but a ___9___ of total amount of information which the teenager has stored. Consider, for example, the number of facts and places that the teenager can recognize on sight. The use of words is the basis of the advanced problem-solving intelligence of human beings. A large part of a person's memory is in terms of words and ___10___ of words.

A) later	I) obviously
B) compare	J) better
C) behaves	K) storing
D) combinations	L) monitoring
E) decisions	M) fraction
F) probably	N) present
G) exists	O) local
H) comes	

◎ **Passage 5**

Money spent on advertising is money spent as well as any I know of. It serves directly to assist a rapid distribution of goods at reasonable ___1___, thereby establishing a firm home market and so making it possible to provide for export at ___2___ prices. By drawing ___3___ to new ideas it helps enormously to raise standards of living. By helping to increase demand it ensures an increased need for labor, and is therefore an ___4___ way to fight unemployment. It ___5___ the costs of many services: without advertisements your daily newspaper would cost four times as much, the price of your television license would need to be doubled, and travel by bus or tube would cost 20 percent ___6___.

And perhaps most important of all, advertising provides a guarantee of reasonable value in the products and ___7___ you buy. Apart from the fact that twenty-seven acts of Parliament govern the terms of advertising, no regular advertiser dare promote a product that fails to live up to the ___8___ of his advertisements. He might fool some people for a little while ___9___ misleading advertising. He will not do so for long, for mercifully the public has the good sense not to buy the inferior article more than once. If you see an article ___10___ advertised, it is the surest proof I know that the article does what is claimed for it, and that it represents good value.

A) covers	I) consistently
B) promise	J) price
C) attention	K) more
D) without	L) lowers
E) effective	M) local
F) fully	N) services
G) useless	O) competitive
H) through	

◎ Passage 6

It was 3:45 in the morning when the vote was finally taken. After six months of __1__ and final 16 hours of hot parliamentary(议会)debates, Australia's Northern Territory became the first legal authority in the world to allow doctors to take the __2__ of incurably ill patients who wish to die. The measure passed by the convincing vote of 15 to 10. Almost __3__ word flashed on the Internet and was picked up, half a __4__ away, by John Hofsess, executive director of the Right to Die Society of Canada. He sent it on via the group's on-line service, Death NET. Says Hofsess: "We posted bulletins all day long, because of course this isn't just something that happened in Australia. It's world history."

The full import may take a while to sink in. The NT Rights of the Terminally Ill law has left physicians and citizens alike trying to deal with its __5__ and practical implications. Some have breathed sighs of relief, others, __6__ churches, right-to-life groups and the Australian Medical Association, bitterly __7__ the bill and the haste of its passage. But the tide is unlikely to __8__ back. In Australia—where an aging population, life-extending technology and changing community attitudes have all played their part—other states are going to __9__ making a similar law to deal with euthanasia. In the US and Canada, where the right-to-die movement is gathering __10__ , observers are waiting for the dominoes to start falling.

A) return	I) immediately
B) arguing	J) including
C) strength	K) lives
D) advantages	L) turn
E) attacked	M) moral
F) stop	N) disagreed
G) world	O) consider
H) openly	

◎ Passage 7

The study of law has been recognized for centuries as a basic intellectual discipline(学科)in European universities. However, only in recent years has it become a feature of undergraduate

programs in Canadian universities. __1__ , legal learning has been __2__ in such institutions as the special preserve of lawyers rather than a __3__ part of the intellectual equipment of a person. Happily, the older and more continental view of legal education is establishing itself in a number of Canadian universities and some have even begun to __4__ undergraduate degrees in law.

If the study of law is beginning to establish itself as part and parcel of a __5__ education, its aims and methods should appeal directly to journalism educators. Law is a discipline which __6__ responsible judgment. On the one hand, it provides __7__ to analyze such ideas as justice, democracy and freedom. On the other, it links these concepts to everyday realities in a manner which is parallel to the links journalists forge on a daily __8__ as they cover and comment on the news. For example, notions of evidence and __9__ , of basic rights and public interest are at work in the process of journalistic judgment and production just as in courts of law. Sharpening judgment by absorbing and reflecting on law is a desirable component of a journalist's intellectual __10__ for his or her career.

A)	educated	I)	cancel
B)	viewed	J)	traditionally
C)	encourages	K)	preparation
D)	general	L)	offer
E)	links	M)	basis
F)	opportunities	N)	higher
G)	necessary	O)	separates
H)	fact		

◎ **Passage 8**

More and more, the operations of our businesses, governments, and financial institutions are controlled by information that exists only inside computer memories. Anyone clever enough to modify this information for his own __1__ can reap substantial rewards. Even worse, a number of people who have done this and been caught at it have managed to get away without __2__ .

It's __3__ for computer crimes to go undetected if no one checks up on what the computer is doing. But even if the crime is detected, the criminal may walk __4__ not only unpunished but with a glowing recommendation from his __5__ employers.

Of course, we have no statistics on crimes that go undetected. But it's disturbing to note how many of the crimes we do know about were detected by __6__ , not by systematic inspections or other security procedures. The computer criminals who have been caught may be the victims of uncommonly bad __7__ .

Unlike other lawbreakers, who must __8__ the country, commit suicide, or go to __9__ , computer criminals sometimes escape punishment, demanding not only that they not be charged but that they be given good recommendations and perhaps other __10__ . All too often, their demands have been met.

Why? Because company executives are afraid of the bad publicity that would result if the public found out that their computer had been misused.

A)	impossible	I)	easy
B)	punishment	J)	jail
C)	out	K)	deed
D)	former	L)	purposes
E)	accident	M)	serve
F)	leave	N)	away
G)	luck	O)	police
H)	benefits		

◎ **Passage 9**

Surprisingly, no one knows how many children receive education in English hospitals, still less the content or ___1___ of that education. Proper records are just not kept. We know that more than 850,000 children go through hospital each year, and that every child of school ___2___ has a legal right to continue to receive education while in hospital. We also know there is only one hospital teacher to ___3___ 1,000 children in hospital.

Little wonder the latest survey concludes that the extent and type of hospital teaching available ___4___ a great deal across the country. It is found that half the hospitals in England which ___5___ children have no teacher. A further quarter has only a part-time teacher. The special children's hospitals in major cities do best; general hospitals in the country and holiday areas are worst off. From this survey, one can estimate that fewer than one in five children have some ___6___ with a hospital teacher—and that contact may be as little as two hours a day. Most children interviewed were 7 _____ to find a teacher in hospital at all.

Reasons for hospital teaching range from ___8___ a child falling behind and maintaining the habit of school to keeping a child occupied, and the latter is often all the teacher can do. The position and influence of many teachers was summed up when parents ___9___ to them as "the library lady" or just "the helper". Children tend to rely on concerned school friends to keep in touch with school work. Several parents spoke of requests for work being ___10___ or refused by the school. Once back at school children rarely get extra teaching, and are told to catch up as best they can.

A)	quality	I)	below
B)	spreading	J)	age
C)	every	K)	surprised
D)	contact	L)	differ
E)	admit	M)	ignored
F)	terrified	N)	adopt
G)	interview	O)	referred
H)	preventing		

◎ **Passage 10**

There must be few questions on which responsible opinion is so utterly divided as on that of how much sleep we ought to have. There are some who think we can leave the body to regulate these matters for itself. "The answer is easy," says Dr. A. Burton. "With the right amount of sleep you should wake up fresh and alert five minutes before the alarm rings." If he is right many people must be undersleeping, including myself. But we must remember that some people are alert at bedtime and ___1___ when it is time to get up, and this may have nothing to do with how fatigued(疲乏的)their bodies are, or how much sleep they must take to lose their fatigue.

Other people feel sure that the present ___2___ is towards too little sleep. To quote one medical opinion, thousands of people drift through life suffering from the effects of too little sleep; the ___3___ is not that they can't sleep. Like advancing colonists, we do seem to be ___4___ ever more of the land of sleep for our waking needs, pushing the boundary back and reaching, apparently, for a point in our evolution where we will sleep no more. This in itself, of course, need not be a ___5___ thing. What could be disastrous(灾难性的), however, is that we should press too ___6___ towards this goal, sacrificing sleep only to gain more time in which to jeopardize(危害)our civilization by actions and ___7___ made weak by fatigue. Then, to ___8___ the picture, there are those who believe that most people are persuaded to sleep too much. One can see the point of this also. It would be a pity to retard our development by holding back those people who are ___9___ enough to work and play well with less than the average amount of sleep, if indeed it does them no ___10___ . If one of the trends of evolution is that more of the life span is to be spent in gainful waking activity, then surely these people are in the van of this advance.

A)	reason	I)	sleepy
B)	released	J)	gifted
C)	decisions	K)	quickly
D)	grasping	L)	harm
E)	draw	M)	trend
F)	bad	N)	promises
G)	complete	O)	itself
H)	hardly		

◎ Passage 11

Traditionally, the woman has held a low position in marriage partnerships. While her husband went his way, she had to wash, stitch and sew. Today the move is to ___1___ the woman, which may in the end ___2___ the marriage union.

Married couples are likely to exert themselves for guests—being ___3___, discussing with passion and point—and then to fall into dull exhausted silence when the guests have ___4___.

As in all friendship, a husband and wife must try to interest each other, and to spend sufficient time sharing absorbing activities to give them ___5___ common interests. But at the same time they must spend ___6___ time on separate interests with separate people to preserve and develop their separate personalities and keep their relationship ___7___.

For too many ___8___ intelligent working women, home represents chore obligations（职责）, because the husband does not participate in household chores. For too many working men, home represents dullness and complaints—from an over-dependent wife who will not gather courage to make her own life.

In such an atmosphere, the partners grow further and further ___9___, both love and liking disappearing. For too many couples with children, the children are allowed to command all time and ___10___, allowing the couple no time to develop liking and friendship, as well as love, allotting（分配）them exclusive parental roles.

A)	actually	I)	amusing
B)	attention	J)	continuing
C)	liberate	K)	strengthen
D)	apart	L)	gone
E)	build	M)	highly
F)	enough	N)	trouble
G)	talkative	O)	fresh
H)	stopped		

◎ Passage 12

Normally a student must attend a certain number of courses in order to graduate, and each course which he attends gives him a credit which he may ___1___ towards a degree. In many American universities the total work for a degree consists of thirty-six courses each lasting for one semester. A ___2___ course consists of three classes per week for fifteen weeks; while attending a university a student will probably attend four or five courses during each semester. ___3___ a student would expect to take four years attending two semesters each year. It is possible to ___4___ the period of work for the degree over a longer period. It is also possible for a student to move ___5___ one university and another during his degree course, though this is not in fact done as a regular practice.

For every course that he follows a student is ___6___ a grade, which is recorded, and the

record is available for the student to show to prospective employers. All this imposes a constant ___7___ and strain of work, but in spite of this some students still find time for great activity in student affairs. Elections to positions in student organizations ___8___ much enthusiasm. The ___9___ world of maintaining discipline is usually performed by students who advise the academic authorities. Any student who is thought to have broken the rules, for example, by cheating has to appear before a student court. A student who has ___10___ one of these positions of authority is much respected and it will be of benefit to him later in his career.

A)	spread	I)	effective
B)	around	J)	handed
C)	count	K)	held
D)	arouse	L)	typical
E)	pressure	M)	between
F)	normally	N)	given
G)	chance	O)	specially
H)	famous		

◎ **Passage 13**

Do you find getting up in the morning so difficult that it's painful? This might be ___1___ laziness, but Dr. Kleitman has a new explanation. He has proved that everyone has a daily energy cycle.

During the hours when you labor through your work you may say that you're "hot". That's true. The time of day when you feel most ___2___ is when your cycle of body temperature is at its peak. For some people the peak comes during the forenoon. For ___3___ it comes in the afternoon or evening. Much family quarrelling ___4___ when husbands and wives realize what these energy cycles mean, and which cycle each member of the family has. You can't change your energy cycle, but you can learn to make your life ___5___ it better. Habit can help, Dr. Kleitman believes. Maybe you're ___6___ in the evening but feel you must stay up late anyway. Counteract(对抗)your cycle to some ___7___ by habitually staying up later than you want to. If our energy is ___8___ in the morning but you have an important job to do early in the day, rise before your usual hour. This won't change your cycle, but you'll get up steam(鼓起干劲)and work better at your low point.

Get off to a slow start which ___9___ your energy. Get up with a leisurely yawn and stretch. Sit on the edge of the bed a minute before putting your feet on the floor. Avoid the troublesome search for ___10___ clothes by laying them out the night before. Whenever possible, do routine work in the afternoon and save tasks requiring more energy or concentration for your sharper hours.

A) judged	I) disappearing
B) most	J) extent
C) fit	K) called
D) saves	L) ends
E) clean	M) others
F) feel	N) spends
G) sleepy	O) energetic
H) low	

参考答案

	1	2	3	4	5	6	7	8	9	10
P1	N	C	H	B	K	A	D	F	E	O
P2	M	C	K	G	J	D	H	F	E	I
P3	O	C	K	M	E	A	B	L	G	H
P4	E	N	A	C	G	K	B	F	M	D
P5	J	O	C	E	L	K	N	B	H	I
P6	B	K	I	G	M	J	E	L	O	C
P7	J	B	G	L	D	C	F	M	H	K
P8	L	B	I	N	D	E	G	F	J	H
P9	A	J	C	L	E	D	K	H	O	M
P10	I	M	A	D	F	K	C	G	J	L
P11	C	K	I	L	J	F	O	M	D	B
P12	C	L	F	A	M	N	E	D	I	K
P13	K	O	M	L	C	G	J	H	D	E

第三章　篇章阅读

第一节　篇章阅读应试技巧

一、测试重点

- 把握文章所叙述的事实与细节；
- 既能读懂字面意思，又能根据文中给出的信息推断隐含之意；
- 能正确理解上下文的逻辑关系，并能根据上下文判断词汇、短句和句子的含义；
- 领会作者的意图、观点和态度；
- 掌握所读材料的主旨。

二、题型分类及答题技巧

1．细节题

细节题是根据文章提供的信息和事实进行提问。这类题是篇章阅读中最为常见的一种题型，所占分值也很大。其最大的特点是往往可以在文章中直接找到答案，所以这种题型相对于其他题型来说较为容易，但是做题时切记不能脱离原文，更不能主观臆测。以下是一些常用的细节题解题技巧：

⊙用略读的方法找到题干或选项中的关键词／线索词，即提取某项信息。

⊙迅速回到原文找到关键词所在处，细读前后句子，寻找答案。如找不到，可继续寻找关键词出现的下一个地方。

⊙正确答案项常常不是原文的原句，答案项的内容与文章中的某一句话的内容最贴近，但用词和句子一般不同。大部分干扰项会使用与原句相同的词汇，但是由于句型和语法关系的变化，表达的意思都不同于原句；另外一种情况是，干扰项与原句内容相似，但往往过于绝对。

2．推断题

这一类问题主要测试考生从已知信息或事实中推断出文章中的隐含意思的能力。这一类问题常常会用 conclude，infer，imply 和 learn 等词进行提问。最常见的问句形式有以下几种：

⊙It can be inferred from the passage that ...

⊙We can learn from the passage that ...

⊙What can be concluded from the passage？

⊙It is implied in the paragraph that ...

⊙It can be concluded from the passage that ...

⊙We can infer from the first two paragraphs that ...

⊙The example of ... indicates that ...

⊙It can be inferred that ...

推断题往往是考生失分最多的题型。在回答这类问题时,关键是不要被显而易见的和简单的信息或事实所误导,也不能凭主观臆想,而要以原文为依据,体会作者话语的隐含意义或表露出来的感情、态度和语气。在解题过程中,应注意吃透题意,把握文章主题,进行合乎逻辑的推理。

3. 词义题

词义题主要考查考生根据上下文判断某些词汇和短语以及某些短句的含义,主要分为三种情况:第一种是考查熟词僻义,在这种情况下,常规含义通常不是解;第二种是考查对超纲词汇的含义的推断,在这种情况下,要根据上下文来判断该词的具体含义;第三种是推断短句的含义,也要放在上下文中,利用前后句的逻辑关系或者段落主题去推理。词义题的常见提问方式有:

⊙The word "..." most probably means....

⊙According to the passage, "..." means "...".

⊙Which of the following is closest in meaning to the phrase "..."?

⊙The word "..." stands for "...".

⊙The word "..." most probably refers to something ....

事实上阅读材料中的每个词与它前后的词语或句子甚至段落都有密不可分的关系。所以,在文章阅读中解决这一类题目最好的办法就是利用语境(各种已知信息)进行推测判断。做词义题的常用技巧有:

→根据合成、转化、派生等构词法,推测出变形、组合形成的整体词义;

→根据上下文中的同义词、反义词猜测词义或根据一些表示对比关系的词语,如:while、but、rather than、far from 等判断词义,也可以利用上下文中因果关系推测词义;

→利用上下文中的定语、同位语等猜测词义;

→根据作者的观点态度和行文逻辑结构来猜测词义;

→对于指代题的猜测,应先根据上下文的逻辑和意义判断其意思,再从语法意义上进行判断。

4. 态度题

此类考题主要考查考生理解作者的观点和态度的能力。其主要要求有:(1)判断作者在整篇文章或某个段落的叙述中所持的观点、态度,或全文的叙述倾向;(2)判断作者对文中某个观点、现象所持的观点、态度,或在陈述某个细节时所流露的语气。前者实际上属于主旨类题型,而后者实质是细节类题型。因此考生解答此类题的关键是首先判断它属于主旨类还是细节类,然后借助这两类题型各自的解题策略,正确理解作者的观点、态度、意图,做出合理推论与判断。态度题常见的提问方式有:

⊙Which of the following is the viewpoint of the ...?

⊙The author's attitude towards ... is....

⊙In the eyes of the author, conventional opinion on ... is....

⊙What's the author's opinion about the ...?

⊙The author's opinion of ... seems to be that....

⊙The author seems to disapprove of....

⊙The author believes that....

⊙What does the writer think about ...?

能否正确把握文章所反映的作者的观点、态度、情绪,以及文章的基调,也是阅读能力的重要方面。解题思路是:一般来说,对作者的总的态度倾向,必须在通读全文,掌握了主题思想和主要事实后,方能做出判断。但在某些情况下,如能根据某些信息一下子领悟作者的意图或抓住问题的实质时,也可很快做出判断。要特别注意,有时候作者先提出了某一观点,却接着在后面又提出了相反的观点。因此,要正确判断作者的观点或态度,必须将上下文联系起来思考。还要注意,有时文章中的有些内容并非都代表作者的观点;有时作者会通过变换词汇,暗示自己对文中某一问题所持的态度和观点。这时,要特别注意仔细琢磨文中所用词汇的特点,弄明白作者的态度是赞成还是反对、是肯定还是否定、以下是表示态度的一些常用词汇:

肯定的	positive	否定的	negative	主观的	subjective
客观的	objective	乐观的	optimistic	悲观的	pessimistic
赞成的	favorable; approving	反对的	disapproving; be against	批评的;批判的	critical
敌视的	hostile	中立的	neutral	宽容的	tolerant
妥协的;折中的	compromising	怀疑的	suspicious; doubtful	讽刺的	ironical; satirical
谨慎的	cautious	武断的	arbitrary	热情的	enthusiastic
同情的	sympathetic	漠不关心的	indifferent	表示怀疑的	questioning

5. 主旨题

主旨题考查考生对文章中心思想的把握。主旨题的常见提问方式有:

⊙The passage is mainly about....

⊙The main idea of the passage is that....

⊙The main purpose of this passage is to....

⊙What is the best title for this passage?

⊙Which of the following titles best summarizes the main idea of the passage?

⊙What is the message the author wants to convey in the passage?

⊙What can we learn from the passage?

⊙What is the author's purpose in writing the passage?

⊙What is the author trying to tell us?

正确把握文章的主题和段落的主旨大意的关键在于找准文章或段落的主题句。主题句是归纳表达文章中心思想的句子。它在文中通常有三种位置:

1) 主题句在开头。主题句出现在段落或文章的开头部分,起着开宗明义、点明主题的作用。它可以使读者一开始就明白文章所讲的内容主旨。

2) 主题句在结尾。用归纳法写的文章,其结构是表述细节的句子放在前面,概述性的句子放在后面,结尾的句子往往起着总结归纳、画龙点睛的作用。

3)主题句位于段落中间。有的文章没有明确的主题句。其中心思想只是通过各个段落的关键字句给出提示,这要求我们通读全文,对文章的层次有清晰的了解,通过逻辑推理和概括来确定文章的主旨。要注意的是,概括出来的文章主旨必须是不同细节所集中论述的要点,而不是只涉及其中的一部分。在做主旨题时,可以此为依据利用排除法对选项进行筛选。

第二节　篇章阅读真题详解

Passage One

Questions 57 to 61 are based on the following passage：

In this age of Internet chat，videogames and reality television，there is no shortage of mindless activities to keep a child occupied. Yet，despite the competition，my 8-year-old daughter Rebecca wants to spend her leisure time writing short stories. She wants to enter one of her stories into a writing contest，a competition she won last year.

As a writer I know about winning contests，and about losing them. I know what it is like to work hard on a story only to receive a rejection slip from the publisher. I also know the pressures of trying to live up to a reputation created by previous victories. What if she doesn't win the contest again？That's the strange thing about being a parent. So many of our own past scars and dashed hopes can surface.

A revelation（启示）came last week when I asked her，"Don't you want to win again？" "No，" she replied，"I just want to tell the story of an angel going to first grade."

I had just spent weeks correcting her stories as she spontaneously（自发地）told them. Telling myself that I was merely an experienced writer guiding the young writer across the hall，I offered suggestions for characters，conflicts and endings for her tales. The story about a fearful angel starting first grade was quickly "guided" by me into the tale of a little girl with a wild imagination taking her first music lesson. I had turned her contest into my contest without even realizing it.

Staying back and giving kids space to grow is not as easy as it looks. Because I know very little about farm animals who use tools or angels who go to first grade，I had to accept the fact that I was co-opting（借用）my daughter's experience.

While stepping back was difficult for me，it was certainly a good first step that I will quickly follow with more steps，putting myself far enough away to give her room but close enough to help if asked. All the while I will be reminding myself that children need room to experiment，grow and find their own voices.

57. What do we learn from the first paragraph？

　　A) A lot of distractions compete for children's time nowadays.

　　B) Children do find lots of fun in many mindless activities.

　　C) Rebecca is much too occupied to enjoy her leisure time.

　　D) Rebecca draws on a lot of online materials for her writing.

58. What did the author say about her own writing experience？

　　A) She was constantly under pressure of writing more.

　　B) Most of her stories had been rejected by publishers.

C) She did not quite live up to her reputation as a writer.

D) Her way to success was full of pains and frustrations.

59. Why did Rebecca want to enter this year's writing contest?

A) She had won a prize in the previous contest.

B) She wanted to share her stories with readers.

C) She was sure of winning with her mother's help.

D) She believed she possessed real talent for writing.

60. The author took great pains to refine her daughter's stories because _____.

A) she wanted to help Rebecca realize her dream of becoming a writer

B) she was afraid Rebecca's imagination might run wild while writing

C) she did not want to disappoint Rebecca who needed her help so much

D) she believed she had the knowledge and experience to offer guidance

61. What's the author's advice for parents?

A) Children should be given every chance to voice their opinions.

B) Parents should keep an eye on the activities their kids engage in.

C) Children should be allowed freedom to grow through experience.

D) A writing career, though attractive, is not for every child to pursue.

Passage Two

Questions 62 to 66 are based on the following passage:

By almost any measure, there is a boom in Internet-based instruction. In just a few years, 34 percent of American universities have begun offering some form of distance learning (DL), and among the larger schools, it's closer to 90 percent. If you doubt the popularity of the trend, you probably haven't heard of the University of Phoenix. It grants degrees entirely on the basis of online instruction. It enrolls 90,000 students, a statistic used to support its claim to be the largest private university in the country.

While the kinds of instruction offered in these programs will differ, DL usually signifies a course in which the instructors post syllabi(课程大纲), reading assignments, and schedules on Websites, and students send in their assignments by e-mail. Generally speaking, face-to-face communication with an instructor is minimized or eliminated altogether.

The attraction for students might at first seem obvious. Primarily, there's the convenience promised by courses on the Net: you can do the work, as they say, in your pajamas(睡衣). But figures indicate that the reduced effort results in a reduced commitment to the course. While dropout rates for all freshmen at American universities is around 20 percent, the rate for online students is 35 percent. Students themselves seem to understand the weaknesses inherent in the setup. In a survey conducted for eCornell, the DL division of Cornell University, less than a third of the respondents expected the quality of the online course to be as good as the classroom course.

Clearly, from the schools' perspective, there's a lot of money to be saved. Although some of the more ambitious programs require new investments in servers and networks to support collaborative software, most DL courses can run on existing or minimally upgraded (升级) systems. The more students who enroll in a course but don't come to campus, the more the school saves on keeping the lights on in the classrooms, paying doorkeepers, and maintaining parking lots. And, while there's evidence that instructors must work harder to run a DL course for a variety of reasons, they won't be paid any more, and might well be paid less.

62. What is the most striking feature of the University of Phoenix?
   A) It boasts the largest number of students on campus.
   B) All its courses are offered online.
   C) Its online courses are of the best quality.
   D) Anyone taking its online courses is sure to get a degree.

63. According to the passage, distance learning is basically characterized by _____.
   A) a minimum or total absence of face-to-face instruction
   B) a considerable flexibility in its academic requirements
   C) the great diversity of students' academic backgrounds
   D) the casual relationship between students and professors

64. Many students take Internet-based courses mainly because they can _____.
   A) save a great deal on traveling and boarding expenses
   B) select courses from various colleges and universities
   C) work on the required courses whenever and wherever
   D) earn their academic degrees with much less effort

65. What accounts for the high drop-out rates for online students?
   A) There is no mechanism to ensure that they make the required effort.
   B) There is no strict control over the academic standards of the courses.
   C) The evaluation system used by online universities is inherently weak.
   D) Lack of classroom interaction reduces the effectiveness of instruction.

66. According to the passage, universities show great enthusiasm for DL programs for the purpose of _____.
   A) building up their reputation
   B) upgrading their teaching facilities
   C) providing convenience for students
   D) cutting down on their expenses

【答案及解析】

57. [A] 细节题。解答本题的关键是要了解作者写作本文的意图,同时要结合原文细节进行筛选。由第一段首句可知，"mindless activities"占据了孩子们的大量时间，但没有提到"find lots of fun"，故选项B不选；选项C"much too occupied"的表述不准确；选项D的内容文中未提及。故本题选A。

58．[D] 推断题。本题问的是作者关于自己的创作经历的描述。从原文第二段中"winning"、"losing"、"rejection slip"、"pressure"等字眼可知其成功之路充满了痛苦与挫折。选项D与文意相符。

59．[B] 细节题。见文章第三段：I just want to tell the story of an angel going to first grade. 可见Rebecca参加写作比赛是为了与读者分享她的故事。因此本题选D。

60．[D] 细节题。据文章第四段第二句可知作者帮助女儿修改作品是因为她认为自己的经验能对女儿创作有所帮助。故本题应选D。

61．[C] 主旨题。文章最后一句作者给出了建议：家长在孩子的成长过程中应给予他们足够的空间去自己体验，去形成主见。因此本题选C。选项A的意思是家长应给予孩子表达其意见的机会，这并非本文主旨；选项B文中未提及；而"写作"只是作者所利用的一个事例，而且文中也没有提到关于选择写作这一职业的建议，故不选D。

62．[B] 细节题。题目问University of Phoenix的最显著特征是什么。文章第一段告诉我们，该校学生所获的学位都是通过在线学习后取得的。因此本题选B。

63．[A] 细节题。见文章第二段末句：Generally speaking, face-to-face communication with an instructor is minimized or eliminated altogether. 可见远程学习的最主要特征是面对面的指导机会被减至最少乃至完全没有。

64．[C] 推断题。见文章第三段：Primarily, there's the convenience promised by courses on the Net：you can do the work, as they say, in your pajamas. 也就是说，许多学生选择此类课程主要是因为其便利性。选项C中的"whenever and wherever"与文中的"convenience"相对应。

65．[B] 推断题。文章第三段指出了这类课程的一个弊端：But figures indicate that the reduced effort results in a reduced commitment to the course. 第三段末句又提到，一项调查显示，认为在线课程跟传统课程一样好的受访者不到三分之一。可见学生退学率高的原因之一是在线课程的学术标准未尽如人意。

66．[D] 推断题。题目问大学为何钟情远程学习项目。文章最后一段开头就提到：从校方的角度来看，开设这类课程与传统课程相比可节省大笔开支。虽然未来可能需要较大的投入，但目前的系统已基本能应付现有的课程要求。同时，学校也不必花费大笔的物业管理费用。由上述分析可知，本题正确答案为D。

★ **2007年6月考题**

Passage One

Questions 57 to 61 are based on the following passage：

I've been writing for most of my life. The book *Writing Without Teachers* introduced me to one distinction and one practice that has helped my writing processes tremendously. The distinction is between the creative mind and the critical mind. While you need to employ both to get to a finished result, they cannot work in parallel no matter how much we might like to think so.

Trying to criticize writing on the fly is possibly the single greatest barrier to writing that most of us encounter—If you are listening to that 5th grade English teacher correct your grammar while you are trying to capture a fleeting (稍纵即逝的) thought, the thought will die. If you capture the fleeting thought and simply share it with the world in raw form, no one is likely to understand. You must learn to create first and then criticize if you want to make writing the tool for thinking that it is.

The practice that can help you past your learned bad habits of trying to edit as you write is what Elbow calls "free writing". In free writing, the objective is to get words down on paper non-stop, usually for 15-20 minutes. No stopping, no going back, no criticizing. The goal is to get the words flowing. As the words begin to flow, the ideas will come out from the shadows and let themselves be captured on your notepad or your screen.

Now you have raw materials that you can begin to work with using the critical mind that you've persuaded to sit on the side and watch quietly. Most likely, you will believe that this will take more time than you actually have and you will end up staring blankly at the page as the deadline draws near.

Instead of staring at a blank screen start filling it with words no matter how bad. Halfway through your available time, stop and rework your raw writing into something closer to finished product. Move back and forth until you run out of time and the final result will most likely be far better than your current practices.

57. When the author says the creative mind and the critical mind "cannot work in parallel" (Line 4, Para. 1) in the writing process, he means _____.
   A) no one can be both creative and critical
   B) they cannot be regarded as equally important
   C) they are in constant conflict with each other
   D) one cannot use them at the same time

58. What prevents people from writing on is _____.
   A) putting their ideal in raw form
   B) attempting to edit as they write
   C) ignoring grammatical soundness
   D) trying to capture fleeting thoughts

59. What is the chief objective of the first stage of writing?
   A) To organize one's thoughts logically.
   B) To choose an appropriate topic.
   C) To get one's ideas down.
   D) To collect raw materials.

60. One common concern of writers about "free writing" is that _____.
   A) it overstresses the role of the creative mind

B) it takes too much time to edit afterwards

C) it may bring about too much criticism

D) it does not help them to think clearly

61. In what way does the critical mind help the writer in the writing process?

A) It refines his writing into better shape.

B) It helps him to come up with new ideas.

C) It saves the writing time available to him.

D) It allows him to sit on the side and observe.

Passage Two

Questions 62 to 66 are based on the following passage:

I don't ever want to talk about being a woman scientist again. There was a time in my life when people asked constantly for stories about what it's like to work in a field dominated by men. I was never very good at telling those stories because truthfully I never found them interesting. What I do find interesting is the origin of the universe, the shape of space, time and the nature of black holes.

At 19, when I began studying astrophysics, it did not bother me in the least to be the only woman in the classroom. But while earning my Ph. D. at MIT and then as a post-doctor doing space research, the issue started to bother me. My every achievement—jobs, research papers, awards—was viewed through the lens of gender (性别) politics. So were my failures. Sometimes, when I was pushed into an argument on left brain versus (相对于) right brain, or nature versus nurture (培育), I would instantly fight fiercely on my behalf and all womankind.

Then one day a few years ago, out of my mouth came a sentence that would eventually become my reply to any and all provocations: I don't talk about that anymore. It took me 10 years to get back the confidence I had at 19 and to realize that I didn't want to deal with gender issues. Why should curing sexism be yet another terrible burden on every female scientist? After all, I don't study sociology or political theory.

Today I research and teach at Barnard, a women's college in New York City. Recently, someone asked me how many of the 45 students in my class were women. You cannot imagine my satisfaction at being able to answer. 45. I know some of my students worry how they will manage their scientific research and a desire for children. And I don't dismiss those concerns. Still, I don't tell them "war" stories. Instead, I have given them this: the visual of their physics professor heavily pregnant doing physics experiments. And in turn they have given me the image of 45 women driven by a love of science. And that's a sight worth talking about.

62. Why doesn't the author want to talk about being a woman scientist again?

A) She feels unhappy working in male-dominated fields.

B) She is fed up with the issue of gender discrimination.

C) She is not good at telling stories of the kind.

D) She finds space research more important.

63. From Paragraph 2，we can infer that people would attribute the author's failures to _____.

A) the very fact that she is a woman

B) her involvement in gender politics

C) her over-confidence as a female astrophysicist

D) the burden she bears in a male-dominated society

64. What did the author constantly fight against while doing her Ph. D. and post-doctoral research?

A) Lack of confidence in succeeding in space science.

B) Unfair accusations from both inside and outside her circle.

C) People's stereotyped attitude towards female scientists.

D) Widespread misconceptions about nature and nurture.

65. Why does the author feel great satisfaction when talking about her class?

A) Female students no longer have to bother about gender issues.

B) Her students' performance has brought back her confidence.

C) Her female students can do just as well as male students.

D) More female students are pursuing science than before.

66. What does the image the author presents to her students suggest?

A) Women students needn't have the concerns of her generation.

B) Women have more barriers on their way to academic success.

C) Women can balance a career in science and having a family.

D) Women now have fewer problems pursuing a science career.

【答案及解析】

57.［D］词义题。in parallel 的意思是"并行的(地)，平行的(地)"。由下文的叙述可知作者认为创造性写作与批判性写作不可兼得。故本题选 D。

58.［B］推断题。据原文第二段的表述可知，作者认为人们在写作过程中往往因为过多地关注语法正确性等方面而无法进行创造性写作。因此本题正确答案是 B。

59.［C］细节题。本文所介绍的写作方法是先进行"free writing"然后对其进行润色。也就是说，第一个阶段的目标是把思想记录下来。

60.［B］细节题。见文章第四段:Most likely, you will believe that this will take more time than you actually have and you will end up staring blankly at the page as the deadline draws near.

61.［A］细节题。见文章最后一段。

62.［B］推断题。根据原文第一段的叙述可知，作者对这类问题已感到十分厌倦。因此本题选 B。

63.［A］.推断题。根据原文第二段可知，人们老是把"我"的成功和失败与"gender politics"扯上关系。故本题选 A。

64. [C] 推断题。见文章第二段最后一句：Sometimes，when I was pushed into an argument on left brain versus right brain，or nature versus nurture，I would instantly fight fiercely on my behalf and all womankind. 从文意可推知这里所说的"left brain versus right brain，or nature versus nurture"等争论其实反映的是人们对女性科学家的陈见，这正是"我"所极力反对的。

65. [D] 推断题。从上文的叙述来看，作者对全班学生均为女性这一事实感到满意的原因正是有越来越多的女性投身科研。因此本题选 D。

66. [C] 推断题。文章最后一段提到有不少女性担心无法平衡家庭与事业的关系。而作者描绘一个孕妇做物理实验这样一幅图景正是为了说明女性科学家完全能够处理好两者的关系。故正确答案为 C。

★ 2006 年 12 月考题

Passage One

Questions 57 to 61 are based on the following passage：

Reaching new peaks of popularity in North America is Iceberg Water which is harvested from icebergs off the coast of Newfoundland，Canada.

Arthur von Wiesenberger，who carries the title Water Master，is one of the few water critics in North America. As a boy，he spent time in the larger cities of Italy，France and Switzerland，Where bottled water is consumed daily. Even then，he kept a water journal，noting the brands he liked best. "My dog could tell the difference between bottled and tap water." He says.

But is plain tap water all that bad? Not at all. In fact，New York's municipal water for more than a century was called the champagne of tap water and until recently considered among the best in the world in terms of both taste and purity. Similarly，a magazine in England found that tap water from the Thames River tasted better than several leading brands of bottled water that were 400 times more expensive.

Nevertheless，soft-drink companies view bottled water as the next battleground for market share—despite the fact that over 25 percent of bottled water comes from tap water：Pepsi Co's Aquafina and Coca-Cola's Dasani are both purified tap water rather than spring water.

As diners thirst for leading brands，bottlers and restaurateurs salivate（垂涎）over the profits. A restaurant's typical mark-up on wine is 100 to 150 percent，whereas on bottled water it's often 300 to 500 percent. But since water is much cheaper than wine，and many of the fancier brands aren't available in stores，most diners don't notice or care.

As a result，some restaurants are turning up the pressure to sell bottled water. According to an article in The Street Journal，some of the more shameless tactics include placing attractive bottles on the table for a visual sell，listing brands on the menu without prices，and pouring bottled water without even asking the diners if they want it.

Regardless of how it's sold，the popularity of bottled water taps into our desire for better health，our wishes to appear cultivated，and even a longing for lost purity.

57. What do we know about Iceberg Water from the passage?
    A) It is a kind of iced water.
    B) It is just plain tap water.
    C) It is a kind of bottled water.
    D) It is a kind of mineral water.

58. By saying "My dog could tell the difference between bottled and tap water" (Line 4, Para. 2), Arthur von Wiesenberger means _____.
    A) plain tap water is certainly unfit for drinking
    B) bottled water is clearly superior to tap water
    C) bottled water often appeals more to dogs taste
    D) dogs can usually detect a fine difference in taste

59. The "fancier brands" (Line 4, Para. 5) refers to _____.
    A) tap water from the Thames River
    B) famous wines not sold in ordinary stores
    C) Pepsi Co's Aquafina and Coca-Cola's Dasani
    D) expensive bottled water with impressive names

60. Why are some restaurants turning up the pressure to sell bottled water?
    A) Bottled water brings in huge profits.
    B) Competition from the wine industry is intense.
    C) Most diners find bottled water affordable .
    D) Bottled water satisfied diners' desire to be fashionable.

61. According to the passage, why is bottled water so popular?
    A) It is much cheaper than wine.
    B) It is considered healthier.
    C) It appeals to more cultivated people.
    D) It is more widely promoted in the market.

Passage Two
Questions 62 to 66 are based on the following passage:

As we have seen, the focus of medical care in our society has been shifting from curing disease to preventing disease—especially in terms of changing our many unhealthy behaviors, such as poor eating habits, smoking, and failure to exercise. The line of thought involved in this shift can be pursued further. Imagine a person who is about the right weight, but does not eat very nutritious(有营养的)foods, who feels OK but exercises only occasionally, who goes to work every day, but is not an outstanding worker, who drinks a few beers at home most nights but does not drive while drunk, and who has no chest pains or abnormal blood counts, but sleeps a lot and often feels tired. This person is not ill. He may not even be at risk for any particular

disease. But we can imagine that this person could be a lot healthier.

The field of medicine has not traditionally distinguished between someone who is merely "not ill" and someone who is in excellent health and pays attention to the body's special needs. Both types have simply been called "well". In recent years, however, some health specialists have begun to apply the terms "well" and "wellness" only to those who are actively striving to maintain and improve their health. People who are well are concerned with nutrition and exercise and they make a point of monitoring their body's condition. Most important, perhaps, people who are well take active responsibility for all matters related to their health. Even people who have a physical disease or handicap(缺陷)may be "well", in this new sense, if they make an effort to maintain the best possible health they can in the face of their physical limitations. "Wellness" may perhaps best be viewed not as a state that people can achieve, but as an ideal that people can strive for. People who are well are likely to be better able to resist disease and to fight disease when it strikes. And by focusing attention on healthy ways of living, the concept of wellness can have a beneficial impact on the ways in which people face the challenges of daily life.

62. Today medical care is placing more stress on _____.
   A) keeping people in a healthy physical condition
   B) monitoring patients' body functions
   C) removing people's bad living habits
   D) ensuring people's psychological well-being

63. In the first paragraph, people are reminded that _____.
   A) good health is more than not being ill
   B) drinking, even if not to excess, could be harmful
   C) regular health checks are essential to keeping fit
   D) prevention is more difficult than cure

64. Traditionally, a person is considered "well" if he _____.
   A) does not have any unhealthy living habits
   B) does not have any physical handicaps
   C) is able to handle his daily routines
   D) is free from any kind of disease

65. According to the author, the true meaning of "wellness" is for people _____.
   A) to best satisfy their body's special needs
   B) to strive to maintain the best possible health
   C) to meet the strictest standards of bodily health
   D) to keep a proper balance between work and leisure

66. According to what the author advocates, which of the following groups of people would be

considered healthy?

A) People who have strong muscles as well as slim figures.

B) People who are not presently experiencing any symptoms of disease.

C) People who try to be as healthy as possible，regardless of their limitations.

D) People who can recover from illness even without seeking medical care.

【答案及解析】

57.［C］推断题。从文章内容来看，本文主要讲的是人们对瓶装水及普通自来水的看法。原文第一段告诉我们，Iceberg Water 现在成为市场新宠，而第三段又笔锋一转：But is plain tap water all that bad？难道普通自来水就真的那么糟糕吗？由以上分析可以推断，Iceberg Water 是某瓶装矿泉水品牌。

58.［B］推断题。题干问 Arthur von Wiesenberger 说"我家的狗也能把瓶装水与自来水区别开来"的用意是什么？从上文可知，他从小就在意大利、法国和瑞士等国家的大城市生活，而在这些地方，瓶装水十分流行。况且，作为一名"品水专家"，他对水的品质自然也是十分敏感的。由此可以推断，他认为瓶装水的水质比普通自来水要好得多。故选项 B 是正确的。

59.［D］推断题。原文第五段告诉我们，就餐者普遍偏爱名牌产品。而在饭店中，销售瓶装水所得的利润比酒要高出很多。不过，由于水比酒便宜，而且那些"fancier brands"又不能在商店中买到，因此就餐者一般不会太过在意价格。由此可知，选项 D 的说法是正确的。

60.［A］细节题。见上题分析。

61.［B］细节题。见文章最后一段：Regardless of how it's sold，the popularity of bottled water taps into our desire for better health，our wish to appear cultivated，and even a longing for lost purity. 可见瓶装水的流行也是人们认为它更有利于健康的一种表现。

62.［C］推断题。见原文首句：As we have seen，the focus of medical care in our society has been shifting from curing disease to preventing disease…故选项 C 是正确的。干扰项 B 不正确是因为今天的 medical care 不仅仅关注 patients。

63.［A］推断题。文章第一段提到一个人可能身体无大碍，自我感觉良好，但事实上他可以使自己更加健康。也就是说，健康不仅仅意味着"不生病"。

64.［D］细节题。见原文的叙述：The field of medicine has not traditionally distinguished between someone who is merely "not ill" and someone who is in excellent health and pays attention to the body's special needs. Both types have simply been called "well".

65.［B］细节题。原文有两处提到"wellness"，一是：In recent years，however，some health specialists have begun to apply the terms "well" and "wellness" only to those who are actively striving to maintain and improve their health. 二是："Wellness" may perhaps best be viewed not as a state that people can achieve，but as an ideal that people can strive for. 可见选项 B 正确。

66.［C］推断题。见原文：Even people who have a physical disease or handicap may be "well"，in this new sense，if they make an effort to maintain the best possible health they can in the face of their physical limitations. 可见本题正确答案为 C。

★ **2006 年 6 月考题**

Passage One

Questions 57 to 61 are based on the following passage:

Communications technologies are far from equal when it comes to conveying the truth. The first study to compare honesty across a range of communications has found that people are twice as likely as to tell lies in phone conversations as they are in emails. The fact that emails are automatically recorded—and can come back to haunt(困扰)you—appears to be the key to the finding.

Jeff Hancock of Cornell University in Ithaca, New York, asked 30 students to keep a communications diary for a week. In it they noted the number of conversations or email exchanges they had lasting more than 10 minutes, and confessed to how many lies they told. Hancock then worked out the number of lies per conversation for each medium. He found that lies made up 14 percent of emails, 21 percent of instant messages, 27 percent of face-to-face interactions and an astonishing 37 percent of phone calls.

His results to be presented at the conference on human-computer interaction in Vienna, Austria, in April, have surprised psychologists. Some expected emailers to be the biggest liars, reasoning that because deception makes people uncomfortable, the detachment(非直接接触)of emailing would make it easier to lie. Others expected people to lie more in face-to-face exchanges because we are most practised at that form of communication.

But Hancock says it is also crucial whether a conversation is being recorded and could be reread, and whether it occurs in real time. People appear to be afraid to lie when they know the communication could later be used to hold them to account, he says. This is why fewer lies appear in email than on the phone.

People are also more likely to lie in real time in an instant message or phone call than if they have time to think of a response, says Hancock. He found many lies are spontaneous(脱口而出的)responses to an unexpected demand, such as: "Do you like my dress?"

Hankcock hopes his research will help companies work out the best ways for their employees to communicate. For instance, the phone might be the best medium for sales where employees are encouraged to stretch the truth. But, given his result, work assessment where honesty is a priority, might be best done using email.

57. Hancock's study focuses on _____.

    A) the consequences of lying in various communications media

    B) the success of communications technologies in conveying ideas

    C) people are less likely to lie in instant messages

    D) people's honesty levels across a range of communications media

58. Hancock's research finding surprised those who believed that _____.

    A) people are less likely to lie in instant messages

    B) people are unlikely to lie in face-to-face interactions

C) people are most likely to lie in email communication

D) People are twice as likely to lie in phone conversations

59. According to the passage, why are people more likely to tell the truth through certain media of communication?

A) They are afraid of leaving behind traces of their lies

B) They believe that honesty is the best policy

C) They tend to be relaxed when using those media

D) They are most practiced at those forms of communication

60. According to Hancock, the telephone is a preferable medium for promoting sales because _____.

A) salesmen can talk directly to their customers

B) salesmen may feel less restrained to exaggerate

C) salesmen can impress customers as being trustworthy

D) salesmen may pass on instant messages effectively

61. It can be inferred from the passage that _____.

A) honesty should be encouraged in interpersonal communications

B) more employers will use emails to communicate with their employees

C) suitable media should be chosen for different communication purposes

D) email is now the dominant medium of communication within a company

Passage Two

Questions 62 to 66 are based on the following passage:

In a country that defines itself by ideals, not by shared blood, who should be allowed to come, work and live here? In the wake of the Sept. 11 attacks, these questions have never seemed more pressing.

On Dec. 11, 2001, as part of the effort to increase homeland security, federal and local authorities in 14 states staged "Operation Safe Travel" —raids on airports to arrest employees with false identification(身份证明). In Salt Lake City there were 69 arrests. But those captured were anything but terrorists, most of them illegal immigrants from central or South America. Authorities said the undocumented workers' illegal status made them open to blackmail(讹诈) by terrorists. Many immigrants in Salt Lake City were angered by the arrests and said they felt as if they were being treated like disposable goods.

Mayor Anderson said those feelings were justified to a certain extent. "We're saying we want you to work in these places, we're going to look the other way in terms of what our laws are, and then when it's convenient for us, or when we can try to make a point in terms of national security, especially after Sept. 11, then you're disposable. There are whole families being uprooted for all of the wrong reasons," Anderson said.

If Sept. 11 had never happened, the airport workers would not have been arrested and could have gone on quietly living in America, probably indefinitely. Ana Castro, a manager at a Ben & Jerry's ice cream shop at the airport, had been working 10 years with the same false Social Security card when she was arrested in the December airport raid. Now she and her family are living under the threat of deportation(驱逐出境). Castro's case is currently waiting to be settled. While she awaits the outcome, the government has granted her permission to work here and she has returned to her job at Ben & Jerry's.

62. According to the author, the United States claims to be a nation _____.
   A) composed of people having different values
   B) encouraging individual pursuits
   C) sharing common interests
   D) founded on shared ideals

63. How did the immigrants in Salt Lake City feel about "Operation Safe Travel"?
   A) Guilty.
   B) Offended.
   C) Disappointed.
   D) Discouraged.

64. Undocumented workers became the target of "Operation Safe Travel" because _____.
   A) evidence was found that they were potential terrorists
   B) most of them worked at airports under threat of terrorists
   C) terrorists might take advantage of their illegal status
   D) they were reportedly helping hide terrorists around the airport

65. By saying ". . . we're going to look the other way in terms of what our laws are" (Lines 2— 3, Para. 3), Mayor Anderson means "_____".
   A) we will turn a blind eye to your illegal status
   B) we will examine the laws in a different way
   C) there are other ways of enforcing the law
   D) the existing laws must not be ignored

66. What do we learn about Ana Castro from the last paragraph?
   A) She will be deported sooner or later.
   B) She is allowed to stay permanently.
   C) Her case has been dropped.
   D) Her fate remains uncertain.

【答案及解析】

57. [D] 细节题。从原文第一、二段可以看出,Hancock 研究的是人们在通过不同的媒介进行交流的时候的诚实程度。因此 D 是正确的。

58. ［C］推断题。文章第三段说,Hancock 的发现令很多心理学家感到惊讶。因为他们中有的人认为人们通过电子邮件等非直接接触的方式交流的时候更容易撒谎,也有人认为人们在面对面交流时更善于掩饰自己。可见 C 是正确的。

59. ［A］细节题。由文章倒数第二、三段可知,人们之所以不敢在以电子邮件等方式沟通时说假话是因为这类方式不像电话交流那样是实时的、转瞬即逝的。

60. ［B］细节题。文章最后一段的 stretch the truth 与选项 B 中的 exaggerate 相吻合。

61. ［C］推断题。文章最后一段提到,由于电话沟通是转瞬即逝的,所以这种方式特别适合于销售等工作,因为即使推销员夸大其词,事后也很难追究;而在需要说真话的工作中,最好采用电子邮件等方式。由此可知选项 C 是正确的。

62. ［D］推断题。文章第一句就说:In a country that defines itself by ideals, not by shared blood, who should be allowed to come, work and live here? 注意句中的 by ideals 后的 not by shared blood。分析该句结构可知,作者认为美国是 a country that defines itself by shared ideals。故本题正确答案是 D。

63. ［B］细节题。见原文第二段最后一句:Many immigrants in Salt Lake City were angered by the arrests and said they felt as if they were being treated like disposable goods. 文中的 angered 与选项 B 中的 offended 相一致。

64. ［C］细节题。答题依据见原文第二段倒数第二句。

65. ［A］推断题。注意题干中 look the other way 的意思是"故意朝另一边看",也就是"睁一只眼闭一只眼",这与 A 中的 turn a blind eye to(熟视无睹)的意思是相符的。Anderson 想说的是如果不是发生了"9·11"这样的事件,美国相关部门可能会对一些非法移民"睁一只眼闭一只眼"。

66. ［D］推断题。见文章最后一句:While she awaits the outcome, the government has granted her permission to work here and she has returned to her job at Ben & Jerry's. 也就是说,在处理结果出来前,她仍然可以在原来的岗位上工作。但是最终是否会被驱逐出境则还不确定。因此正确答案是 D。

★ **2005 年 12 月考题**

Passage One

Questions 21 to 25 are based on the following passage:

Just five one-hundredths of an inch thick, light golden in color and with a perfect "saddle curl", the Lay's potato chip seems an unlikely weapon for global domination. But its maker, Frito-Lay, thinks otherwise. "Potato chips are a snack food for the world," said Salman Amin, the company's head of global marketing. Amin believes there is no corner of the world that can resist the charms of a Frito-Lay potato chip.

Frito-Lay is the biggest snack maker in America, owned by Pepsi Co., and accounts for over half of the parent company's $3 billion annual profits. But the U.S. snack food market is largely saturated, and to grow, the company has to look overseas.

Its strategy rests on two beliefs: first a global product offers economies of scale with which local brands cannot compete. And second, consumers in the 21st century are drawn to "global" as a concept. "Global" does not mean products that are consciously identified as American, but ones that consumers—especially young people—see as part of a modern, innovative(创新的) world in which people are linked across cultures by shared beliefs and tastes. Potato chips are an American invention, but most Chinese, for instance, do not know that Frito-Lay is an American company. Instead, Riskey, the company's research and development head, would hope they associate the brand with the new world of global communications and business.

With brand perception a crucial factor, Riskey ordered a redesign of the Frito-Lay logo(标志). The logo, along with the company's long-held marketing image of the "irresistibility" of its chips, would help facilitate the company's global expansion.

The executives acknowledge that they try to swing national eating habits to a food created in America, but they deny that amounts to economic imperialism. Rather, they see Frito-Lay as spreading the benefits of free enterprise across the world. "We're making products in those countries, we're adapting them to the tastes of those countries, building businesses and employing people and changing lives," said Steve Reinemund, Pepsi Co.'s chief executive.

21. It is the belief of Frito-Lay's head of global marketing that _____.
    A) potato chips can hardly be used as a weapon to dominate the world market
    B) their company must find new ways to promote domestic sales
    C) the light golden color enhances the charm of their company's potato chips
    D) people the world over enjoy eating their company's potato chips

22. What do we learn about Frito-Lay from Paragraph 2?
    A) Its products used to be popular among overseas consumers.
    B) Its expansion has caused fierce competition in the snack market.
    C) It gives half of its annual profits to its parent company.
    D) It needs to turn to the world market for development.

23. One of the assumptions on which Frito-Lay bases its development strategy is that _____.
    A) consumers worldwide today are attracted by global brands
    B) local brands cannot compete successfully with American brands
    C) products suiting Chinese consumers' needs bring more profits
    D) products identified as American will have promising market value

24. Why did Riskey have the Frito-Lay logo redesigned?
    A) To suit changing tastes of young consumers.
    B) To promote the company's strategy of globalization.
    C) To change the company's long-held marketing image.
    D) To compete with other American chip producers.

25. Frito-Lay's executives claim that the promoting of American food in the international market _____.
    A) won't affect the eating habits of the local people

B) will lead to economic imperialism

C) will be in the interest of the local people

D) won't spoil the taste of their chips

Passage Two

Questions 26 to 30 are based on the following passage:

In communities north of Denver, residents are pitching in to help teachers and administrators as the Vrain school district tries to solve a $13.8 million budget shortage blamed on mismanagement. "We're worrying about our teachers and principals, and we really don't want to lose them because of this," one parent said. "If we can help ease their financial burden, we will."

Teachers are grateful, but know it may be years before the district is solvent(有综合能力的). They feel really good about the parent support, but they realize it's impossible for them to solve this problem.

The 22,000-student district discovered the shortage last month. "It's extraordinary. Nobody would have imagined something happening like this at this level," said State Treasurer Mike Coffman.

Coffman and district officials last week agreed on a state emergency plan freeing a $9.8 million loan that enabled the payroll(工资单)to be met for 2,700 teachers and staff in time for the holidays.

District officials also took $1.7 million from student-activity accounts of its 38 schools.

At Coffman's request, the District Attorney has begun investigating the district's finances. Coffman says he wants to know whether district officials hid the budget shortage until after the November election, when voters approved a $212 million bond issue for schools.

In Frederick, students' parents are buying classroom supplies and offering to pay for groceries and utilities to keep first-year teachers and principals in their jobs.

Some $36,000 has been raised in donations from Safeway. A Chevrolet dealership donated $10,000 and forgave the district's $10,750 bill for renting the driver educating cars. IBM contributed 4,500 packs of paper.

"We employ thousands of people in this community," said Mitch Carson, a hospital chief executive, who helped raise funds. "We have children in the school, and we see how they could be affected."

At Creek High School, three students started a website that displays newspaper articles, district information and an email forum(论坛). "Rumors about what's happening to the district are moving at lightning speed," said a student. "We wanted to know the truth, and spread that around instead."

26. What has happened to the Vrain School District?

A) A huge financial problem has arisen.

B) Many schools there are mismanaged.

C) Lots of teachers in the district are planning to quit.

D) Many administrative personnel have been laid off.

27. How did the residents in the Vrain School District respond to the budget shortage?
    A) They felt somewhat helpless about it.
    B) They accused those responsible for it.
    C) They pooled their efforts to help solve it.
    D) They demanded a thorough investigation.

28. In the view of State Treasurer Mike Coffman, the educational budget shortage is _____.
    A) unavoidable
    B) unthinkable
    C) insolvable
    D) irreversible

29. Why did Coffman request an investigation?
    A) To see if there was a deliberate cover-up of the problem.
    B) To find out the extent of the consequences of the case.
    C) To make sure that the school principals were innocent.
    D) To stop the voters approving the $212 million bond issue.

30. Three high school students started a website in order to _____.
    A) attract greater public attention to their needs
    B) appeal to the public for contributions and donations
    C) expose officials who neglected their duties
    D) keep people properly informed of the crisis

Passage Three

Questions 31 to 35 are based on the following passage:

"Humans should not try to avoid stress any more than they would shun food, love or exercise." said Dr. Hans Selye, the first physician to document the effects of stress on the body. While there's no question that continuous stress is harmful, several studies suggest that challenging situations in which you're able to rise to the occasion can be good for you.

In a 2001 study of 158 hospital nurses, those who faced considerable work demands but coped with the challenge were more likely to say they were in good health than those who felt they couldn't get their work done.

Stress that you can manage also boost immune(免疫的)function. In a study at the Academic Center for Dentistry in Amsterdam, researchers put volunteers through two stressful experiences. In the first, a timed task that required memorizing a list followed by a short test, subjects believed they had control over the outcome. In the second, they were't in control: they had to sit through a gory(血淋淋的)video on surgical procedures. Those who did well on the memory test had an increase in levels of immunoglobulin A, an antibody that's the body's first

line of defense against germs. The video-watchers experienced a downturn in the antibody.

Stress prompts the body to produce certain stress hormones. In short bursts these hormones have a positive effect, including improved memory function. "They can help nerve cells handle information and put it into storage," says Dr. Bruce McEwen of Rockefeller University in New York, "But in the long run these hormones can have a harmful effect on the body and brain."

"Sustained stress is not good for you," says Richard Morimoto, a researcher at Northwestern University in Illinois studying the effects of stress on longevity, "It's the occasional burst of stress or brief exposure to stress that could be protective."

31. The passage is mainly about _____.
   A) the benefits of manageable stress
   B) how to avoid stressful situations
   C) how to cope with stress effectively
   D) the effect of stress hormones on memory

32. The word "shun" (Line 1, Para. 1) most probably means _____.
   A) cut down on
   B) stay away from
   C) run out of
   D) put up with

33. We can conclude from the study of the 158 nurses in 2001 that _____.
   A) people under stress tend to have a poor memory
   B) people who can't get their job done experience more stress
   C) doing challenging work may be good for one's health
   D) stress will weaken the body's defense against germs

34. In the experiment described in Paragraph 3, the video-watchers experienced a downturn in the antibody because _____.
   A) the video was not enjoyable at all
   B) the outcome was beyond their control
   C) they knew little about surgical procedures
   D) they felt no pressure while watching the video

35. Dr. Bruce McEwen of Rockefeller University believes that _____.
   A) a person's memory is determined by the level of hormones in his body
   B) stress hormones have lasting positive effects on the brain
   C) short bursts of stress hormones enhance memory function
   D) a person's memory improves with continued experience of stress

Passage Four

Questions 36 to 40 are based on the following passage:

If you want to teach your children how to say sorry, you must be good at saying it yourself, especially to your own children. But how you say it can be quite tricky.

If you say to your children "I'm sorry I got angry with you, but. . . " what follows that "but" can render the apology ineffective: "I had a bad day" or "your noise was giving me a headache" leaves the person who has been injured feeling that he should be apologizing for his bad behavior in expecting an apology.

Another method by which people appear to apologize without actually doing so is to say "I'm sorry you're upset"; this suggests that you are somehow at fault for allowing yourself to get upset by what the other person has done.

Then there is the general, all-covering apology, which avoids the necessity of identifying a specific act that was particularly hurtful or insulting, and which the person who is apologizing should promise never to do again. Saying "I'm useless as a parent" does not commit a person to any specific improvement.

These pseudo-apologies are used by people who believe saying sorry shows weakness. Parents who wish to teach their children to apologize should see it as a sign of strength, and therefore not resort to these pseudo-apologies.

But even when presented with examples of genuine contrition, children still need help to become aware of the complexities of saying sorry. A three-year-old might need help in understanding that other children feel pain just as he does, and that hitting a playmate over the head with a heavy toy requires an apology. A six-year-old might need reminding that spoiling other children's expectations can require an apology. A 12-year-old might need to be shown that raiding the biscuit tin without asking permission is acceptable, but that borrowing a parent's clothes without permission is not.

36. If a mother adds "but" to an apology, _____.

    A) she doesn't feel that she should have apologized

    B) she does not realize that the child has been hurt

    C) the child may find the apology easier to accept

    D) the child may feel that he owes her an apology

37. According to the author, saying "I'm sorry you're upset" most probably means "_____".

    A) You have good reason to get upset

    B) I'm aware you're upset, but I'm not to blame

    C) I apologize for hurting your feelings

    D) I'm at fault for making you upset

38. It is not advisable to use the general, all-covering apology because _____.

    A) it gets one into the habit of making empty promises

    B) it may make the other person feel guilty

C) it is vague and ineffective

D) it is hurtful and insulting

39. We learn from the last paragraph that in teaching children to say sorry _____.

A) the complexities involved should be ignored

B) their ages should be taken into account

C) parents need to set them a good example

D) parents should be patient and tolerant

40. It can be inferred from the passage that apologizing properly is _____.

A) a social issue calling for immediate attention

B) not necessary among family members

C) a sign of social progress

D) not as simple as it seems

【答案及解析】

21. [D] 细节题。见原文第一段："Potato chips are a snack food for the world," said Salman Amin, the company's head of global marketing. Amin believes there is no corner of the world that can resist the charms of a Frito-Lay potato chip. 可见 Salman Amin 相信世界各地的人都会喜欢该公司的炸土豆片。

22. [D] 推断题。从文章第二段可以看出，虽然 Frito-Lay 在美国获利颇丰，但由于美国市场已经饱和，要继续发展就必须拓展海外市场。因此本题正确答案为 D。

23. [A] 细节题。原文第三段告诉我们，这种策略是基于两种观点：一是与地方品牌相比，国际品牌具有规模经济优势；二是现在越来越多的消费者开始被"国际品牌"这一概念所吸引。

24. [B] 推断题。联系上下文可知，Frito-Lay 公司重新设计公司标志显然是为其国际市场上的扩张服务的。

25. [C] 推断题。由文章最后一段可以看出，该公司认为他们拓展国际市场时会调整产品生产使其符合当地人的品味，而且，他们还会在各方面促进当地经济的发展。故选项 C 是正确的。

26. [A] 细节题。见原文首句。

27. [C] 细节题。题干问当地居民对这起事件的反应如何。从文中的叙述来看，他们都在尽其所能地协助解决这次危机。因此 C 是正确的。

28. [B] 细节题。从原文可知 Coffman 对此事件的表态是：It's extraordinary. Nobody would have imagined something happening like this at this level. 可见他认为这是不可思议的（unthinkable）。

29. [A] 细节题。见文章倒数第五段：Coffman says he wants to know whether district officials hid the budget shortage until after the November election, when voters approved a $212 million bond issue for schools. 文中的 hide 即 to cover up。故选 A。

30. [D] 细节题。由文章最后一段可知，他们建立网站的目的是为了让人们了解事情的真相。

31. [A] 主旨题。文章第一段末句点出了全文的主旨：While there's no question that continuous stress is harmful, several studies suggest that challenging situations in which you're able to

rise to the occasion can be good for you. 即本文的主要内容是可以应付的压力带来的好处。

32. [B] 词义题。原文是：Humans should not try to avoid stress any more than they would shun food, love or exercise. 从句中的 avoid 可以推断出 shun 也是"避免，逃避"的意思。因此选项 B stay away from 是正确的。

33. [C] 推断题。由原文第二段可知，对这些护士的研究表明，那些能够应付工作中的挑战的护士健康状况比那些在压力下不堪重负的护士要好。故本题正确答案为 C。

34. [B] 细节题。见原文第三段：In the second, they were't in control: they had to sit through a gory video on surgical procedures.

35. [C] 细节题。见原文倒数第二段：In short bursts these hormones have a positive effect, including improved memory function.

36. [D] 推断题。由文章第二段可以看出，类似的话会：... leaves the person who has been injured feeling that he should be apologizing for his bad behavior in expecting an apology. 也就是说，似乎首先该道歉的是对方。故选项 D 是正确的。

37. [B] 细节题。见原文第三段：... this suggests that you are somehow at fault for allowing yourself to get upset by what the other person has done.

38. [C] 推断题。从文章第四段可知，这种"万能的"、无所不包的道歉方式其实是含糊的、无效的。

39. [B] 推断题。文章最后一段在建议家长如何教导孩子学会道歉时举了几个例子，这些例子中的孩子属于不同的年龄段。由此可见选项 B 是正确的。

40. [D] 主旨题。文章先析了人们道歉的常用语，指出这些话其实不能真正起到作用。文章的后半部分又指出：But even when presented with examples of genuine contrition, children still need help to become aware of the complexities of saying sorry. 从而可以推知要学会恰当地道歉其实没有人们所认为的那么简单。

★ 2005 年 6 月考题

Passage One

Questions 21 to 25 are based on the following passage：

Is there enough oil beneath the Arctic National Wildlife Refuge(保护区)(ANWR) to help secure America's energy future? President Bush certainly thinks so. He has argued that tapping ANWR's oil would help ease California's electricity crisis and provide a major boost to the country's energy independence. But no one knows for sure how much crude oil lies buried beneath the frozen earth with the last government survey, conducted in 1998, projecting output anywhere from 3 billion to 16 billion barrels.

The oil industry goes with the high end of the range, which could equal as much as 10% of U.S. consumption for as long as six years. By pumping more than 1 million barrels a day from the reserve for the next two to three decades, lobbyists claim, the nation could cut back on imports equivalent to all shipments to the U.S. from Saudi Arabia. Sounds good. An oil boom would also mean a multibillion-dollar windfall(意外之财)in tax revenues, royalties(开采权使用费)and leasing fees for Alaska and the Federal Government. Best of all, advocates of drilling say, damage to the environment would be insignificant. "We've never had a document case of oil rig chasing deer out onto the pack ice." says Alaska State Representative Scott Ogan.

Not so fast, say environmentalists. Sticking to the low end of government estimates, the National Resources Defense Council says there may be no more than 3. 2 billion barrels of economically recoverable oil in the coastal plain of ANWR, a drop in the bucket that would do virtually nothing to ease America's energy problems. And consumers would wait up to a decade to gain any benefits, because drilling could begin only after much bargaining over leases, environmental permits and regulatory review. As for ANWR's impact on the California power crisis, environmentalists point out that oil is responsible for only 1% of the Golden State's electricity output—and just 3% of the nation's.

21. What does President Bush think of tapping oil in ANWR?
    A) It will exhaust the nation's oil reserves.
    B) It will help secure the future of ANWR.
    C) It will help reduce the nation's oil imports.
    D) It will increase America's energy consumption.

22. We learn from the second paragraph that the American oil industry _____.
    A) believes that drilling for oil in ANWR will produce high yields
    B) tends to exaggerate America's reliance on foreign oil
    C) shows little interest in tapping oil in ANWR
    D) expects to stop oil imports from Saudi Arabia

23. Those against oil drilling in ANWR argue that _____.
    A) it can cause serious damage to the environment
    B) it can do little to solve U.S. energy problems
    C) it will drain the oil reserves in the Alaskan region
    D) it will not have much commercial value

24. What do the environmentalists mean by saying "Not so fast" (Line 1, Para. 3)?
    A) Oil exploitation takes a long time.
    B) The oil drilling should be delayed.
    C) Don't be too optimistic.
    D) Don't expect fast returns.

25. It can be learned from the passage that oil exploitation beneath ANWR's frozen earth

    _____.
    A) remains a controversial issue
    B) is expected to get under way soon
    C) involves a lot of technological problems
    D) will enable the U.S. to be oil independent

Passage Two

Questions 26 to 30 are based on the following passage:

"Tear 'em apart!" "Kill the fool!" " Murder the referee(裁判)!"

These are common remarks one may hear at various sporting events. At the time they are made, they may seem innocent enough. But let's not kid ourselves. They have been known to influence behavior in such a way as to lead to real bloodshed. Volumes have been written about the way words affect us. It has been shown that words having certain connotations(含义)may cause us to react in ways quite foreign to what we consider to be our usual humanistic behavior. I see the term "opponent" as one of those words. Perhaps the time has come to delete it from sports terms.

The dictionary meaning of the term "opponent" is "adversary"; "enemy"; "one who opposes your interests". Thus, when a player meets an opponent, he or she may tend to treat that opponent as an enemy. At such times, winning may dominate one's intellect, and every action, no matter how gross, may be considered justifiable. I recall an incident in a handball game when a referee refused a player's request for a time out for a glove change because he did not consider them wet enough. The player proceeded to rub his gloves across his wet T-shirt and then exclaimed. "Are they wet enough now?"

In the heat of battle, players have been observed to throw themselves across the court without considering the consequences that such a move might have on anyone in their way. I have also witnessed a player reacting to his opponent's intended and illegal blocking by deliberately hitting him with the ball as hard as he could during the course of play. Off the court, they are good friends. Does that make any sense? It certainly gives proof of a court attitude which departs from normal behavior.

Therefore, I believe it is time we elevated(提升)the game to the level where it belongs thereby setting an example to the rest of the sporting world. Replacing the term "opponent" with "associate" could be an ideal way to start.

The dictionary meaning of the term "associate" is "colleague"; "friend"; "companion". Reflect a moment! You may soon see and possibly feel the difference in your reaction to the term "associate" rather than "opponent".

26. Which of the following statements best expresses the author's view?

    A) Aggressive behavior in sports can have serious consequences.

    B) The words people use can influence their behavior.

    C) Unpleasant words in sports are often used by foreign athletes.

    D) Unfair judgments by referees will lead to violence on the sports field.

27. Harsh words are spoken during games because the players _____.

    A) are too eager to win

    B) are usually short-tempered and easily offended

    C) cannot afford to be polite in fierce competition

    D) treat their rivals as enemies

28. What did the handball player do when he was not allowed a time out to change his gloves?

    A) He refused to continue the game.

    B) He angrily hit the referee with a ball.

    C) He claimed that the referee was unfair.

    D) He wet his gloves by rubbing them across his T-shirt.

29. According to the passage, players, in a game, may _____.

    A) deliberately throw the ball at anyone illegally blocking their way

    B) keep on screaming and shouting throughout the game

    C) lie down on the ground as an act of protest

    D) kick the ball across the court with force

30. The author hopes to have the current situation in sports improved by _____.

    A) calling on players to use clean language on the court

    B) raising the referee's sense of responsibility

    C) changing the attitude of players on the sports field

    D) regulating the relationship between players and referees

Passage Three

Questions 31 to 35 are based on the following passage:

Consumers are being confused and misled by the hodge-podge(大杂烩) of environmental claims made by household products, according to a "green labeling" study published by *Consumers International Friday*.

Among the report's more outrageous(令人无法容忍的)findings—a German fertilizer described itself as "earthworm friendly", a brand of flour said it was "non-polluting" and a British toilet paper claimed to be "environmentally friendlier".

The study was written and researched by Britain's National Consumer Council (NCC) for lobby group Consumer International. It was funded by the German and Dutch governments and the European Commission.

"While many good and useful claims are being made, it is clear there is a long way to go in ensuring shoppers are adequately informed about the environmental impact of products they buy," said Consumers International director Anna Fielder.

The 10-country study surveyed product packaging in Britain, Western Europe, Scandinavia and the United States. It found that products sold in Germany and the United Kingdom made the most environmental claims on average.

The report focused on claims made by specific products, such as detergent(洗涤剂), insect sprays and by some garden products. It did not test the claims, but compared them to labeling guidelines set by the International Standards Organization (ISO) in September, 1999.

Researchers documented claims of environmental friendliness made by about 2,000 products and found many too vague or too misleading to meet ISO standards.

"Many products had specially-designed labels to make them seem environmentally friendly, but in fact many of these symbols mean nothing," said report researcher Philip Page.

"Laundry detergents made the most number of claims with 158. Household cleaners were second with 145 separate claims, while paints were third on our list with 73. The high numbers show how very confusing it must be for consumers to sort the true from the misleading." he said.

The ISO labeling standards ban vague or misleading claims on product packaging, because terms such as "environmentally friendly" and "non-polluting" cannot be verified. "What we are now pushing for is to have multinational corporations meet the standards set by the ISO," said Page.

31. According to the passage, the NCC found it outrageous that _____.
   A) all the products surveyed claim to meet ISO standards
   B) the claims made by products are often unclear or deceiving
   C) consumers would believe many of the manufacturers' claim
   D) few products actually prove to be environment friendly

32. As indicated in this passage, with so many good claims, the consumers _____.
   A) are becoming more cautious about the products they are going to buy
   B) are still not willing to pay more for products with green labeling
   C) are becoming more aware of the effects different products have on the environment
   D) still do not know the exact impact of different products on the environment

33. A study was carried out by Britain's NCC to _____.
   A) find out how many claims made by products fail to meet environmental standards
   B) inform the consumers of the environmental impact of the products they buy
   C) examine claims made by products against ISO standards
   D) revise the guidelines set by the International Standards Organization

34. What is one of the consequences caused by the many claims of household products?
   A) They are likely to lead to serious environmental problems.
   B) Consumers find it difficult to tell the true from the false.
   C) They could arouse widespread anger among consumer.
   D) Consumers will be tempted to buy products they don't need.

35. It can be inferred from the passage that the lobby group Consumer International wants to

   _____.
   A) make product labeling satisfy ISO requirements
   B) see all household products meet environmental standards
   C) warn consumers of the danger of so-called green products
   D) verify the efforts of non-polluting products

Passage Four

Questions 36 to 40 are based on the following passage:

Two hours from the tall buildings of Manhattan and Philadelphia live some of the world's largest black bears. They are in northern Pennsylvania's Pocono Mountains, a home they share with an abundance of other wildlife.

The streams, lakes, meadows(草地), mountain ridges and forests that make the Poconos an ideal place for black bears have also attracted more people to the region. Open spaces are threatened by plans for housing estates and important habitats(栖息地) are endangered by highway construction. To protect the Poconos' natural beauty from irresponsible development, the Nature Conservancy(大自然保护协会) named the area one of America's "Last Great Places".

Operating out of a century-old schoolhouse in the village of Long Pond, Pennsylvania, the conservancy's Bud Cook is working with local people and business leaders to balance economic growth with environmental protection. By forging partnerships with people like Francis Altemose, the Conservancy has been able to protect more than 14,000 acres of environmentally important land in the area.

Altemose's family has farmed in the Pocono area for generations. Two years ago Francis worked with the Conservancy to include his farm in a county farmland protection program. As a result, his family's land can be protected from development and the Altemoses will be better able to provide a secure financial future for their 7-year-old grandson.

Cook attributes the Conservancy's success in the Poconos to having a local presence and a commitment to working with local residents.

"The key to protecting these remarkable lands is connecting with the local community," Cook said. "The people who live there respect the land. They value quiet forests, clear streams and abundant wildlife. They are eager to help with conservation effort."

For more information on how you can help The Nature Conservancy protect the Poconos and the world's other "Last Great Places", please call 1-888-564 6864, or visit us on the World Wide Web at www. tnc. org.

36. The purpose in naming the Poconos as one of America's "Last Great Places" is to _____.
   A) gain support from the local community
   B) protect it from irresponsible development
   C) make it a better home for black bears
   D) provide financial security for future generations

37. We can learn from the passage that _____.
   A) the population in the Pocono area is growing
   B) wildlife in the Pocono area is dying out rapidly
   C) the security of the Pocono residents is being threatened
   D) farmlands in the Pocono area are shrinking fast

38. What is important in protecting the Poconos according to Cook?

    A) The setting up of an environmental protection website.

    B) Support from organizations like The Nature Conservancy.

    C) Cooperation with the local residents and business leaders.

    D) Inclusion of farmlands in the region's protection program.

39. What does Bud Cook mean by "having a local presence" (Line 1, Para. 5)?

    A) Financial contributions from local business leaders.

    B) Consideration of the interests of the local residents.

    C) The establishment of a wildlife protection foundation in the area.

    D) The setting up of a local Nature Conservancy branch in the Pocono area.

40. The passage most probably is _____.

    A) an official document

    B) a news story

    C) an advertisement

    D) a research report

【答案及解析】

21. [C] 细节题。根据文章第一段：He has argued that tapping ANWR's oil would help ease California's electricity crisis and provide a major boost to the country's energy independence. 可知布什总统认为对该地区的石油开采能使美国减轻对外国的能源依赖。故本题选 C。

22. [A] 推断题。由文章第二段第一、二句可知 A 正确。

23. [B] 推断题。见第三段第二句。

24. [C] 推断题。上文列举了石油开采的种种好处,该句下文则是反对者的观点。据此不难推断"Not so fast"的意思是"不要过于乐观"。故本题正确答案为 C。

25. [A] 推断题。由上述分析可知人们对在北极圈野生动物保护区开采石油这一问题还没有达成一致意见。因此选项 A 是正确的。

26. [B] 态度题。见原文第二段：They have been known to influence behavior in such a way as to lead to real bloodshed. 以及 It has been shown that words having certain connotations may cause us to react in ways quite foreign to what we consider to be our usual humanistic behavior.

27. [D] 细节题。见原文第三段：Thus, when a player meets an opponent, he or she may tend to treat that opponent as an enemy. 选项 D 的说法与文意相符。

28. [D] 细节题。选项 D 的表述与文中 rub his gloves across his wet T-shirt 的表述相符,故为正确选项。

29. [A] 细节题。见原文第四段：I have also witnessed a player reacting to his opponent's intended and illegal blocking by deliberately hitting him with the ball as hard as he could during the course of play.

30. [C] 推断题。作者列举了在运动场上的种种不文明行为,并提出了自己的看法和建议。作者说要把"opponent"改为"associate",事实上就是说要改变运动员在运动场上的态度。故本题正确答案为C。

31.[B] 推断题。见文章第二、四段。

32.[D] 细节题。见原文第四段:While many good and useful claims are being made,it is clear there is a long way to go in ensuring shoppers are adequately informed about the environmental impact of products they buy.

33.[A] 细节题。见原文第六段:It did not test the claims,but compared them to labeling guidelines set by the International Standards Organization(ISO)in September,1999.

34.[B] 细节题。见原文倒数第二段:The high numbers show how very confusing it must be for consumers to sort the true from the misleading.

35.[A] 细节题。见原文最后一段末句。

36.[B] 细节题。见原文第二段最后一句。

37.[A] 细节题。依据见原文第二段首句:The streams,lakes,meadows,mountain ridges and forests that make the Poconos an ideal place for black bears have also attracted more people to the region.

38.[C] 推断题。见文章第三段:Operating out of a century-old schoolhouse in the village of Long Pond,Pennsylvania,the conservancy's Bud Cook is working with local people and business leaders to balance economic growth with environmental protection. 可见在Cook看来,与当地居民和商界人士的合作是很重要的。

39.[B] 由第六段Cook所说的话可以推断"having a local presence"的意思是要考虑当地居民的利益,因此本题正确答案为B。

40.[D] 推断题。从本文的叙述方式及最后一段来看,本文很可能是一份研究报告,而不是一份官方文件或一则广告,更不会是一则新闻故事。故本题正确答案为D。

★2005年1月考题

Passage One

Questions 11 to 15 are based on the following passage:

Scratchy throats, stuffy noses and body aches all spell misery, but being able to tell if the cause is a cold or flu(流感)may make a difference in how long the misery lasts.

The American Lung Association(ALA)has issued new guidelines on combating colds and the flu, and one of the keys is being able to quickly tell the two apart. That's because the prescription drugs available for the flu need to be taken soon after the illness sets in. As for colds, the sooner a person starts taking over-the-counter remedy, the sooner relief will come.

The common cold and the flu are both caused by viruses. More than 200 viruses can cause cold symptoms, while the flu is caused by three viruses—flu A, B and C. There is no care for either illness, but the flu can be prevented by the flu vaccine(疫苗), which is, for most people, the best way to fight the flu, according to the ALA.

But if the flu does strike, quick action can help. Although the flu and common cold have many similarities, there are some obvious signs to look for.

Cold symptoms such as stuffy nose, runny nose and scratchy throat typically develop gradually, and adults and teens often do not get a fever. On the other hand, fever is one of the characteristic features of the flu for all ages. And in general, flu symptoms including fever and chills, sore throat and body aches come, hit suddenly and are more severe than cold symptoms.

The ALA notes that it may be particularly difficult to tell when infants and preschool age children have the flu. It advises parents to call the doctor if their small children have flu-like symptoms.

Both cold and flu symptoms can be eased with over-the-counter medications as well. However, children and teens with a cold or flu should not take aspirin for pain relief because of the risk of Reye syndrome(综合征), a rare but serious condition of the liver and central nervous system.

There is, of course, no vaccine for the common cold. But frequent hand washing and avoiding close contact with people who have colds can reduce the likelihood of catching one.

11. According to the author, knowing the cause of the misery will help _____.
    A) shorten the duration of the illness
    B) the patient buy medicine over the counter
    C) the patient obtain cheaper prescription drugs
    D) prevent the people from catching colds and the flu

12. We can learn from the passage that _____.
    A) one doesn't need to take any medicine if he has a cold or the flu
    B) aspirin should not be included in over-the-counter medicines for the flu
    C) delayed treatment of the flu will harm the liver and central nervous system
    D) over-the-counter drugs can be taken to ease the misery caused by a cold or the flu

13. According to the passage, to combat the flu effectively, one should _____.
    A) identify the virus which causes it
    B) consult a doctor as soon as possible
    C) take medicine upon catching the disease
    D) remain alert when the disease is spreading

14. Which of the following symptoms will distinguish the flu from a cold?
    A) A stuffy nose.   B) A high temperature.
    C) A sore throat.   D) A dry cough.

15. If children have flu-like symptoms, their parents _____.
    A) are advised not to give them aspirin
    B) should watch out for signs of Reye syndrome
    C) are encourage to take them to hospital for vaccination
    D) should prevent them from mixing with people running a fever

Passage Two

Questions 16 to 20 are based on the following passage:

In a time of low academic achievement by children in the United States, many Americans are turning to Japan, a country of high academic achievement and economic success, for possible answers. However, the answers provided by Japanese preschools are not the ones Americans expected to find. In most Japanese preschools, surprisingly little emphasis is put on academic instruction. In one investigation, 300 Japanese and 210 American preschool teachers, child development specialists, and parents were asked about various aspects of early childhood education. Only 2 percent of the Japanese respondents(答问卷者)listed "to give children a good start academically" as one of their top three reasons for a society to have preschools. In contrast, over half the American respondents chose this as one of their top three choices. To prepare children for successful careers in first grade and beyond, Japanese schools do not teach reading, writing, and mathematics, but rather skills such as persistence, concentration, and the ability to function as a member of a group. The vast majority of young Japanese children are taught to read at home by their parents.

In recent comparison of Japanese and American preschool education, 91 percent of Japanese respondents chose providing children with a group experience as one of their top three reasons for a society to have preschools. Sixty-two percent of the more individually oriented(强调个体发展的)Americans listed group experience as one of their top three reasons. An emphasis on the importance of the group seen in Japanese early childhood education continues into elementary school education.

Like in America, there is diversity in Japanese early childhood education. Some Japanese kindergartens have specific aims, such as early musical training or potential development. In large cities, some kindergartens are attached to universities that have elementary and secondary schools. Some Japanese parents believe that if their young children attend a university-based program, it will increase the children's chances of eventually being admitted to top-rated schools and universities. Several more progressive programs have introduced free play as a way out for the heavy intellectualizing in some Japanese kindergartens.

16. We can learn from the first paragraph that many Americans believe _____.
   A) Japanese parents are more involved in preschool education than American parents
   B) Japan's economic success is a result of its scientific achievements
   C) Japanese preschool education emphasizes academic instruction
   D) Japan's higher education in superior to theirs

17. Most Americans surveyed believe that preschools should also attach importance to _____.
   A) problem solving   B) group experience
   C) parental guidance   D) individually-oriented development

18. In Japan's preschool education, the focus is on _____.
   A) preparing children academically

B) developing children's artistic interests

C) tapping children's potential

D) shaping children's character

19. Free play has been introduced in some Japanese kindergartens in order to _____.

A) broaden children's horizon   B) cultivate children's creativity

C) lighten children's study load   D) enrich children's knowledge

20. Why do some Japanese parents send their children to university-based kindergartens?

A) They can do better in their future studies.

B) They can accumulate more group experience there.

C) They can be individually oriented when they grow up.

D) They can have better chances of getting a first-rate education.

Passage Three

Questions 21 to 25 are based on the following passage:

Lead deposits, which accumulated in soil and snow during the 1960's and 70's, were primarily the result of leaded gasoline emissions originating in the United States. In the twenty years that the Clean Air Act has mandated unleaded gas use in the United States, the lead accumulation worldwide has decreased significantly.

A study published recently in the journal Nature shows that air-borne leaded gas emissions from the United States were the leading contributor to the high concentration of lead in the snow in Greenland. The new study is a result of the continued research led by Dr. Charles Boutron, an expert on the impact of heavy metals on the environment at the National Center for Scientific Research in France. A study by Dr. Boutron published in 1991 showed that lead levels in arctic (北极的)snow were declining.

In his new study, Dr. Boutron found the ratios of the different forms of lead in the leaded gasoline used in the United States were different from the ratios of European, Asian and Canadian gasolines and thus enabled scientists to differentiate(区分)the lead sources. The dominant lead ratio found in Greenland snow matched that found in gasoline from the United States.

In a study published in the journal Ambio, scientists found that lead levels in soil in the Northeastern United States had decreased markedly since the introduction of unleaded gasoline.

Many scientists had believed that the lead would stay in soil and snow for a longer period.

The authors of the Ambio study examined samples of the upper layers of soil taken from the same sites of 20 forest floors in New England, New York and Pennsylvania in 1980 and in 1990. The forest environment processed and redistributed the lead faster than the scientists had expected.

Scientists say both studies demonstrate that certain parts of the ecosystem(生态系统) respond rapidly to reductions in atmospheric pollution, but that these findings should not be used as a license to pollute.

21. The study published in the journal Nature indicated that _____.

    A) the Clean Air Act has not produced the desired results

    B) lead deposits in arctic snow are on the increase

    C) lead will stay in soil and snow longer than expected

    D) the US is the major source of lead pollution in arctic snow

22. Lead accumulation worldwide decreased significantly after the use of unleaded gas in the US

    _____.

    A) was discouraged   B) was enforced by law

    C) was prohibited by law   D) was introduced

23. How did scientists discover the source of lead pollution in Greenland?

    A) By analyzing the data published in journals like Nature and Ambio.

    B) By observing the lead accumulations in different parts of the arctic area.

    C) By studying the chemical elements of soil and snow in Northeastern America.

    D) By comparing the chemical compositions of leaded gasoline used in various countries.

24. The authors of the Ambio study have found that _____.

    A) forests get rid of lead pollution faster than expected

    B) lead accumulations in forests are more difficult to deal with

    C) lead deposits are widely distributed in the forests of the US

    D) the upper layers of soil in forests are easily polluted by lead emissions

25. It can be inferred from last paragraph that scientists _____.

    A) are puzzled by the mystery of forest pollution

    B) feel relieved by the use of unleaded gasoline

    C) still consider lead pollution a problem

    D) lack sufficient means to combat bad pollution

Passage Four

Questions 26 to 30 are based on the following passage:

    Exercise is one of the few factors with a positive role in long-term maintenance of body weight. Unfortunately, that message has not gotten through to the average American, who would rather try switching to "light" beer and low-calorie bread than increase physical exertion. The Centers for Disease Control, for example, found that fewer than one-fourth of overweight adults who were trying to shed pounds said they were combining exercise with their diet.

    In rejecting exercise, some people may be discouraged too much by caloric-expenditure charts; for example, one would have to briskly walk three miles just to work off 275 calories in one delicious Danish pastry(小甜饼). Even exercise professionals concede half a point here. "Exercise by itself is a very tough way to lose weight," says York Onnen, program director of the President's Council on Physical Fitness and Sports.

Still, exercise's supporting role in weight reduction is vital. A study at the Boston University Medical Center of overweight police officers and other public employees confirmed that those who dieted without exercise regained almost all their old weight, while those who worked exercise into their daily routine maintained their new weight.

If you have been sedentary(极少活动的) and decide to start walking one mile a day, the added exercise could burn an extra 100 calories daily. In a year's time, assuming no increase in food intake, you could lose ten pounds. By increasing the distance of your walks gradually and making other dietary adjustments, you may lose even more weight.

26. What is said about the average American in the passage?
    A) They tend to exaggerate the healthful effect of "light" beer.
    B) They usually ignore the effect of exercise on losing weight.
    C) They prefer "light" beer and low-calorie bread to other drinks and food.
    D) They know the factors that play a positive role in keeping down body weight.

27. Some people dislike exercise because they _____.
    A) think it is physically exhausting
    B) find it hard to exercise while on a diet
    C) don't think it possible to walk 3 miles every day
    D) find consulting caloric-expenditure charts troublesome

28. "Even exercise professionals concede half a point here" (Line 3, Para. 2) means "They _____."
    A) agree that the calories in a small piece of pastry can be difficult to work off by exercise
    B) partially believe diet plays a supporting role in weight reduction
    C) are not fully convinced that dieting can help maintain one's new weight
    D) are not sufficiently informed of the positive role of exercise in losing weight

29. What was confirmed by the Boston University Medical Center's study?
    A) Controlling one's calorie intake is more important than doing exercise.
    B) Even occasional exercise can help reduce weight.
    C) Weight reduction is impossible without exercise.
    D) One could lose ten pounds in a year's time if there's no increase in food intake.

30. What is the author's purpose in writing this article? To _____.
    A) justify the study of the Boston University Medical Center
    B) stress the importance of maintaining proper weight
    C) support the statement made by York Onnen
    D) show the most effective way to lost weight

【答案及解析】

11. [A] 细节题。见原文第一段及第二段末句。

12. [D] 细节题。文章第七段提到：Both cold and flu symptoms can be eased with over-the-counter medications as well. 可见感冒和流感的症状都可以通过服用非处方药来缓解。

13. [C] 细节题。见文章第二段：That's because the prescription drugs available for the flu need to be taken soon after the illness sets in.

14. [B] 细节题。答案见原文第五段。

15. [A] 细节题。文章倒数第二段说：However, children and teens with a cold or flu should not take aspirin for pain relief because of the risk of Reye syndrome, a rare but serious condition of the liver and central nervous system. 可见当孩子有流感症状的时候，父母不要让其用阿司匹林来缓解。因此 A 是正确的。

16. [C] 细节题。由原文开头部分的叙述可知，很多美国人认为日本的学前教育对孩子的学术能力培养十分重视。故本题选 C。

17. [B] 细节题。由原文：Sixty-two percent of the more individually oriented(强调个体发展的) Americans listed group experience as one of their top three reasons. 可以看出，虽然其重视程度不如日本家长，但美国家长还是很看重孩子们成长中的团队经验。选项 B 符合文意。

18. [D] 推断题。见原文第一段后半部分的叙述：To prepare children for successful careers in first grade and beyond, Japanese schools do not teach reading, writing, and mathematics, but rather skills such as persistence, concentration, and the ability to function as a member of a group. 可见日本的学前教育注重孩子们性格品质的培养。

19. [C] 细节题。由文章末句：Several more progressive programs have introduced free play as a way out for the heavy intellectualizing in some Japanese kindergartens. 可以看出 free play 的引入是为了减轻孩子们的学业负担。

20. [D] 细节题。见文章倒数第二句：Some Japanese parents believe that if their young children attend a university-based program, it will increase the children's chances of eventually being admitted to top-rated schools and universities.

21. [D] 细节题。见原文第二段首句：A study published recently in the journal Nature shows that air-borne leaded gas emissions form the United States were the leading contributor to the high concentration of lead in the snow in Greenland.

22. [B] 细节题。文章第一段提到：In the twenty years that the Clean Air Act has mandated unleaded gas use in the United States, the lead accumulation worldwide has decreased significantly. 可见美国颁布并实施了空气洁净法令来强制推广无铅汽油。

23. [D] 细节题。由文章第三段可知，由于欧洲、亚洲及加拿大等地汽油含铅比例与美国不同，科学家可以找出污染的真正来源。

24. [A] 细节题。答案依据见文章倒数第二段。

25. [C] 推断题。从文章最后两段可知，在科学家看来，虽然铅污染得到了控制，环境自净能力也比人们预料的要强，但是不能以此为借口继续污染环境。因此选项 C 的表述是正确的。

26. [B] 细节题。文章第一段和第二段都谈到了很多美国人往往忽视体育锻炼对减肥的作用。故本题正确答案是 B。

27. [A] 推断题。从文章第二段可以看出，很多人觉得体育锻炼减肥的方式很辛苦而且效果不佳。

28. [D] 推断题。从文章第二段的叙述来看,人们因为觉得锻炼这种减肥方法太辛苦而不愿采用,可见他们对其作用还没有足够的了解。因此选项 D 是正确的。

29. [C] 推断题。文章第三段告诉我们,该研究表明,只节食而不锻炼的减肥方式收效甚微,这也说明了体育锻炼在减肥过程中的必要性。

30. [D] 主旨题。本文详细讨论了节食和体育锻炼对减肥的作用,可见作者写作此文的目的是为了说明减肥的最有效的方法。故 D 为正确选项。

★**2004 年 6 月考题**

Passage One

Questions 11 to 15 are based on the following passage:

A is for always getting to work on time.

B is for being extremely busy.

C is for the conscientious(勤勤恳恳的)way you do your job.

You may be all these things at the office, and more. But when it comes to getting ahead, experts say, the ABCs of business should include a P, for politics, as in office politics.

Dale Carnegie suggested as much more than 50 years ago hard work alone doesn't ensure career advancement. You have to be able to sell yourself and your ideas, both publicly and behind the scenes. Yet, despite the obvious rewards of engaging in office politics—a better job, a raise, praise—many people are still unable—or unwilling—to "play the game."

"People assume that office politics involves some manipulative(工于心计的)behavior," says Deborah Comer, an assistant professor of management at Hofstra University. "But politics derives from the word 'polite'. It can mean lobbying and forming associations. It can mean being kind and helpful, or even trying to please your superior, and then expecting something in return."

In fact, today, experts define office politics as proper behavior used to pursue one's own self-interest in the workplace. In many cases, this involves some form of socializing within the office environment—not just in large companies, but in small workplaces as well.

"The first thing people are usually judged on is their ability to perform well on a consistent basis," says Neil P. Lewis, a management psychologist. "But if two or three candidates are up for a promotion, each of whom has reasonably similar ability, a manager is going to promote the person he or she likes best. It's simple human nature."

Yet, psychologists say, many employees and employers have trouble with the concept of politics in the office. Some people, they say, have an idealistic vision of work and what it takes to succeed. Still others associate politics with flattery(奉承), fearful that, if they speak up for themselves, they may appear to be flattering their boss for favors. Experts suggest altering this negative picture by recognizing the need for some self-promotion.

11. Office politics (Line 2, Para. 4) is used in the passage to refer to _____.

    A) the code of behavior for company staff

    B) the political views and beliefs of office workers

C) the interpersonal relationships within a company

D) the various qualities required for a successful career

12. To get promoted, one must not only be competent but _____.

A) give his boss a good impression

B) honest and loyal to his company

C) get along well with his colleagues

D) avoid being too outstanding

13. Why are many people unwilling to play the game (Line 4, Para. 5)?

A) They believe that doing so is impractical.

B) They feel that such behavior is unprincipled.

C) They are not good at manipulating colleagues.

D) They think the effort will get them nowhere.

14. The author considers office politics to be _____.

A) unwelcome at the workplace

B) bad for interpersonal relationships

C) indispensable to the development of company culture

D) an important factor for personal advancement

15. It is the author's view that _____.

A) speaking up for oneself is part of human nature

B) self-promotion does not necessarily mean flattery

C) hard work contributes very little to one's promotion

D) many employees fail to recognize the need of flattery

Passage Two

Questions 16 to 20 are based on the following passage:

As soon as it was revealed that a reporter for Progressive magazine had discovered how to make a hydrogen bomb, a group of firearm (火器) fans formed the National Hydrogen Bomb Association, and they are now lobbying against any legislation to stop Americans from owning one.

"The Constitution," said the association's spokesman, "gives everyone the right to own arms. It doesn't spell out what kind of arms. But since anyone can now make a hydrogen bomb, the public should be able to buy it to protect themselves."

"Don't you think it's dangerous to have one in the house, particularly where there are children around?"

"The National Hydrogen Bomb Association hopes to educate people in the safe handling of this type of weapon. We are instructing owners to keep the bomb in a locked cabinet and the fuse (导火索) separately in a drawer."

"Some people consider the hydrogen bomb a very fatal weapon which could kill somebody."

The spokesman said, "Hydrogen bombs don't kill people—people kill people. The bomb is for self-protection and it also has a deterrent effect. If somebody knows you have a nuclear weapon in your house, they're going to think twice about breaking in."

"But those who want to ban the bomb for American citizens claim that if you have one locked in the cabinet, with the fuse in a drawer, you would never be able to assemble it in time to stop an intruder(侵入者)."

"Another argument against allowing people to own a bomb is that at the moment it is very expensive to build one. So what your association is backing is a program which would allow the middle and upper classes to acquire a bomb while poor people will be left defenseless with just handguns."

16. According to the passage, some people started a national association so as to _____.
    A) block any legislation to ban the private possession of the bomb
    B) coordinate the mass production of the destructive weapon
    C) instruct people how to keep the bomb safe at home
    D) promote the large-scale sale of this newly invented weapon

17. Some people oppose the ownership of H-bombs by individuals on the grounds that _____.
    A) the size of the bomb makes it difficult to keep in a drawer
    B) most people don't know how to handle the weapon
    C) people's lives will be threatened by the weapon
    D) they may fall into the hands of criminals

18. By saying that the bomb also has a deterrent effect the spokesman means that it _____.
    A) will frighten away any possible intruders
    B) can show the special status of its owners
    C) will threaten the safety of the owners as well
    D) can kill those entering others' houses by force

19. According to the passage, opponents of the private ownership of H-bombs are very much worried that _____.
    A) the influence of the association is too powerful for the less privileged to overcome
    B) poorly-educated Americans will find it difficult to make use of the weapon
    C) the wide use of the weapon will push up living expenses tremendously
    D) the cost of the weapon will put citizens on an unequal basis

20. From the tone of the passage we know that the author is _____.
    A) doubtful about the necessity of keeping H-bombs at home for safety
    B) unhappy with those who vote against the ownership of H-bombs
    C) not serious about the private ownership of H-bombs

D) concerned about the spread of nuclear weapons

Passage Three
Questions 21 to 25 are based on the following passage：

Sign has become a scientific hot button. Only in the past 20 years have specialists in language study realized that sign languages are unique—a speech of the hand. They offer a new way to probe how the brain generates and understands language, and throw new light on an old scientific controversy whether language, complete with grammar, is something that we are born with, or whether it is a learned behavior. The current interest in sign language has roots in the pioneering work of one rebel teacher at Gallaudet University in Washington, D. C., the world's only liberal arts university for deaf people.

When Bill Stokoe went to Gallaudet to teach English, the school enrolled him in a course in signing. But Stokoe noticed something odd among themselves, students signed differently from his classroom teacher.

Stokoe had been taught a sort of gestural code, each movement of the hands representing a word in English. At the time, American Sign Language (ASL) was thought to be no more than a form of pidgin English(混杂英语). But Stokoe believed the hand talk his students used looked richer. He wondered：Might deaf people actually have a genuine language? And could that language be unlike any other on Earth? It was 1955, when even deaf people dismissed their signing as "substandard". Stokoe's idea was academic heresy(异端邪说).

It is 37 years later. Stokoe—now devoting his time to writing and editing books and journals and to producing video materials on ASL and the deaf culture—is having lunch at a café near the Gallaudet campus and explaining how he started a revolution. For decades educators fought his idea that sign languages are natural languages like English, French and Japanese. They assumed language must be based on speech, the modulation(调节)of sound. But sign language is based on the movement of hands, the modulation of space. "What I said," Stokoe explains, "is that language is not mouth stuff—it's brain stuff."

21. The study of sign language is thought to be _____.
    A) a new way to look at the learning of language
    B) a challenge to traditional views on the nature of language
    C) an approach to simplifying the grammatical structure of a language
    D) an attempt to clarify misunderstanding about the origin of language

22. The present growing interest in sign language was stimulated by _____.
    A) a famous scholar in the study of the human brain
    B) a leading specialist in the study of liberal arts
    C) an English teacher in a university for the deaf
    D) some senior experts in American Sign Language

23. According to Stokoe, sign language is _____.

A) a substandard language

B) a genuine language

C) an artificial language

D) an international language

24. Most educators objected to Stokoe's idea because they thought _____.

A) sign language was not extensively used even by deaf people

B) sign language was too artificial to be widely accepted

C) a language should be easy to use and understand

D) a language could only exist in the form of speech sounds

25. Stokoe's argument is based on his belief that _____.

A) sign language is as efficient as any other language

B) sign language is derived from natural language

C) language is a system of meaningful codes

D) language is a product of the brain

Passage Four

Questions 26 to 30 are based on the following passage：

It came as something of a surprise when Diana, Princess of Wales, made a trip to Angola in 1997, to support the Red Cross's campaign for a total ban on all anti-personnel landmines. Within hours of arriving in Angola, television screens around the world were filled with images of her comforting victims injured in explosions caused by landmines. "I knew the statistics," she said. "But putting a face to those figures brought the reality home to me; like when I met Sandra, a 13-year-old girl who had lost her leg, and people like her."

The Princess concluded with a simple message："We must stop landmines." And she used every opportunity during her visit to repeat this message.

But, back in London, her views were not shared by some members of the British government, which refused to support a ban on these weapons. Angry politicians launched an attack on the Princess in the press. They described her as very "ill-informed" and "a loose cannon(乱放炮的人)."

The Princess responded by brushing aside the criticisms ："This is a distraction(干扰)we do not need. All I'm trying to do is help."

Opposition parties, the media and the public immediately voiced their support for the Princess. To make matters worse for the government, it soon emerged that the Princess's trip had been approved by the Foreign Office, and that she was in fact very well-informed about both the situation in Angola and the British government's policy regarding landmines. The result was a severe embarrassment for the government.

To try and limit the damage, the Foreign Secretary, Malcolm Rifkidnd, claimed that the Princess's views on landmines were not very different from government policy, and that it was working towards a worldwide ban. The Defence Secretary, Michael Portillo, claimed the matter was a misinterpretation or misunderstanding.

For the Princess, the trip to this war-torn country was an excellent opportunity to use her popularity to show the world how much destruction and suffering landmines can cause. She said that the experience had also given her the chance to get closer to people and their problems.

26. Princess Diana paid a visit to Angola in 1997 _____.
    A) to voice her support for a total ban of landmines
    B) to clarify the British government's stand on landmines
    C) to investigate the sufferings of landmine victims there
    D) to establish her image as a friend of landmine victims

27. What did Diana mean when she said "... putting a face to those figures brought the reality home to me" (Line 5, Para.1)?
    A) She just couldn't bear to meet the landmine victims face to face.
    B) The actual situation in Angola made her feel like going back home.
    C) Meeting the landmine victims in person made her believe the statistics.
    D) Seeing the pain of the victims made her realize the seriousness of the situation.

28. Some members of the British government criticized Diana because _____.
    A) she was ill-informed of the government's policy
    B) they were actually opposed to banning landmines
    C) she had not consulted the government before the visit
    D) they believed that she had misinterpreted the situation in Angola

29. How did Diana respond to the criticisms?
    A) She paid no attention to them.
    B) She made more appearances on TV.
    C) She met the 13-year-old girl as planned.
    D) She rose to argue with her opponents.

30. What did Princess Diana think of her visit to Angola?
    A) It had caused embarrassment to the British government.
    B) It had brought her closer to the ordinary people.
    C) It had greatly promoted her popularity.
    D) It had affected her relations with the British government.

【答案及解析】

11. [C] 细节题。见原文第六段：It can mean lobbying and forming associations. It can mean being kind and helpful, or even trying to please your superior, and then expecting something in return...和原文第七段：In many cases, this involves some form of socializing within the office environment...由此可知,文中的"办公室政治"说的就是公司内部的人际关系。

12. [A] 推断题。见原文第八段：But if two or three candidates are up for a promotion, each of whom has reasonably similar ability, a manager is going to promote the person he or she likes best. 可见如果想要获得晋升，一个人不仅要有能力，还要给老板一个好的印象。故选 A。

13. [B] 细节题。从原文第五、六段及最后一段可以看出，人们不愿意这样做是因为他们觉得这种行为显得工于心计、阿谀奉承，是不光彩、不道德的。选项 B 中的 unprincipled 意思就是"不道德的，无原则的"。

14. [D] 细节题。依据见文章第四段及最后两段。

15. [B] 态度题。本文指出了人们对"办公室政治"的普遍的看法，又引用了专家的观点对其进行评价。不难看出，作者是赞同专家的观点的，因此选项 B 是正确答案。

16. [A] 细节题。见原文第一段：... they are now lobbying against any legislation to stop Americans from owning one.

17. [C] 细节题。解题依据见原文第三段及第五段。

18. [A] 细节题。题干问为什么该发言人认为这种炸弹能起到威慑作用。见原文第二段：But since anyone can now make a hydrogen bomb, the public should be able to buy it to protect themselves. 也就是说他认为这种炸弹能用于自我防卫。

19. [D] 原文最后一段提到有人担心由于这种新型的炸弹价格高昂，最后会导致有钱人用得起，而穷人则只能用手枪这类杀伤力相对较小的武器来保护自己，这无疑又是一种新的不平等。

20. [D] 态度题。从整篇文章来看，作者用大量篇幅引述了正反两方的观点，而自己却没有明确表态。但从其行文可以看出，作者对此事件是十分关注的。

21. [A] 推断题。原文第一段提到，手语使人们以一种全新的方式去探索大脑是如何产生语言和理解语言的，同时还使人们对语言能力是天生的还是后天习得的这一古老的科学论争有了更多的了解。由此可见，只有选项 A 的说法与原文相符。

22. [C] 细节题。题干问是谁激发了人们对手语的兴趣。从原文第一段：The current interest in sign language has roots in the pioneering work of one rebel teacher at Gallaudet University in Washington, D. C. , the world's only liberal arts university for deaf people. 可知选项 C 是正确的。

23. [B] 推断题。见原文第三段：He wondered：Might deaf people actually have a genuine language? And could that language be unlike any other on Earth? 及第四段：For decades educators fought his idea that sign languages are natural languages like English, French and Japanese. 由此可知，在 Stokoe 看来，手语也是一种真正的语言。

24. [D] 细节题。见原文第四段：They assumed language must be based on speech, the modulation of sound. 反对 Stokoe 的人认为语言必须以语音为基础，而手语则不符合这个条件，故手语不是真正的语言。因此选项 D 是正确的。

25. [D] 细节题。从文章最后一句可知，Stokoe 的观点是语言是大脑的产物，故选 D。

26. [A] 细节题。文章开头就提到戴安娜王妃出访安哥拉的目的正是"to support the Red Cross's campaign for a total ban on all anti-personnel landmines"。

27. [D] 推断题。解答此题的关键是要理解"bring sth. home to sb."的意思是"使……明白……"，该短语与选项 D 中的 realize 相吻合。

28. [B] 细节题。见原文第三段：But, back in London, her views were not shared by some members of the British government, which refused to support a ban on these weapons. 可见他们实际上反对禁用地雷。

29. ［A］细节题。文中的"brush aside"的意思是"扫除，漠视"，也就是 pay no attention，即"置之不理"之意。

30. ［B］细节题。见文章末句。

★ 2003 年 12 月考题

Passage One

Questions 21 to 25 are based on the following passage：

I'm usually fairly skeptical about any research that concludes that people are either happier or unhappier or more or less certain of themselves than they were 50 years ago. While any of these statements might be true，they are practically impossible to prove scientifically. Still，I was struck by a report which concluded that today's children are significantly more anxious than children in the 1950s. In fact，the analysis showed，normal children ages 9 to 17 exhibit a higher level of anxiety today than children who were treated for mental illness 50 years ago.

Why are America's kids so stressed? The report cites two main causes：increasing physical isolation—brought on by high divorce rates and less involvement in community，among other things—and a growing perception that the world is a more dangerous place.

Given that we can't turn the clock back，adults can still do plenty to help the next generation cope.

At the top of the list is nurturing（培育）a better appreciation of the limits of individualism. No child is an island. Strengthening social ties helps build communities and protect individuals against stress.

To help kids build stronger connections with others，you can pull the plug on TVs and computers. Your family will thank you later. They will have more time for face-to-face relationships，and they will get more sleep.

Limit the amount of virtual（虚拟的）violence your children are exposed to. It's not just video games and movies；children see a lot of murder and crime on the local news. Keep your expectations for your children reasonable. Many highly successful people never attended Harvard or Yale.

Make exercise part of your daily routine. It will help you cope with your own anxieties and provide a good model for your kids. Sometimes anxiety is unavoidable. But it doesn't have to ruin your life.

21. The author thinks that the conclusions of any research about people's state of mind are

_____。

    A) surprising   B) confusing   C) illogical   D) questionable

22. What does the author mean when he says，"we can't turn the clock back"（Line 1，Para. 3）？

    A) It's impossible to slow down the pace of change.

    B) The social reality children are facing cannot be changed.

    C) Lessons learned from the past should not be forgotten.

D) It's impossible to forget the past.

23. According to an analysis, compared with normal children today, children treated as mentally ill 50 years ago _____ .
    A) were less isolated physically
    B) were probably less self-centered
    C) probably suffered less from anxiety
    D) were considered less individualistic

24. The first and most important thing parents should do to help their children is _____ .
    A) to provide them with a safer environment
    B) to lower their expectations for them
    C) to get them more involved socially
    D) to set a good model for them to follow

25. What conclusion can be drawn from the passage?
    A) Anxiety, though unavoidable, can be coped with.
    B) Children's anxiety has been enormously exaggerated.
    C) Children's anxiety can be eliminated with more parental care.
    D) Anxiety, if properly controlled, may help children become mature.

Passage Two
Questions 26 to 30 are based on the following passage:

It is easier to negotiate initial salary requirement because once you are inside, the organizational constraints(约束)influence wage increases. One thing, however, is certain: your chances of getting the raise you feel you deserve are less if you don't at least ask for it. Men tend to ask for more, and they get more, and this holds true with other resources, not just pay increases. Consider Beth's story:

I did not get what I wanted when I did not ask for it. We had cubicle(小隔间)offices and window offices. I sat in the cubicles with several male colleagues. One by one they were moved into window offices, while I remained in the cubicles. Several males who were hired after me also went to offices. One in particular told me he was next in line for an office and that it had been part of his negotiations for the job. I guess they thought me content to stay in the cubicles since I did not voice my opinion either way.

It would be nice if we all received automatic pay increases equal to our merit, but "nice" isn't a quality attributed to most organizations. If you feel you deserve a significant raise in pay, you'll probably have to ask for it.

Performance is your best bargaining chip(筹码)when you are seeking a raise. You must be able to demonstrate that you deserve a raise. Timing is also a good bargaining chip. If you can give your boss something he or she needs (a new client or a sizable contract, for example) just before merit pay decisions are being made, you are more likely to get the raise you want.

Use information as a bargaining chip too. Find out what you are worth on the open market. What will someone else pay for your services?

Go into the negotiations prepared to place your chips on the table at the appropriate time and prepared to use communication style to guide the direction of the interaction.

26. According to the passage, before taking a job, a person should _____.
    A) demonstrate his capability
    B) give his boss a good impression
    C) ask for as much money as he can
    D) ask for the salary he hopes to get

27. What can be inferred from Beth's story?
    A) Prejudice against women still exists in some organizations.
    B) If people want what they deserve, they have to ask for it.
    C) People should not be content with what they have got.
    D) People should be careful when negotiating for a job.

28. We can learn from the passage that _____.
    A) unfairness exists in salary increases
    B) most people are overworked and underpaid
    C) one should avoid overstating one's performance
    D) most organizations give their staff automatic pay raises

29. To get a pay raise, a person should _____.
    A) advertise himself on the job market
    B) persuade his boss to sign a long-term contract
    C) try to get inside information about the organization
    D) do something to impress his boss just before merit pay decisions

30. To be successful in negotiations, one must _____.
    A) meet his boss at the appropriate time
    B) arrive at the negotiation table punctually
    C) be good at influencing the outcome of the interaction
    D) be familiar with what the boss likes and dislikes

Passage Three
Questions 31 to 35 are based on the following passage:

When families gather for Christmas dinner, some will stick to formal traditions dating back to Grandma's generation. Their tables will be set with the good dishes and silver, and the dress code will be Sunday-best.

But in many other homes, this china-and-silver elegance has given way to a stoneware(粗

陶)-and-stainless informality, with dresses assuming an equally casual-Friday look. For hosts and guests, the change means greater simplicity and comfort. For makers of fine china in Britain, it spells economic hard times.

Last week Royal Doulton, the largest employer in Stoke-on-Trent, announced that it is eliminating 1,000 jobs—one-fifth of its total workforce. That brings to more than 4,000 the number of positions lost in 18 months in the pottery(陶瓷)region. Wedgwood and other pottery factories made cuts earlier.

Although a strong pound and weak markets in Asia play a role in the downsizing, the layoffs in Stoke have their roots in earthshaking social shifts. A spokesman for Royal Doulton admitted that the company "has been somewhat slow in catching up with the trend" toward casual dining. Families eat together less often, he explained, and more people eat alone, either because they are single or they eat in front of television.

Even dinner parties, if they happen at all, have gone casual. In a time of long work hours and demanding family schedules, busy hosts insist, rightly, that it's better to share a takeout pizza on paper plates in the family room than to wait for the perfect moment or a "real" dinner party. Too often, the perfect moment never comes. Iron a fine-patterned tablecloth? Forget it. Polish the silver? Who has time?

Yet the loss of formality has its down side. The fine points of etiquette(礼节)that children might once have learned at the table by observation or instruction from parents and grandparents ("Chew with your mouth closed." "Keep your elbows off the table.") must be picked up elsewhere. Some companies now offer etiquette seminars for employees who may be competent professionally but clueless socially.

31. The trend toward casual dining has resulted in _____.
    A) bankruptcy of fine china manufacturers
    B) shrinking of the pottery industry
    C) restructuring of large enterprises
    D) economic recession in Great Britain

32. Which of the following may be the best reason for casual dining?
    A) Family members need more time to relax.
    B) Busy schedules leave people no time for formality.
    C) People want to practice economy in times of scarcity.
    D) Young people won't follow the etiquette of the older generation.

33. It can be learned from the passage that Royal Doulton is _____.
    A) a retailer of stainless steel tableware
    B) a dealer in stoneware
    C) a pottery chain store
    D) a producer of fine china

34. The main cause of the layoffs in the pottery industry is _____.
    A) the increased value of the pound
    B) the economic recession in Asia
    C) the change in people's way of life
    D) the fierce competition at home and abroad

35. Refined table manners, though less popular than before in current social life _____.
    A) are still a must on certain occasions
    B) are bound to return sooner or later
    C) are still being taught by parents at home
    D) can help improve personal relationships

Passage Four

Questions 36 to 40 are based on the following passage:

Some houses are designed to be smart. Others have smart designs. An example of the second type of house won an Award of Excellence from the American Institute of Architects.

Located on the shore of Sullivan's Island off the coast of South Carolina, the award-winning cube-shaped beach house was built to replace one smashed to pieces by Hurricane(飓风)Hugo 10 years ago. In September 1989, Hugo struck South Carolina, killing 18 people and damaging or destroying 36,000 homes in the state.

Before Hugo, many new houses built along South Carolina's shoreline were poorly constructed, and enforcement of building codes wasn't strict, according to architect Ray Huff, who created the cleverly-designed beach house. In Hugo's wake, all new shoreline houses are required to meet stricter, better-enforced codes. The new beach house on Sullivan's Island should be able to withstand a Category 3 hurricane with peak winds of 179 to 209 kilometers per hour.

At first sight, the house on Sullivan's Island looks anything but hurricane-proof. Its redwood shell makes it resemble "a large party lantern(灯笼)" at night, according to one observer. But looks can be deceiving. The house's wooden frame is reinforced with long steel rods to give it extra strength.

To further protect the house from hurricane damage, Huff raised it 2.7 meters off the ground on timber pilings—long, slender columns of wood anchored deep in the sand. Pilings might appear insecure, but they are strong enough to support the weight of the house. They also elevate the house above storm surges. The pilings allow the surges to run under the house instead of running into it. "These swells of water come ashore at tremendous speeds and cause most of the damage done to beach-front buildings," said Huff.

Huff designed the timber pilings to be partially concealed by the house's ground-to-roof shell. "The shell masks the pilings so that the house doesn't look like it's standing with its pant legs pulled up," said Huff. In the event of a storm surge, the shell should break apart and let the waves rush under the house, the architect explained.

36. After the tragedy caused by Hurricane Hugo，new houses built along South Carolina's shore line are required _____.
    A) to be easily reinforced
    B) to look smarter in design
    C) to meet stricter building standards
    D) to be designed in the shape of cubes

37. The award-winning beach house is quite strong because _____.
    A) it is strengthened by steel rods
    B) it is made of redwood
    C) it is in the shape of a shell
    D) it is built with timber and concrete

38. Huff raised the house 2.7 meters off the ground on timber pilings in order to _____.
    A) withstand peak winds of about 200 km/hr
    B) anchor stronger pilings deep in the sand
    C) break huge sea waves into smaller ones
    D) prevent water from rushing into the house

39. The main function of the shell is _____.
    A) to strengthen the pilings of the house
    B) to give the house a better appearance
    C) to protect the wooden frame of the house
    D) to slow down the speed of the swelling water

40. It can be inferred from the passage that the shell should be _____.
    A) fancy-looking   B) waterproof
    C) easily breakable   D) extremely strong

【答案及解析】

21. [D] 态度题。从第一段第一句可以看出,作者对当前所做的关于人们心理状态的研究结论都持怀疑态度。skeptical(怀疑)与 questionable 同义。

22. [B] 推断题。使时光倒流是不可能的,比喻社会现实不可改变。其他几项文中均没有提及。

23. [C] 推断题。见第一段最后一句:In fact, the analysis showed, normal children ages 9 to 17 exhibit a higher level of anxiety today than children who were treated for mental illness 50 years ago. 即今天 9 到 15 岁的正常的孩子的焦虑程度比 50 年前那些需要接受心理治疗的孩子还要高。反过来说,50 年前需要接受心理治疗的孩子的焦虑程度要轻一些。

24. [C] 推断题。本题问及家长们帮助孩子缓解压力的首要措施,即考查对文章第四段要点的理解。在该段中,作者指出:要充分认识个人主义的局限性;孩子也是社会的一分子,而不是一座孤岛;加强与外界社会的沟通有助于缓解压力。

25. [A] 推断题。见最后一段。焦虑有时是不可避免的,但它不至于会摧毁你的生活。也就是

说,可以采取有效的措施来应对。B、D 两项文中均未提及,C 项与文意相悖。

26. [D] 细节题。见第一段第一句。意即接受工作前谈工资条件比进入机构后容易得多,因为那时不用受机构中条条框框的制约。所以工作前要提出你的期望薪资。

27. [B] 推断题。文中该故事的前后两段都有提及自己主动提出要求的重要性。

28. [A] 推断题。第三段。就是说如果能根据我们业绩自动加薪,那真是最好不过了。但现实中并没有这样美好的事情。如果你觉得自己应该获得加薪,那很可能要你自己提出。从这点可以看出,现实中在加薪这一事情上显然存在不公平的地方。

29. [D] 细节题。第四段中作者列举了几点加薪的"筹码"。总的来说是要在适当时机,特别是在提出加薪要求前有所表现。

30. [A] 细节题。见最后一段。作者指出,要在加薪谈判中获胜,就要准备好与老板讨价还价的筹码,并事先做好准备以使谈判朝有利于自己的方向进行。可见,与老板见面的时机的选择是最重要的。

31. [B] 细节题。这道题问的是人们就餐方式日趋随意的趋势已导致了什么后果。文中第三段指出了就餐方式的改变对英国的陶瓷工业的影响。

32. [B] 推断题。由第四、五段可知,人们选择随意的就餐方式是由于家庭生活及工作方式的转变。

33. [D] 推断题。第二段最后一句说陶瓷业不景气,紧接着第三段又说 Royal Doulton 裁员,可见 Royal Doulton 是瓷器制造商。

34. [C] 推断题。注意题目问的是陶瓷行业萧条的主要原因。通观全文,整篇文章都在谈论人们就餐方式的变化导致的后果,因此选项 C 最符合题意。

35. [A] 推断题。文章最后一句告诉我们,一些公司对社交能力不强的员工提供礼仪培训,可见用餐礼仪在某些场合还是十分必要的。

36. [C] 推断题。回答此题的关键是要知道第三段中的"in…wake"指的是"在……之后"。该句意思是在飓风袭击后,有关部门对当地新建的房屋提出了更为严格的标准。

37. [A] 细节题。从第四段可以直接找到答案。

38. [D] 细节题。见第五段第三句。可见把房屋建在木桩上的目的是使洪水从房屋底下流走而不是涌进屋里。

39. [B] 细节题。见文章最后一段第二句。用框架罩住木桩就是为了让房子看上去更加美观。

40. [C] 细节题。见最后一段末句。一旦洪水来袭,罩在外面的框架就会破裂以让洪水从房屋底下流过。可见它是"easily breakable"。

★ 2003 年 9 月考题

Passage One

Questions 21 to 25 are based on the following passage:

About six years ago I was eating lunch in a restaurant in New York City when a woman and a young boy sat down at the next table, I couldn't help overhearing parts of their conversation. At one point the woman asked: "So, how have you been?" And the boy—who could not have been more than seven or eight years old—replied. "Frankly, I've been feeling a little depressed lately."

This incident stuck in my mind because it confirmed my growing belief that children are changing. As far as I can remember, my friends and I didn't find out we were "depressed" until we were in high school.

The evidence of a change in children has increased steadily in recent years. Children don't seem childlike anymore. Children speak more like adults, dress more like adults and behave more like adults than they used to.

Whether this is good or bad is difficult to say, but it certainly is different. Childhood as it once was no longer exists. Why?

Human development is based not only on innate(天生的)biological states, but also on patterns of access to social knowledge. Movement from one social role to another usually involves learning the secrets of the new status. Children have always been taught adult secrets, but slowly and in stages: traditionally, we tell sixth graders things we keep hidden from fifth graders.

In the last 30 years, however, a secret-revelation(揭示)machine has been installed in 98 percent of American homes. It is called television. Television passes information, and indiscriminately(不加区分地), to all viewers alike, be they children or adults. Unable to resist the temptation, many children turn their attention from printed texts to the less challenging, more vivid moving pictures.

Communication through print, as a matter of fact, allows for a great deal of control over the social information to which children have access. Reading and writing involve a complex code of symbols that must be memorized and practiced. Children must read simple books before they can read complex materials.

21. According to the author, feeling depressed is _____.

   A) something hardly to be expected in a young child

   B) a mental scale present in all humans, including children

   C) an inevitable stage of children's mental development

   D) a sure sign of a psychological problem in a child

22. Traditionally, a child is supposed to learn about the adult world _____.

   A) through contact with society

   B) gradually and under guidance

   C) through exposure to social information

   D) naturally and by biological instinct

23. The phenomenon that today's children seem adultlike is attributed by the author to _____.

   A) the constantly rising standard of living

   B) the widespread influence of television

   C) the poor arrangement of teaching content

   D) the fast pace of human intellectual development

24. Why is the author in favor of communication through print for children?

    A) It can control what children are to learn.

    B) It helps children to memorize and practice more.

    C) It enables children to gain more social information.

    D) It develops children's interest in reading and writing.

25. What does the author think of the change in today's children?

    A) He seems to be upset about it.

    B) He considers it a positive development.

    C) He feels amused by child premature behavior.

    D) He thinks it is a phenomenon worthy of note.

Passage Two

Questions 26 to 30 are based on the following passage:

"Opinion" is a word that is used carelessly today. It is used to refer to matters of taste, belief, and judgment. This casual use would probably cause little confusion if people didn't attach too much importance to opinion. Unfortunately, most do attach great importance to it. "I have as much right to my opinion as you to yours", and "Everyone's entitled to his opinion", are common expressions. In fact, anyone who would challenge another's opinion is likely to be branded intolerant.

Is that label accurate? Is it intolerant to challenge another's opinion? It depends on what definition of opinion you have in mind. For example, you may ask a friend "What do you think of the new Ford cars?" And he may reply, "In my opinion, they're ugly." In this case, it would not only be intolerant to challenge his statement, but foolish. For it is obvious that by opinion he means his personal preference, a matter of taste. And as the old saying goes, "It's pointless to argue about matters of taste."

But consider this very different use of the term, a newspaper reports that the Supreme Court has delivered its opinion in a controversial case. Obviously the justices did not share their personal preferences, their mere likes and dislikes. They stated their considered judgment, painstakingly arrived at after thorough inquiry and deliberation.

Most of what is referred to as opinion falls somewhere between these two extremes. It is not an expression of taste. Nor is it careful judgment. Yet it may contain elements of both. It is a view or belief more or less casually arrived at, with or without examining the evidence.

Is everyone entitled to his opinion? Of course, this is not only permitted, but guaranteed. We are free to act on our opinions only so long as, in doing so, we do not harm others.

26. Which of the following statements is TRUE, according to the author?

    A) Casual use of the word "opinion" often brings about quarrels.

    B) Most people tend to be careless in forming their opinions.

    C) Free expression of opinions often leads to confusion.

    D) Everyone has a right to hold his own opinion.

第三章 篇章阅读

27. According to the author, who of the following would be labeled as intolerant?

    A) Someone whose opinions harm other people.

    B) Someone who values only their own opinions.

    C) Someone who can't put up with others' tastes.

    D) Someone who turns a deaf ear to others' opinions.

28. The new Ford cars are cited as an example to show that _____.

    A) it is foolish to criticize a famous brand

    B) personal tastes are not something to be challenged

    C) it is unwise to express one's likes and dislikes in public

    D) one should not always agree to others' opinions

29. Considered judgment is different from personal preference in that _____.

    A) it is based on careful thought

    B) it is stated by judges in the court

    C) it reflects public likes and dislikes

    D) it is a result of a lot of controversy

30. As indicated in the passage, being free to act on one's opinion _____.

    A) doesn't mean that one has the right to charge others without evidence

    B) means that one can impose his preferences on others

    C) doesn't mean that one has the right to do things at will

    D) means that one can ignore other people's criticism

Passage Three

Questions 31 to 35 are based on the following passage:

A recent study, published in last week's Journal of the American Medical Association, offers a picture of how risky it is to get a lift from a teenage driver. Indeed, a 16-year-old driver with three or more passengers is three times as likely to have a fatal accident as a teenager driving alone. By contrast, the risk of death for drivers between 30 and 59 decreases with each additional passenger.

The author also found that the death rates for teenage drivers increased dramatically after 10 p.m., and especially after midnight. With passengers in the car, the driver was even more likely to die in a late-night accident.

Robert Foss, a scientist at the University of North Carolina Highway Safety Research Center, says the higher death rates for teenage drivers have less to do with "really stupid behavior" than with just a lack of driving experience. "The basic issue," He says, "is that adults who are responsible for issuing licenses fail to recognize how complex and skilled a task driving is."

Both he and the author of the study believe that the way to mitigate(使……缓解)the problem is to have states institute so-called graduated licensing systems, in which getting a license is a multistage process. A graduated license requires that a teenager first prove himself capable of driving in the presence of an adult, followed by a period of driving with night passenger restrictions, before graduating to full driving privileges.

Graduated licensing systems have reduced teenage driver crashes, according to recent studies. About half of the states now have some sort of graduated licensing system in place, but only 10 of those states have restrictions on passengers. California is the strictest, with a novice (新手) driver prohibited from carrying any passenger under 20 (without the presence of an adult over 25) for the first six months.

31. Which of the following situations is most dangerous according to the passage?
    A) A teenager getting a lift from a stranger on the highway at midnight.
    B) Adults driving with three or more teenage passengers late at night.
    C) Adults giving a lift to teenagers on the highway after 10 p.m.
    D) A teenager driving after midnight with passengers in the car.

32. According to Robert Foss. The high death rate of teenage drivers is mainly due to _____.
    A) their frequent driving at night
    B) their driving with passengers
    C) their improper way of driving
    D) their lack of driving experience

33. According to Paragraph 3, which of the following statements is TRUE?
    A) Restrictions should be imposed on teenagers applying to take driving lessons.
    B) Teenagers should spend more time learning to drive.
    C) Driving is a skill too complicated for teenagers to learn.
    D) The licensing authorities are partly responsible for teenagers driving accidents.

34. A suggested measure to be taken to reduce teenagers driving accidents is that _____.
    A) the licensing system should be improved
    B) they should not be allowed to drive after 10 p.m.
    C) they should be prohibited from taking on passengers
    D) driving in the presence of an adult should be made a rule

35. The present situation in about half of the states is that the graduated licensing system _____.
    A) has been perfected   B) is under discussion
    C) has been put into effect   D) is about to be set up

Passage Four

Questions 36 to 40 are based on the following passage:

If you know exactly what you want, the best route to a job is to get specialized training. A recent survey shows that companies like graduates in such fields as business and health care who can go to work immediately with very little on-the-job training.

That's especially true of booming fields that are challenging for workers. At Cornell's School of Hotel Administration, for example, bachelor's degree graduates get an average of four or five job offers with salaries ranging from the high teens to the low 20s and plenty of chances for rapid advancement. Large companies, especially, like a background of formal education coupled with work experience.

But in the long run, too much specialization doesn't pay off. Business, which has been flooded with MBAs, no longer considers the degree an automatic stamp of approval. The MBA may open doors and command a higher salary initially, but the impact of a degree washes out after five years.

As further evidence of the erosion(销蚀)of corporate(公司的)faith in specialized degrees, Michigan State's Scheetz cites a pattern in corporate hiring practices, Although companies tend to take on specialists as new hires, they often seek out generalists for middle and upper-level management. "They want someone who isn't constrained(限制)by nuts and bolts to look at the big picture," says Scheetz.

This sounds suspiciously like a formal statement that you approve of the liberal-arts graduate. Time and again labor-market analysts mention a need for talents that liberal-arts majors are assumed to have: writing and communication skills, organizational skills, open-mindedness and adaptability, and the ability to analyze and solve problems, David Birch claims he does not hire anybody with an MBA or an engineering degree, "I hire only liberal-arts people because they have a less-than-canned way of doing things," says Birch. Liberal-arts means an academically thorough and strict program that includes literature, history, mathematics, economics, science, human behavior—plus a computer course or two. With that under your belt, you can feel free to specialize, "A liberal-arts degree coupled with an MBA or some other technical training is a very good combination in the marketplace," says Scheetz.

36. What kinds of people are in high demand on the job market?
    A) People with special training in engineering.
    B) Students with a bachelor's degree in humanities.
    C) People with an MBA degree from top universities.
    D) People with formal schooling plus work experience.

37. By saying "...but the impact of a degree washes out after five years" (Line 3, Para. 3), the author means _____.
    A) in five years people will forget about the degree the MBA graduates have got
    B) MBA programs will not be as popular in five years' time as they are now
    C) an MBA degree does not help promotion to managerial positions

D) most MBA programs fail to provide students with a solid foundation

38. According to Scheetz's statement (Lines 4—5, Para. 4), companies prefer _____.
    A) people who have received training in mechanics
    B) people who have a strategic mind
    C) people who are talented in fine arts
    D) people who are ambitious and aggressive

39. David Birch claims that he only hires liberal-arts people because _____.
    A) they have attended special programs in management
    B) they can stick to established ways of solving problems
    C) they are more capable of handling changing situations
    D) they are thoroughly trained in a variety of specialized fields

40. Which of the following statements does the author support?
    A) Generalists will outdo specialists in management.
    B) On-the-job training is, in the long run, less costly.
    C) Formal schooling is less important than job training.
    D) Specialists are more expensive to hire than generalists.

【答案及解析】

21. [A] 推断题。见文章第二段。

22. [B] 细节题。见原文第五段最后一句:Children have always been taught about adult secrets, but slowly and in stages ...

23. [B] 细节题。见文章倒数第二段。

24. [A] 细节题。见文章最后一段首句:Communication through print, as a matter of fact, allows for a great deal of control over the social information to which children have access. 可见印刷形式的交流能够较好地控制孩子所获取的信息。

25. [D] 作者首先对这一问题表示震惊,然后把自己及自己的同龄人的经历与小男孩进行对比,追溯其原因,从孩子的教育出发进行讨论,并指出了电视的不良影响及读书的好处。从这些叙述足见作者对该问题的重视。因此本题选 D。

26. [A] 推断题。见原文第一段。

27. [B] 细节题。依据见第一段末句:In fact, anyone who would challenge another's opinion is likely to be branded intolerant.

28. [B] 推断题。从上下文来看,福特车的例子是为了说明关于个人喜好的争论是没有意义的。故本题选 B。

29. [A] 细节题。见文章倒数第二段:They stated their considered judgment, painstakingly arrived at after thorough inquiry and deliberation. 可见 considered judgment 是经过深入研究和探讨得出的。

30. [C] 推断题。文章最后一句说:We are free to act on our opinions only so long as, in doing so, we do not harm others. 只要是我们所说的不会对他人造成危害,我们就可以自由地表

达自己的意见。也就是说,我们做事情不能随心所欲。

31. [D] 细节题。由文章第一段分析可知,选项 D 所说的情况是最危险的。

32. [D] 细节题。由文章第三段可知 Robert Foss 的观点是:... the higher death rates for teenage drivers have less to do with "really stupid behavior" than with just a lack of driving experience. 可见青少年驾驶事故的高死亡率是主要是由于他们缺乏驾驶经验。故本题选 D。

33. [D] 推断题。第三段最后一句话说,负责发放驾照的成年人没有充分认识到驾驶的复杂性和技术性,也就是说他们没有对青少年进行严格的考核,从这个角度来看,他们对青少年驾驶事故也是负有部分责任的。

34. [A] 推断题。见上题分析。

35. [C] 细节题。见文章最后一段:About half of the states now have some sort of graduated licensing system in place...

36. [D] 细节题。见文章第二段最后一句话:Large companies, especially, like a background of formal education coupled with work experience.

37. [C] 细节题。见第四段:Although companies tend to take on specialists as new hires, they often seek out generalists for middle and upper-level management. 可见 MBA 学位对于提升到管理层没有帮助。而公司也经常挑选出全才做中上层的管理工作。

38. [B] 推断题。原文是:They want someone who isn't constrained by nuts and bolts to look at the big picture. 也就是说,公司需要能从全局考虑问题的人。

39. [C] 见文章第五段第二句:Time and again labor-market analysts mention a need for talents that liberal-arts majors are assumed to have: writing and communication skills, organizational skills, open-mindedness and adaptability, and the ability to analyze and solve problems. 句中的 adaptability 指的是适应性,即灵活应对变化的能力。故选项 C 是正确答案。

40. [A] 主旨题。通读全文可知,本文讲的是那些知识面广、应变能力强的全才更受用人单位的欢迎。故选项 A 正确。

★ 2002 年 12 月考题

Passage One

Questions 11 to 15 are based on the following passage:

Like many of my generation, I have a weakness for hero worship. At some point, however, we all begin to question our heroes and our need for them. This leads us to ask: What is a hero?

Despite immense differences in cultures, heroes around the world generally share a number of characteristics that instruct and inspire people.

A hero does something worth talking a about. A hero has a story of adventure to tell and a community who will listen. But a hero goes beyond mere fame.

Heroes serve powers or principles larger than themselves. Like high-voltage transformers, heroes take the energy of higher powers and step it down so that it can be used by ordinary people.

The hero lives a life worthy of imitation. Those who imitate a genuine hero experience life with new depth, enthusiasm, and meaning. A sure test for would-be heroes is what or whom do they serve? What are they willing to live and die for? If the answer or evidence suggests they serve only their own fame, they may be famous persons but not heroes. Madonna and Michael Jackson are famous, but who would claim that their fans find life more abundant?

Heroes are catalysts(催化剂) for change. They have a vision from the mountain top. They have the skill and the charm to move the masses. They create new possibilities. Without Gandhi, India might still be part of the British Empire. Without Rosa Parks and Martin Luther King, Jr., we might still have segregated(隔离的) buses, restaurants, and parks. It may be possible for large scale change to occur without leaders with magnetic personalities, but the pace of change would be slow, the vision uncertain, and the committee meetings endless.

11. Although heroes may come from different cultures, they _____.
    A) generally possess certain inspiring characteristics
    B) probably share some weaknesses of ordinary people
    C) are often influenced by previous generations
    D) all unknowingly attract a large number of fans

12. According to the passage, heroes are compared to high-voltage transformers in that _____.
    A) they have a vision from the mountaintop
    B) they have warm feelings and emotions
    C) they can serve as concrete examples of noble principles
    D) they can make people feel stronger and more confident

13. Madonna and Michael Jackson are not considered heroes because _____.
    A) they are popular only among certain groups of people
    B) their performances do not improve their fans morally
    C) their primary concern is their own financial interests
    D) they are not clear about the principles they should follow

14. Gandhi and Martin Luther King are typical examples of outstanding leaders who _____.
    A) are good at demonstrating their charming characters
    B) can move the masses with their forceful speeches
    C) are capable of meeting all challenges and hardships
    D) can provide an answer to the problems of their people

15. The author concludes that historical changes would _____.
    A) be delayed without leaders with inspiring personal qualities
    B) not happen without heroes making the necessary sacrifices
    C) take place if there were heroes to lead the people

D) produce leaders with attractive personalities

Passage Two

Questions 16 to 20 are based on the following passage:

According to a survey, which was based on the responses of over 188,000 students, today's traditional-age college freshmen are "more materialistic and less altruistic(利他主义的)" than at any time in the 17 years of the poll.

Not surprising in these hard times, the student's major objective "is to be financially well off. Less important than ever is developing a meaningful philosophy of life." It follows then that today the most popular course is not literature or history but accounting.

Interest in teaching, social service and the "altruistic" fields is at a low. On the other hand, enrollment in business programs, engineering and computer science is way up.

That's no surprise either. A friend of mine (a sales representative for a chemical company) was making twice the salary of her college instructors her first year on the job—even before she completed her two-year associate degree.

While it's true that we all need a career, it is equally true that our civilization has accumulated an incredible amount of knowledge in fields far removed from our own and that we are better for our understanding of these other contributions—be they scientific or artistic. It is equally true that, in studying the diverse wisdom of others, we learn how to think. More important, perhaps, education teaches us to see the connections between things, as well as to see beyond our immediate needs.

Weekly we read of unions who went on strike for higher wages, only to drive their employer out of business. No company, no job. How shortsighted in the long run!

But the most important argument for a broad education is that in studying the accumulated wisdom of the ages, we improve our moral sense. I saw a cartoon recently which shows a group of businessmen looking puzzled as they sit around a conference table; one of them is talking on the intercom(对讲机): "Miss Baxter," he says, "could you please send in someone who can distinguish right from wrong?"

From the long-term point of view, that's what education really ought to be about.

16. According to the author's observation, college students _____.
    A) have never been so materialistic as today
    B) have never been so interested in the arts
    C) have never been so financially well off as today
    D) have never attached so much importance to moral sense

17. The students' criteria for electing majors today have much to do with _____.
    A) the influences of their instructors
    B) the financial goals they seek in life
    C) their own interpretations of the courses
    D) their understanding of the contributions of others

18. By saying "While it's true that... be they scientific or artistic" (Lines 1—3, Para. 5), the
    author means that _____.
    A) business management should be included in educational programs
    B) human wisdom has accumulated at an extraordinarily high speed
    C) human intellectual development has reached new heights
    D) the importance of a broad education should not be overlooked

19. Studying the diverse wisdom of others can _____.
    A) create varying artistic interests
    B) help people see things in their right perspective
    C) help improve connections among people
    D) regulate the behavior of modern people

20. Which of the following statements is true according to the passage?
    A) Businessmen absorbed in their career are narrow-minded.
    B) Managers often find it hard to tell right from wrong.
    C) People engaged in technical jobs lead a more rewarding life.
    D) Career seekers should not focus on immediate interests only.

Passage Three
Questions 21 to 25 are based on the following passage:

New technology links the world as never before. Our planet has shrunk. It's now a "global
village" where countries are only seconds away by fax or phone satellite link. And, of course,
our ability to benefit from this high-tech communications equipment is greatly enhanced by
foreign language skills.

Deeply involved with this new technology is a breed of modern businesspeople who have a
growing respect for the economic value of doing business abroad. In modern markets, success
overseas often helps support domestic business efforts.

Overseas assignments are becoming increasingly important to advancement within executive
ranks. The executive stationed in another country no longer need fear being "out of sight and out
of mind." He or she can be sure that the overseas effort is central to the company's plan for
success, and that promotions often follow or accompany an assignment abroad. If an employee
can succeed in a difficult assignment overseas, superiors will have greater confidence in his or
her ability to cope back in the United Sates where cross-cultural considerations and foreign
language issues are becoming more and more prevalent(普遍的).

Thanks to a variety of relatively inexpensive communications devices with business
applications, even small businesses in the United States are able to get into international
markets.

English is still the international language of business. But there is an ever-growing need for
people who can speak another language. A second language isn't generally required to get a job

in business, but having language skills gives a candidate the edge when other qualifications appear to be equal.

The employee posted abroad who speaks the country's principal language has an opportunity to fast-forward certain negotiations, and can have the cultural insight to know when it is better to move more slowly. The employee at the home office who can communicate well with foreign clients over the telephone or by fax machine is an obvious asset to the firm.

21. What is the author's attitude toward high-tech communications equipment?

A) Critical.   B) Indifferent.

C) Prejudiced.   D) Positive.

22. With the increased use of high-tech communications equipment, business people _____.

A) have to get familiar with modern technology

B) are gaining more economic benefits from domestic operations

C) are attaching more importance to their overseas business

D) are eager to work overseas

23. In this passage, "out of sight and out of mind" (Lines 2 — 3, Para. 3) probably means

_____.

A) being unable to think properly for lack of insight

B) being totally out of touch with business at home

C) missing opportunities for promotion when abroad

D) leaving all care and worth bchind

24. According to the passage, what is an important consideration of international corporations in employing people today?

A) Connections with business overseas.

B) Ability to speak the client's language.

C) Technical know-how.

D) Business experience.

25. The advantage of employees having foreign language skills is that they can _____.

A) better control the whole negotiation process

B) easily find new approaches to meet market needs

C) fast-forward their proposals to headquarters

D) easily make friends with businesspeople abroad

Passage Four

Questions 26 to 30 are based on the following passage:

In recent years, Israeli consumers have grown more demanding as they've become wealthier and more worldly-wise. Foreign travel is a national passion; this summer alone, one in 10 citizens will go abroad. Exposed to higher standards of service elsewhere, Israelis are returning home expecting the same. American firms have also begun arriving in large numbers. Chains such as KFC, McDonald's and Pizza Hut are setting a new standard of customer service, using strict employee training and constant monitoring to ensure the friendliness of frontline staff. Even the American habit of telling departing customers to "Have a nice day" has caught on all over Israel. "Nobody wakes up in the morning and say, 'Let's be nicer,'" says Itsik Cohen, director of a consulting firm. "Nothing happens without competition."

Privatization, or the threat of it, is a motivation as well. Monopolies(垄断者)that until recently have been free to take their customers for granted now fear what Michael Perry, a marketing professor, calls "the revengeful(报复的)consumer." "When the government opened up competition with Bezaq, the phone company, its international branch lost 40% of its market share, even while offering competitive rates," Says Perry, "People wanted revenge for all the years of bad service." The electric company, whose monopoly may be short-lived, has suddenly stopped requiring users to wait half a day for a repairman. Now, appointments are scheduled to the half-hour. The graceless EI Al Airlines, which is already at auction(拍卖), has retrained its employees to emphasize service and is boasting about the results in an ad campaign with the slogan, "You can feel the change in the air." For the first time, praise outnumbers complaints on customer survey sheets.

26. It may be inferred from the passage that _____.
   A) customer service in Israel is now improving
   B) wealthy Israeli customers are hard to please
   C) the tourist industry has brought chain stores to Israel
   D) Israel customers prefer foreign products to domestic ones

27. In the author's view, higher service standards are impossible in Israel _____.
   A) if customer complaints go unnoticed by the management
   B) unless foreign companies are introduced in greater numbers
   C) if there's no competition among companies
   D) without strict routine training of employees

28. If someone in Israel today needs a repairman in case of a power failure, _____.
   A) they can have it fixed in no time
   B) it's no longer necessary to make an appointment
   C) the appointment takes only half a day to make
   D) they only have to wait half an hour at most

29. The example of El Al Airlines shows that _____.
   A) revengeful customers are a threat to the monopoly of enterprises
   B) an ad campaign is a way out for enterprises in financial difficulty
   C) a good slogan has great potential for improving service

D) staff retraining is essential for better service

30. Why did Bezaq's international branch lose 40% of its market share?

A) Because the rates it offered were not competitive enough.

B) Because customers were dissatisfied with its past service.

C) Because the service offered by its competitors was far better.

D) Because it no longer received any support from the government.

【答案及解析】

11. [A] 细节题。答案见文章第二段。

12. [C] 推断题。文章第四段把英雄人物比作变压器,他们本身能量强大,同时又能把这种能量调整到普通人都能用得上的程度。也就是说,他们能成为大众的楷模。

13. [B] 推断题。第五段有一个反问句:谁能说他们那些追星族由此发现生活更加充实了呢?即这些明星并没有从精神层面给他们有益的引导。可见选项 B 正确。

14. [D] 细节题。文章最后一段指出了这两位英雄人物的事迹,旨在说明他们对于变革的巨大作用,而实际上这种变革就是解决人民所面临的问题。故本题选 D。

15. [A] 细节题。文章最后一句话是结论:如果没有富有魅力的领袖,历史仍会进步,但其步伐可能会放慢。

16. [A] 细节题。答案见原文第一、二段。

17. [B] 推断题。第二段提到由于今天的学生更倾向于追求物质上的富有,造成今天最流行的不是文学、历史而是会计学等实用性较强的学科。文中的 to be financially well off 与 the financial goals they seek in life 相吻合。

18. [D] 推断题。原文第五段指出,职业对一个人来说固然十分重要,但是我们不能忽视人类文明史上积累下来的各类知识财富的作用。

19. [B] 细节题。文中的 learn how to think 与选项中的 help people see things in their right perspective 相对应。

20. [D] 主旨题。联系全文来看,作者的观点是人们不能仅仅关心眼前的利益,而应注意吸收各方面的知识以完善自我。

21. [D] 态度题。文章第一段指出,随着科技的发展,世界已变成了一个"地球村",人们之间的联系变得更为便捷。可见作者对高科技通信设备持肯定态度。

22. [C] 细节题。原文第二段说新科技使得人们对海外业务更加重视。选项 C 中的话其实就是第二段第一句话的另一种表述方式。attach to 的意思是"认为……有意义(重要性);归因于,适用于"。

23. [C] 推断题。联系上下文来看,文章的意思是由于通信的日益发达,驻外的员工也不必担心自己的业绩会因为不被总部所知晓而失去晋升的机会。可见选项 C 符合文意。

24. [B] 细节题。文章后半部分都在论述懂外语的重要性。而第一段也提到在通信科技日益发达的今天,外语技能十分重要。

25. [A] 细节题。文章最后一段说懂外语的人能够加快或放慢谈判的进度,也就是说能较好地控制整个谈判的过程。

26. [A] 推断题。从文章第一段及文中所列举的例子来看,以色列的公司、企业的服务质量正在不断提高。

27. ［C］细节题。从第一段末及第二段开头的叙述来看，作者认为引入竞争机制有助于服务质量的提高。

28. ［D］细节题。文章第二段有这么一句话：Now, appointments are scheduled to the half-hour. 由此可见，现在在以色列如果出现电力故障，最多不过半小时就可以得到维修服务。故 D 为正确选项。其余选项的表述均不符合文意。

29. ［A］推断题。该航空公司的事例出现在第二段后半部分。文中还提到了该公司培训员工的举措和积极的口号。再看该段的前半部分，提到"the revengeful consumer"一词。可见饱受劣质服务折磨的消费者的报复对这类公司的生存构成了威胁。

30. ［B］细节题。第二段说的是以色列国内的部分公司因以前服务不佳而开始遭到消费者的"报复"，Bezaq 的经历就是一个很好的例子，由此可知 B 为正确选项。

★ 2002 年 6 月考题

Passage One

Questions 21 to 25 are based on the following passage：

In the 1960s medical researchers Thomas Holmes and Richard Rahe developed a checklist of stressful events. They appreciated the tricky point that any major change can be stressful. Negative events like "serious illness of a family member" were high on the list—but so were some positive life-changing events, like marriage. When you take the Holmes-Rahe test you must remember that the score does not reflect how you deal with stress—it only shows how much you have to deal with. And we now know that the way you handle these events dramatically affects your chances of staying healthy.

By the early 1970s, hundreds of similar studies had followed Holmes and Rahe. And millions of Americans who work and live under stress worried over the reports. Somehow the research got boiled down to a memorable message. Women's magazines ran headlines like "Stress causes illness!" If you want to stay physically and mentally healthy, the articles said, avoid stressful events.

But such simplistic advice is impossible to follow. Even if stressful events are dangerous—many—like the death of a loved one—are impossible to avoid. Moreover, any warning to avoid all stressful events is a prescription(处方)for staying away from opportunities as well as trouble. Since any change can be stressful, a person who wanted to be completely free of stress would never marry, have a child, take a new job or move.

The notion that all stress makes you sick also ignores a lot of what we know about people. It assumes we're all vulnerable(脆弱的)and passive in the face of adversity(逆境). But what about human initiative and creativity? Many come through periods of stress with more physical and mental vigor than they had before. We also know that a long time without change or challenge can lead to boredom and physical and mental strain.

21. The result of Holmes-Rahe's medical research tells us _____.

A) the way you handle major events may cause stress

B) what should be done to avoid stress

C) what kind of event would cause stress

D) how to cope with sudden changes in life

22. The studies on stress in the early 1970's led to _____ .

A) widespread concern over its harmful effects

B) great panic over the mental disorder it could cause

C) an intensive research into stress-related illnesses

D) popular avoidance of stressful jobs

23. The score of the Holmes-Rahe test shows _____ .

A) how much pressure you are under

B) how positive events can change you life

C) how stressful a major event can be

D) how you can deal with life-changing events

24. Why is "such simplistic advice"(Line 1, Para. 3) impossible to follow?

A) No one can stay on the same job for long.

B) No prescription is effective in relieving stress.

C) People have to get married someday.

D) You could be missing opportunities as well.

25. According to the passage people who have experienced ups and downs may become

_____ .

A) nervous when faced with difficulties

B) physically and mentally strained

C) more capable of coping with adversity

D) indifferent toward what happens to them

Passage Two

Questions 26 to 30 are based on the following passage:

Most episodes of absent-mindedness—forgetting where you left something or wondering why you just entered a room—are caused by a simple lack of attention, says Schacter. "You're supposed to remember something, but you haven't encoded it deeply."

Encoding, Schacter explains, is a special way of paying attention to an event that has a major impact on recalling it later. Failure to encode properly can create annoying situations. If you put your mobile phone in a pocket, for example, and don't pay attention to what you did because you're involved in a conversation, you'll probably forget that the phone is in the jacket now hanging in your wardrobe(衣柜). "Your memory itself isn't failing you," says Schacter. "Rather, you didn't give your memory system the information it needed."

Lack of interest can also lead to absent-mindedness. "A man who can recite sports statistics from 30 years ago," says Zelinski, "may not remember to drop a letter in the mailbox." Women have slightly better memories than men, possibly because they pay more attention to their environment, and memory relies on just that.

Visual cues can help prevent absent-mindedness, says Schacter. "But be sure the cue is clear and available," he cautions. If you want to remember to take a medication(药物)with lunch, put the pill bottle on the kitchen table—don't leave it in the medicine chest and write yourself a note that you keep in a pocket.

Another common episode of absent-mindedness: walking into a room and wondering why you're there. Most likely, you were thinking about something else. "Everyone does this from time to time," says Zelinski. The best thing to do is to return to where you were before entering the room, and you'll likely remember.

26. Why does the author think that encoding properly is very important?
    A) It helps us understand our memory system better.
    B) It enables us to recall something from our memory.
    C) It expands our memory capacity considerably.
    D) It slows down the process of losing our memory.

27. One possible reason why women have better memories than men is that _____.
    A) they have a wider range of interests
    B) they are more reliant on the environment
    C) they have an unusual power of focusing their attention
    D) they are more interested in what's happening around them

28. A note in the pocket can hardly serve as a reminder because _____.
    A) it will easily get lost
    B) it's not clear enough for you to read
    C) it's out of your sight
    D) it might get mixed up with other things

29. What do we learn from the last paragraph?
    A) If we focus our attention on one thing, we might forget another.
    B) Memory depends to a certain extent on the environment.
    C) Repetition helps improve our memory.
    D) If we keep forgetting things, we'd better return to where we were.

30. What is the passage mainly about?
    A) The process of gradual memory loss.
    B) The causes of absent-mindedness.
    C) The impact of the environment on memory.
    D) A way of encoding and recalling.

Passage Three

Questions 31 to 35 are based on the following passage:

It is hard to track the blue whale, the ocean's largest creature, which has almost been killed off by commercial whaling and is now listed as an endangered species. Attaching radio devices to it is difficult, and visual sightings are too unreliable to give real insight into its behavior.

So biologists were delighted early this year when with the help of the Navy they were able to track a particular blue whale for 43 days monitoring its sounds. This was possible because of the Navy's formerly top-secret system of underwater listening devices spanning the oceans.

Tracking whales is but one example of an exciting new world just opening to civilian scientists after the cold war as the Navy starts to share and partly uncover its global network of underwater listening system built over the decades to track the ships of potential enemies.

Earth scientists announced at a news conference recently that they had used the system for closely monitoring a deep-sea volcanic eruption(爆发)for the first time and that they plan similar studies.

Other scientists have proposed to use the network for tracking ocean currents and measuring changes in ocean and global temperatures.

The speed of sound in water is roughly one mile a second—slower than through land but faster than through air. What is most important, different layers of ocean water can act as channels for sounds, focusing them in the same way a stethoscope(听诊器)does when it carries faint noises from a patient's chest to a doctor's ear. This focusing is the main reason that even relatively weak sounds in the ocean, especially low-frequency ones, can often travel thousands of miles.

31. The passage is chiefly about _____.
    A) an effort to protect an endangered marine species
    B) the civilian use of a military detection system
    C) the exposure of a U.S. Navy top-secret weapon
    D) a new way to look into the behavior of blue whales

32. The underwater listening system was originally designed _____.
    A) to trace and locate enemy vessels
    B) to monitor deep-sea volcanic eruptions
    C) to study the movement of ocean currents
    D) to replace the global radio communications network

33. The deep-sea listening system makes use of _____.
    A) the sophisticated technology of focusing sounds under water
    B) the capability of sound to travel at high speed
    C) the unique property of layers of ocean water in transmitting sound
    D) low-frequency sounds traveling across different layers of water

34. It can be inferred from the passage that _____.

    A) new radio devices should be developed for tracking the endangered blue whales

    B) blue whales are no longer endangered with the use of the new listening system

    C) opinions differ as to whether civilian scientists should be allowed to use military technology

    D) military technology has great potential in civilian use

35. Which of the following is true about the U.S. Navy underwater listening network?

    A) It is now partly accessible to civilian scientists.

    B) It has been replaced by a more advanced system.

    C) It became useless to the military after the cold war.

    D) It is indispensable in protecting endangered species.

Passage Four

Questions 36 to 40 are based on the following passage:

The fitness movement that began in the late 1960s and early 1970s centered around aerobic exercise(有氧操). Millions of individuals became engaged in a variety of aerobic activities, and literally thousands of health spas developed around the country to capitalize(获利)on this emerging interest in fitness, particularly aerobic dancing for females. A number of fitness spas existed prior to this aerobic fitness movement, even a national chain with spas in most major cities. However, their focus was not on aerobics, but rather on weight-training programs designed to develop muscular mass strength and endurance in their primarily male enthusiasts. These fitness spas did not seem to benefit financially from the aerobic fitness movement to better health, since medical opinion suggested that weight-training programs offered few, if any, health benefits. In recent years, however, weight training has again become increasingly popular for males and for females. Many current programs focus not only on developing muscular strength and endurance but on aerobic fitness as well.

Historically, most physical-fitness tests have usually included measures of muscular strength and endurance, not for health-related reasons, but primarily because such fitness components have been related to performance in athletics. However, in recent years, evidence has shown that training programs designed primarily to improve muscular strength and endurance might also offer some health benefits as well. The American College of Sports Medicine now recommends that weight training be part of a total fitness program for healthy Americans. Increased participation in such training is one of the specific physical activity and fitness objectives of Healthy People 2000 National Health Promotion and Disease Prevention Objectives.

36. The word "spas"(Line 3, Para.1) most probably refers to _____.

    A) sports activities

    B) places for physical exercise

    C) recreation centers

D）athletic training programs

37. Early fitness spas were intended mainly for _____.
    A) the promotion of aerobic exercise
    B) endurance and muscular development
    C) the improvement of women's figures
    D) better performance in aerobic dancing

38. What was the attitude of doctors towards weight training in health improvement?
    A) Positive.   B) Indifferent.
    C) Negative.   D) Cautious.

39. People were given physical fitness tests in order to find out _____.
    A) how well they could do in athletics
    B) what their health condition was like
    C) what kind of fitness center was suitable for them
    D) whether they were fit for aerobic exercise

40. Recent studies have suggested that weight training _____.
    A) has become an essential part of people's life
    B) may well affect the health of the trainees
    C) will attract more people in the days to come
    D) contributes to health improvement as well

【答案及解析】

21. [C] 细节题。由文章第一段可知,该研究发现,生活中任何大的改变都会带来压力,像"家庭成员患重疾"这类不幸的事情高居榜首,但像"结婚"这样的喜事也榜上有名。故本题应选C。

22. [A] 由文章第二段开头部分可知这些研究引发了公众的忧虑。

23. [A] 细节题。依据见第一段倒数第二句:When you take the Holmes-Rahe test you must remember that the score does not reflect how you deal with stress—it only shows how much you have to deal with.

24. [D] 推断题。第二段反复说明了逃避压力的方法不可取。在该段末尾作者更是指出,一味地逃避压力的做法会让一个人失去很多机会。故本题选D。

25. [C] 细节题。见文章最后一段:Many come through periods of stress with more physical and mental vigor than they had before.

26. [B] 细节题。见文章第二段:Encoding, Schacter explains，is a special way of paying attention to an event that has a major impact on recalling it later. Failure to encode properly can create annoying situations.

27. [D] 细节题。见文章第三段末句:Women have slightly better memories than men, possibly because they pay more attention to their environment, and memory relies on just that. 缺乏

兴趣会使人健忘。女性的记忆力略强于男性,很可能是因为女性对周围的事物更感兴趣。

28. [C] 推断题。文章第四段开头告诉我们,Schacter认为视觉提示有助于克服健忘。下文的这个例子正是为了说明这一点。因此正确答案为C。

29. [A] 推断题。文章最后一段给出了一个常见的情景:你进入了一个房间,又突然发现自己忘记了为什么要进来。这很可能是因为你当时脑子里正想着其他事情。也就是说,如果我们把注意力集中在一件事上,就有可能忘记其他事情。故本题选A。

30. [B] 主旨题。通读全文可知,本文引述了专家的观点,并举了一些日常生活中常见的事例,其目的都是为了说明健忘的原因。

31. [B] 主旨题。本文论述了生物学家和地球科学家利用美国海军水下监听系统,使其科学研究取得了很多新的成果。因此,"军事探测系统的民用"正是本文论述的主题。

32. [A] 细节题。依据见原文第三段:... the Navy starts to share and partly uncover its global network of underwater listening system built over the decades to track the ships of potential enemies.

33. [C] 推断题。见文章最后一段。

34. [D] 推断题。由文中所举的两个例子可知军事技术在民用方面可以发挥很大作用。

35. [A] 细节题。由文章第三段可知,美国海军水下监听系统现已部分用于民用。故选项A正确。

36. [B] 词义题。文章第一段提到,参加各种有氧健身运动的人有数百万之众,而人们对健身运动的热情使得全国出现了数以千计的"health spas"。由此不难推断,该词指的是健身场所。因此本题选B。

37. [B] 细节题。见第一段中间部分:However, their focus was not on aerobics, but rather on weight-training programs designed to develop muscular mass strength and endurance in their primarily male enthusiasts.

38. [C] 态度题。见第一段:These fitness spas did not seem to benefit financially from the aerobic fitness movement to better health, since medical opinion suggested that weight-training programs offered few, if any, health benefits. 可见以前,医生对这类训练的态度是否定的。

39. [A] 细节题。见文章第二段首句:Historically, most physical-fitness tests have usually included measures of muscular strength and endurance, not for health-related reasons, but primarily because such fitness components have been related to performance in athletics.

40. [D] 细节题。依据见文章第二段第二句:However, in recent years, evidence has shown that training programs designed primarily to improve muscular strength and endurance might also offer some health benefits as well. 这句话的意思是,最近的研究表明这些肌肉力量和耐力的训练对健康也有好处。

第四章 简 答 题

第一节 简答题应试技巧

一、什么是简答题

　　简答题(Short Answer Questions)是 1997 年起全国大学英语四、六级考试中开始采用的一种题型。其阅读材料一般为一篇 300 个词左右的文章,题材与难易程度与阅读理解的文章近似。问题设置有两种形式,一种为完全形式,以一个完整的问句提问;另一种为不完全形式,问题为一个不完整的句子,要求考生根据文章内容把句子补充完整。回答既可以是句子,也可以是短语或单词。

　　1997 年以前的全国英语四、六级考试的阅读理解部分都是采用单项选择题的形式进行考查。尽管这种形式具有客观、可靠等优点,但也存在很多不足。而简答题除了考查考生的阅读能力之外,还能考查其概括能力和语言表达能力。

二、简答题的评分标准

　　首先要注意的是答案的字数。从过去的试题来看,一般都要求答案字数不能超过 10 个词,否则要扣 0.5 分。

　　具体的评分标准如下:

　　· 考生应在读懂文章的基础上,用正确简短的语言回答问题。在评分时应同时考虑内容和语言。每题满分为 2 分,最低分为 0 分。

　　· 给分标准:

　　　　＊2 分:答出全部内容,语言正确;

　　　　＊1 分:答出部分内容,语言正确;

　　　　＊0 分:没有答对问题。

　　· 扣分标准:

　　　　＊语言有错误扣 0.5 分(不包括引起歧义的、可以辨识的拼写错误)。每题由于语言错误扣分不能超过 0.5 分。

　　　　＊涉及无关内容者扣 0.5 分;答案中有相互矛盾的内容,则内容矛盾部分不得分。

　　　　＊整句原封不动照搬应扣分;照搬一句扣 0.5 分;照搬两句及两句以上者扣 2 分。

三、简答题问题类型归纳

　　⊙具体细节题

　　具体细节题是简答题中出现最多的题型。这类题目考查考生能否了解或理解文章中给出的各种信息,如事实、时间、地点、人物、起因、结果等。这类问题的答案往往可以直接在文章中找到。

　　⊙推断题

　　这类题型主要包括在事实基础上的推理和在逻辑基础上的推理。但简答题中的推断题不但

要求掌握文章所表达的字面含义,而且还要用自己的话进行概括。

⊙词义题

这类题的目的在于考查考生转述或解释某个词或短语在特定场合下的含义的能力。该类题要求考生不仅要读懂原文,而且要能准确、清晰地表达出来。

⊙态度题

态度题主要考查对作者或文中涉及的人或机构的观点、态度的把握。如 1997 年 1 月第 74 题:What is the opinion of British authorities concerning speeding laws? 和 2002 年 6 月第 2 题:What do researchers conclude about children's learning patterns? 都属于这类题型。

⊙主旨题

这类题型主要考查考生对整文章的理解和概括能力。这类题目难度较大,在以往的简答题中出现频率也不高。由于考查的文章以记叙文居多,通常没有明确的可以概括全文的主旨句。事实上,考查对文章主旨的理解的题目往往已转化为以具体细节题的形式出现。

四、简答题解题技巧

⊙认真审题。明确问题是解题的关键。首先,考生应快速地浏览问题。了解问题后,确定原文中该题的题眼,然后仔细分析题眼处的相关信息,这样可以避免答非所问。注意要结合上下文全面而又综合地考虑问题和作答,切不可断章取义。

⊙找准答案,即找出与问题相关的关键词(线索词)在文章中的大体位置,并尽可能缩小概括范围,不要瞻前顾后,眉毛胡子一把抓。否则答案涉及无关内容要扣分。

⊙认真核对,避免错误。做完题后应仔细检查以下几点:答案是否切题,是否完整;是否有时态与原文不符、主谓不一致、词语用法不当等语法错误;拼写(包括大小写)、标点是否正确。同时还要注意提问方式与答案的协调性。不同的问题要求不同形式的回答。如问目的时,答案就应当用表示目的的用语,如 for 短语、不定式短语,而用名词性或形容词性的答案就不合适。掌握这一原则有助于增强答题的针对性。例如 1999 年 6 月考题中的一道题:Which word in the first two paragraphs best explains why many women have to work? 这个问题不仅限定了范围,而且也规定了答案的形式。做这类题目时必须十分小心,以免因为不按要求作答而失分。

第二节 简答题真题详解

★2005 年 6 月考题

Part Ⅳ Short Answer Questions(15 minutes)

Directions:In this part there is a short passage with five questions or incomplete statements. Read the passage carefully. Then answer the questions or complete the statements in the fewest possible words (not exceeding 10 words).

We commonly think of sportsmanship in connection with athletic contests, but it also applies to individual outdoor sports. Not everyone who picks up a fishing rod or goes out with a gun is a sportsman. The sportsman first of all obeys the fish and game laws, not because he is liable to be punished as a violator, but because he knows that in the main these laws are made for his best interests.

The following are some of the things that those who would qualify for membership in the sportsmanship fraternity(圈内人)will do.

1. Take no more game than the bag limit provided for by the fish and game laws. The person who comes back from a trip boasting about the large number of fish or game taken is not a sportsman but a game hog(贪得无厌的捕猎者).

2. Observe the unwritten rules of fair play. This means shooting game birds only when the birds are "on the wing". For the same reason, do not use a shotgun to shoot a rabbit or similar animal while it is sitting or standing still.

3. Be careful in removing illegal or undersized fish from the hook. This should be done only after wetting the hands. This is necessary because the body of the fish is covered with a thin, protective film which will stick to your dry hands. If the hands are dry when the fish is handled, the film is torn from the body of the fish. Without the protective film, the fish is more easily attacked by diseases. If you wish to release a fish that is hooked in such a way that it will be impossible to close to the hook as convenient. In a remarkably short time, the hook will break down and the fish will remain almost unharmed. Fish has been known to feed successfully while hooks were still in their lips.

4. Be sure of the identity of your target before you shoot. Many useful and harmless species of wildlife are thoughtlessly killed by the uninformed person who is out with a gun to kill whatever flies within range.

Questions:(注意:答题尽量简短,超过 10 个词要扣分。每条横线限写一个英语单词,标点符号不占格。)

S1. In what respect does the author think individual outdoor sports are similar to athletic contests?

____ ____ ____ ____ ____ ____ ____ ____ ____ .

S2. A person who goes out fishing with a fishing rod or hunting with a gun is not necessarily

____ ____ ____ ____ ____ ____ ____ ____ ____ .

S3. What's the most important thing a true sportsman should bear in mind when he goes fishing or hunting?

____ ____ ____ ____ ____ ____ ____ ____ ____ .

S4. Those who violate the fish and game laws will not be ____ ____
____ ____ ____ for membership in the sportsmanship fraternity.

S5. What are people called when they break the bag limit and boast about their big catch?

____ ____ ____ ____ ____ ____ ____ ____ ____ .

S6. A true sportsman will not shoot an animal which is not ____ ____

_____ _____ _____ _____ _____ .

S7. What are people advised to do before they remove illegal or undersized fish from the hook?

_____ _____ _____ _____ _____ _____ _____ _____ _____ .

S8. What should sportsman do to avoid killing rare species of wildlife?

_____ _____ _____ _____ _____ _____ _____ _____ _____ .

【答案及解析】

S1. Sportsmanship

【答题依据】We commonly think of sportsmanship in connection with athletic contests，but it also applies to individual outdoor sports.

S2. a sportsman

【答题依据】Not everyone who picks up a fishing rod or goes out with a gun is a sportsman.

S3. Obeying the fish and game laws

【答题依据】The sportsman first of all obeys the fish and game laws，not because he is liable to be punished as a violator，but because he knows that in the main these laws are made for his best interests.

S4. qualified

【答题依据】The following are some of the things that those who would qualify for membership in the sportsmanship fraternity will do.

S5. Game hogs

【答题依据】The person who comes back from a trip boasting about the large number of fish or game taken is not a sportsman but a game hog.

S6. moving

【答题依据】This means shooting game birds only when the birds are "on the wing". For the same reason，do not use a shotgun to shoot a rabbit or similar animal while it is sitting or standing still.

S7. To wet the hands

【答题依据】Be careful in removing illegal or undersized fish from the hook. This should be done only after wetting the hands.

S8. Be sure of the identity of the target before shooting

【答题依据】Be sure of the identity of your target before you shoot. Many useful and harmless species of wildlife are thoughtlessly killed by the uninformed person who is out with a gun to kill whatever flies within range.

★2003 年 9 月考题

Sports is one of the world's largest industries, and most athletes are professionals who are paid for their efforts. Because an athlete succeeds by achievement only—not by economic background or family connections—sports can be a fast route to wealth, and many athletes play only for money than for love.

This has not always been true. In the ancient Olympics the winner got only a wreath of olive leaves(橄榄叶花环). Even though the winners became national heroes, the games remained amateur for centuries. Athletes won fame, but no money. As time passed, however, the contests became increasingly less amateur and cities began to hire athletes to represent them. By the fourth century A. D. , the Olympics were ruined, and they were soon ended.

In 1896, the Olympic Games were revived(使再度兴起)with the same goal of pure amateur competition. The rules bar athletes who have ever received a $ 50 prize or an athletic scholar or who have spent four weeks in a training camp. At least one competitor in the 1896 games met these qualifications. He was Spiridon Loues, a water carrier who won the marathon race. After race, a rich Athenian offered him anything he wanted. A true amateur, Loues accepted only a cart and a horse. Then he gave up running forever. But Loues was an exception and now, as the Chairman of the German Olympic Committee said, "Nobody pays any attention to these rules. " Many countries pay their athletes to train year-round, and Olympic athletes are eager to sell their names to companies that make everything from ski equipment to fast food.

Even the games themselves have become a huge business. Countries fight to hold the Olympics not only for honor, but for money. The 1972 games in Munich cost the Germans 545 million dollars, but by selling medal symbols, TV rights, food, drink, hotel rooms, and souvenirs(纪念品), they managed to make a profit. Appropriately, the symbol of victory in the Olympic Games is no longer a simple olive wreath—it is a gold medal.

S1. To many people, sports today is nothing but ＿＿＿ ＿＿＿ ＿＿＿ ＿＿＿ ＿＿＿ ＿＿＿ ＿＿＿ ＿＿＿ ＿＿＿ ＿＿＿ .

S2. What do most athletes of today go after?

＿＿＿ ＿＿＿ ＿＿＿ ＿＿＿ ＿＿＿ ＿＿＿ ＿＿＿ ＿＿＿

S3. What reward could an ancient Greek athlete expect?

＿＿＿ ＿＿＿ ＿＿＿ ＿＿＿ ＿＿＿ ＿＿＿ ＿＿＿ ＿＿＿ .

S4. By the fourth century A. D. , Olympic contests became increasingly more ＿＿＿ ＿＿＿

＿＿＿ ＿＿＿ ＿＿＿ ＿＿＿ ＿＿＿ ＿＿＿ ＿＿＿ ＿＿＿ .

S5. When the Olympic Games were revived in 1896, athletes who had received special training

in camps would be ___ ___ ___ ___ ___ ___ ___ ___
___ .

S6. What did Spiridon Loues do after he accepted the Athenian's gift?

___ ___ ___ ___ ___ ___ ___ ___ ___ ___

S7. According to the author, some athletes are even willing to advertise for businesses which sell things like ___ ___ ___ ___ ___ ___ ___ ___ ___ .

S8. The 1972 Munich games managed to make a big profit mainly by ___ ___ ___
___ ___ ___ ___ ___ ___ ___ services and selling ___ ___
___ .

【答案及解析】

S1. a fast route to wealth

【答题依据】Because an athlete succeeds by achievement only—not by economic background or family connections—sports can be a fast route to wealth, and many athletes play only for money than for love.

S2. Money

【答题依据】... sports can be a fast route to wealth, and many athletes play only for money than for love.

S3. A wreath of olive leaves / Olive wreath

【答题依据】In the ancient Olympics the winner got only a wreath of olive leaves.

S4. professional

【答题依据】As time passed, however, the contests became increasingly less amateur and cities began to hire athletes to represent them. By the fourth century A.D. , the Olympics were ruined, and they were soon ended.

S5. barred

【答题依据】The rules bar athletes who have ever received a $50 prize or an athletic scholars or who have spent four weeks in a training camp.

S6. He gave up running forever / Giving up running forever

【答题依据】A true amateur, Loues accepted only a cart and a horse. Then he gave up running forever.

S7. ski equipment and fast food

【答题依据】Many countries pay their athletes to train year-round, and Olympic athletes are eager to sell their names to companies that make everything from ski equipment to fast food.

S8. (1) hotel souvenirs, food and drinks

(2) medal symbols, TV rights,

【答题依据】The 1972 games in Munich cost the Germans 545 million dollars, but by selling medal symbols, TV rights, food, drink, hotel rooms, and souvenirs, they managed to make a profit.

★2003 年 6 月考题

What personal qualities are desirable in a teacher? I think the following would be generally accepted.

First, the teacher's personality should be lively and attractive. This does not rule out people who are plain-looking, or even ugly, because many such people have great personal charm. But it does rule out such types as the over-excitable, sad, cold, and frustrated.

Secondly, it is not merely desirable but essential for a teacher to have a genuine capacity for sympathy, a capacity to understand the minds and feelings of other people, especially, since most teachers are school teachers, the minds and feelings of children. Closely related with this is the capacity to be tolerant—not, indeed, of what is wrong, but of the weaknesses and immaturity of human nature which induce people, and again especially children, to make mistakes.

Thirdly, I hold it essential for a teacher to be both intellectually and morally honest. This means that he will be aware of his intellectual strengths and limitations, and will have thought about and decided upon the moral principles by which his life shall be guided. There is no contradiction in my going on to say that a teacher should be a bit of an actor. That is part of the technique of teaching, which demands that every now and then a teacher should be able to put on an act to enliven(使生动) a lesson, correct a fault, or award praise. Children, especially young children, live in a world that is rather larger than life.

A teacher must be capable of infinite patience. This, I may say, is largely a matter of self-discipline and self-training, for we are none of us born like that.

Finally, I think a teacher should have the kind of mind which always wants to go on learning. Teaching is a job at which one will never be perfect; there is always something more to learn about it. There are three principal objects of study: the subjects which the teacher is teaching; the methods by which the subjects can best be taught to the particular pupils in the classes he is teaching; and—by far the most important—the children, young people, or adults to whom the subjects are to be taught. The two fundamental principles of British education today are that education is education of the whole person, and that it is best acquired through full and active co-operation between two persons, the teacher and the learner.

S1. Plain-looking teachers can also be admired by their students if they have _____ _____

S2. The author says it is ＿＿＿＿ ＿＿＿＿ ＿＿＿＿ ＿＿＿＿ ＿＿＿＿ ＿＿＿＿ ＿＿＿＿ that teachers be sympathetic with their students.

S3. A teacher should be tolerant because humans tend to have ＿＿＿＿ ＿＿＿＿ ＿＿＿＿ ＿＿＿＿ ＿＿＿＿ ＿＿＿＿ and to be ＿＿＿＿ ＿＿＿＿ ＿＿＿＿ ＿＿＿＿ ＿＿＿＿.

S4. A teacher who is ＿＿＿＿ ＿＿＿＿ ＿＿＿＿ ＿＿＿＿ ＿＿＿＿ will be able to make his lessons more lively.

S5. How can a teacher acquire infinite patience?

＿＿＿＿ ＿＿＿＿ ＿＿＿＿ ＿＿＿＿ ＿＿＿＿ ＿＿＿＿ ＿＿＿＿ ＿＿＿＿ ＿＿＿＿ .

S6. Since teaching is a job no one can be perfect at, it is necessary for teachers to keep improving their knowledge of the subjects they teach and their ＿＿＿＿ ＿＿＿＿ ＿＿＿＿ ＿＿＿＿ ＿＿＿＿ ＿＿＿＿ ＿＿＿＿ ＿＿＿＿ ＿＿＿＿ ＿＿＿＿ .

S7. Teachers' most important object of study is ＿＿＿＿ ＿＿＿＿ ＿＿＿＿ ＿＿＿＿ ＿＿＿＿ ＿＿＿＿ ＿＿＿＿ ＿＿＿＿ .

S8. Education cannot be best acquired without ＿＿＿＿ ＿＿＿＿ ＿＿＿＿ ＿＿＿＿ ＿＿＿＿ ＿＿＿＿ ＿＿＿＿ between the teacher and the learner.

【答案及解析】

S1. great personal charm

【答题依据】This does not rule out people who are plain-looking, or even ugly, because many such people have great personal charm.

S2. desirable and essential

【答题依据】Secondly, it is not merely desirable but essential for a teacher to have a genuine capacity for sympathy, a capacity to understand the minds and feelings of other people, especially, since most teachers are school teachers, the minds and feelings of children.

S3. (1) weakness and immaturity (2) wrong

【答题依据】Closely related with this is the capacity to be tolerant—not, indeed, of what is wrong, but of the weaknesses and immaturity of human nature which induce people, and again especially children, to make mistakes.

S4. a bit of an actor

【答题依据】There is no contradiction in my going on to say that a teacher should be a bit of an actor. That is part of the technique of teaching, which demands that every now and then a teacher should be able to put on an act to enliven a lesson, correct a fault, or award praise.

S5. By self-discipline and self-training

【答题依据】A teacher must be capable of infinite patience. This, I may say, is largely a matter of self-discipline and self-training, for we are none of us born like that.

S6. methods by which the subjects can best be taught

【答题依据】There are three principal objects of study: the subjects which the teacher is teaching; the methods by which the subjects can best be taught to the particular pupils in the classes he is teaching...

S7. the learners to whom the subjects are to be taught

【答题依据】There are three principal objects of study: the subjects which the teacher is teaching; the methods by which the subjects can best be taught to the particular pupils in the classes he is teaching; and—by far the most important—the children, young people, or adults to whom the subjects are to be taught.

S8. full and active co-operation

【答题依据】The two fundamental principles of British education today are that education is education of the whole person, and that it is best acquired through full and active co-operation between two persons, the teacher and the learner.

★2002 年 6 月考题

As researchers learn more about how children's intelligence develops, they are increasingly surprised by the power of parents. The power of the school has been replaced by the home. To begin with, all the factors which are part of intelligence—the child's understanding of language learning patterns curiosity—are established well before the child enters school at the age of six. Study after study has shown that even after school begins, children's achievements have been far more influenced by parents than by teachers. This is particularly true about learning that is language-related. The school rather than the home is given credit for variations in achievement in subjects such as science.

In view of their power it's sad to see so many parents not making the most of their child's intelligence. Until recently parents had been warned by educators who asked them not to educate their children. Many teachers now realize that children cannot be educated only at school and parents are being asked to contribute both before and after the child enters school.

Parents have been particularly afraid to teach reading at home. Of course children shouldn't be pushed to read by their parents but educators have discovered that reading is best taught individually—and the easiest place to do this is at home. Many four and five-year-old who have been shown a few letters and taught their sounds will compose single words of their own with them even before they have been taught to read.

S1. What have researchers found out about the influence of parents and the school on children's intelligence?

＿＿＿＿＿＿＿＿＿＿＿＿＿＿＿＿＿＿＿＿＿＿＿＿＿＿＿＿＿＿＿＿＿.

S2. What do researchers conclude about children's learning patterns?

＿＿＿＿＿＿＿＿＿＿＿＿＿＿＿＿＿＿＿＿＿＿＿＿＿＿＿＿＿＿＿＿＿.

S3. In which area may school play a more important role?

＿＿＿＿＿＿＿＿＿＿＿＿＿＿＿＿＿＿＿＿＿＿＿＿＿＿＿＿＿＿＿＿＿.

S4. Why did many parents fail to make the most of their children's intelligence?

＿＿＿＿＿＿＿＿＿＿＿＿＿＿＿＿＿＿＿＿＿＿＿＿＿＿＿＿＿＿＿＿＿.

S5. The author suggests in the last paragraph that parents should be encouraged to ＿＿＿＿

＿＿＿＿＿＿＿＿＿＿＿＿＿.

【答案及解析】

S1. Parents have greater influence than the school / Parents' influence is greater than the school's
【答题依据】The power of the school has been replaced by the home.

S2. They are established well before the age of six / They are established well before the children enter school
【答题依据】To begin with，all the factors which are part of intelligence—the child's understanding of language learning patterns curiosity—are established well before the child enters school at the age of six.

S3. In science subjects / In subjects such as science
【答题依据】The school rather than the home is given credit for variations in achievement in subjects such as science.

S4. They were told not to educate their children / They had been warned not to educate their children
【答题依据】Until recently parents had been warned by educators who asked them not to educate their children.

S5. teach reading at home

【答题依据】Of course children shouldn't be pushed to read by their parents but educators have discovered that reading is best taught individually—and the easiest place to do this is at home.

★1999 年 6 月考题

For many women choosing whether to work or not to work outside their home is a luxury; they must work to survive. Others face a hard decision.

Perhaps the easiest choice has to do with economics. One husband said, "Marge and I decided after careful consideration that for her to go back to work at this moment was an extravagance(奢侈)we couldn't afford." With two preschool children, it soon became clear in their figuring that with babysitters(临时照看小孩的人), transportation, and increased taxes, rather than having more money, they might actually end up with less.

Economic factors are usually the first to be considered, but they are not the most important. The most important aspects of the decision have to do with the emotional needs of each member of the family. It is in this area that husbands and wives find themselves having to face many confusing and conflicting feelings.

There are many women who find that homemaking is boring or who feel imprisoned(被囚人)if they have to stay home with a young child or several children. On the other hand, there are women who think that homemaking gives them the deepest satisfaction.

From my own experience, I would like to suggest that sometimes the decision to go back to work to is made in too much haste. There are few decisions that I now regret more. I wasn't mature enough to see how much I could have gained at home. I regret my impatience to get on with my career. I wish I had allowed myself the luxury of watching the world through my little girl's eyes.

S1. Which word in the first two paragraphs best explains why many women have to work?

_____ _____ _____ _____ _____ _____ _____ _____ .

S2. Why did Marge and her husband think it an extravagance for Marge to go back to work?

_____ _____ _____ _____ _____ _____ _____ _____ _____ _____ .

S3. What are the two major considerations in deciding whether women should go out to work?

_____ _____ _____ _____ _____ _____ _____ _____ .

S4. Some women would rather do housework and take care of their children than pursue a career because they feel _____ _____ _____ _____ _____ _____ _____ _____ _____ _____ .

S5. If given a second chance, the writer would probably choose to _____ _____ _____ _____

_____ _____ _____ _____ _____ _____ .

【答案及解析】

S1. Survive

【答题依据】For many women choosing whether to work or not to work outside their home is a luxury; they must work to survive.

S2. Because the increased cost will be more than Marge's income / Because they might actually end up with less money

【答题依据】With two preschool children, it soon became clear in their figuring that with babysitters, transportation, and increased taxes, rather than having more money, they might actually end up with less.

S3. Economic factors and emotional needs

【答题依据】Economic factors are usually the first to be considered, but they are not the most important. The most important aspects of the decision have to do with the emotional needs of each member of the family.

S4. that homemaking gives them the deepest satisfaction

【答题依据】On the other hand, there are women who think that homemaking gives them the deepest satisfaction.

S5. stay at home / stay at home and enjoy family life

【答题依据】I regret my impatience to get on with my career. I wish I had allowed myself the luxury of watching the world through my little girl's eyes.

★1999 年 1 月考题

Would-be language teachers everywhere have one thing in common: they all want some recognition of their professional status and skills, and a job. The former requirement is obviously important on a personal level, but it is vital if you are to have any chance of finding work.

Ten years ago, the situation was very different. In virtually every developing country, and in many developed countries as well, being a native English speaker was enough to get you employed as an English teacher.

Now employers will only look at teachers who have the knowledge, the skills and attitudes to teach English effectively. The result of this has been to raise non-native English teachers to the same status as their native counterparts(相对应的人)—something they have always deserved but seldom enjoyed. Non-natives are now happy—linguistic discrimination(语言上的歧视)is a thing of the past.

An ongoing research project, funded by the University of Cambridge, asked a sample of teachers, educators and employers in more than 40 countries whether they regard the native/

non-native speakers distinction as being at all important. "NO" was the answer. As long as candidates could teach and had the required level of English, it didn't matter who they were and where they came from. Thus, a new form of discrimination—this time justified because it singled out the unqualified—liberated the linguistically oppressed(受压迫的). But the Cambridge project did more than just that: it confirmed that the needs of native and non-native teachers are extremely similar.

S1. The selection of English teachers used to be mainly based on _____ _____ _____ _____ _____ .

S2. What did non-native English teachers deserve but seldom enjoy?
_____ _____ _____ _____ _____ _____ _____ _____ _____ .

S3. What kind of people can now find a job as an English teacher?
_____ _____ _____ _____ _____ _____ _____ _____ .

S4. What is the result of the "new form of discrimination"(Line 5, Para. 4)?
_____ _____ _____ _____ _____ _____ _____ _____ _____ .

S5. The phrase "the linguistically oppressed"(Line 6, Para. 4) refers to those who were
_____ _____ _____ _____ _____ _____ _____ _____ .

【答案及解析】
S1. whether the person is a native speaker or not
【答题依据】In virtually every developing country, and in many developed countries as well, being a native English speaker was enough to get you employed as an English teacher.

S2. The same status as their counterparts
【答题依据】The result of this has been to raise non-native English teachers to the same status as their native counterparts—something they have always deserved but seldom enjoyed.

S3. One who can teach and have the required English level
【答题依据】Now employers will only look at teachers who have the knowledge, the skills and attitudes to teach English effectively.

S4. Non-native English teachers have been liberated / It singled out the unqualified
【答题依据】Thus, a new form of discrimination—this time justified because it singled out the unqualified—liberated the linguistically oppressed.

S5. non-native English speakers

【答题依据】As long as candidates could teach and had the required level of English, it didn't matter who they were and where they came from.

★1997 年 1 月考题

In Britain, the old Road Traffic Act restricted speeds to 2 m. p. h. (miles per hour) in towns and 4 m. p. h. in the country. Later Parliament increased the speed limit to 14 m. p. h. But by 1903 the development of the car industry had made it necessary to raise the limit to 20 m. p. h. By 1930, however, the law was so widely ignored that speeding restrictions were done away with altogether. For five years motorists were free to drive at whatever speed they like. Then in 1935 the Road Traffic Act imposed a 30 m. p. h. speed limit in built-up areas, along with the introduction of driving tests and pedestrian crossing.

Speeding is now the most common motoring offence in Britain. Offences for speeding fall into three classes: exceeding the limit on a restricted road, exceeding on any road the limit for the vehicle you are driving, and exceeding the 70 m. p. h. limit on any road. A restricted road is one where the street lamps are 200 yards apart, or more.

The main controversy(争论)surrounding speeding laws is the extent of their safety value. The Ministry of Transport maintains that speed limits reduce accidents. It claims that when the 30 m. p. h. limit was introduced in 1935 there was a fall of 15 percent in fatal accidents. Likewise, when the 40 m. p. h. speed limit was imposed on a number of roads in London in the late fifties, there was a 28 percent reduction in serious accidents. There were also fewer casualties(伤亡)in the year after the 70 m. p. h. motorway limit was imposed in 1966.

In America, however, it is thought that the reduced accident figures are due rather to the increase in traffic density. This is why it has even been suggested that the present speed limits should be done away with completely, or that a guide should be given to inexperienced drivers and the speed limits made advisory, as is done in parts of the USA.

S1. During which period could British motorists drive without speed limits?

_____ _____ _____ _____ _____ _____ _____ _____ _____ _____ .

S2. What measures were adopted in 1935 in addition to the speeding restrictions?

S3. Speeding is a motoring offence a driver commits when he _____ _____

_____ _____ _____ _____ _____ _____ _____ _____ .

S4. What is the opinion of British authorities concerning speeding laws?

_____ _____ _____ _____ _____ _____ _____ _____ _____ _____

S5. What reason do Americans give for the reduction in traffic accidents?

【答案及解析】

S1. 1930—1935 / From 1930 to 1935 / Between 1930 and 1935

【答题依据】By 1930, however, the law was so widely ignored that speeding restrictions were done away with altogether. For five years motorists were free to drive at whatever speed they like. Then in 1935 the Road Traffic Act imposed a 30 m. p. h. speed limit in built-up areas, along with the introduction of driving tests and pedestrian crossing.

S2. The introduction of driving tests and pedestrian crossing / Driving tests and pedestrian crossing

【答题依据】Then in 1935 the Road Traffic Act imposed a 30 m. p. h. speed limit in built-up areas, along with the introduction of driving tests and pedestrian crossing.

S3. exceeds the speed limits / breaks speeding laws

【答题依据】Speeding is now the most common motoring offence in Britain. Offences for speeding fall into three classes: exceeding the limit on a restricted road, exceeding on any road the limit for the vehicle you are driving, and exceeding the 70 m. p. h. limit on any road.

S4. Speed limits reduce accidents / Speed limits help reduce accidents / Reducing accidents

【答题依据】The Ministry of Transport maintains that speed limits reduce accidents.

S5. The increase in traffic density

【答题依据】In America, however, it is thought that the reduced accident figures are due rather to the increase in traffic density.

第三节　简答题强化训练

◎ **Passage 1**

This is the "designer" age. People in the West talk of designer labels and designer violence. The word "designer" has become an adjective loaded with the symbolism and imagery of the consumer society. For the first time in history, it is possible to live a "designer lifestyle"—if you can afford it.

But what does the word "design" mean? The subject of design covers a wide range of activities, from materials technology at the hard end to styling and marketing at the soft end. The number of people who have made a contribution to the history of design at any of these levels is vast. Actually the term can also be confined to meaning the people who had the ideas and who invented the forms which changed our taste.

The term "design" as we now use it is a modern invention, a product of the division of labor

and other economic changes thrown up by the Industrial Revolution in the 18th and 19th centuries. With the rise of mechanized production and standardized products, there came the need for disciplined product planning. No longer did the person who had an idea for something go on to make it. The new order, in which the designer had the idea and the factory-worker manufactured it, meant the designer achieved a new and unprecedented(空前的)status in the system.

The 20th century design has had an important influence on the Western way of life. Objects have acquired not only culture status, but massive symbolic significance through people's perceptions of them. The Coca-Cola bottle—the most famous bottle in the world and the classic piece of modern package design now symbolizes the power of the 20th century Western civilization to penetrate and erode other cultures. From modern painters such as Warhol to many contemporary films, Coca-Cola has become a symbol of cultural imperialism, and is such a familiar part of the consumer landscape that it is almost invisible.

The possibility that the Coca-Cola bottle was too familiar worried the company so much that several years ago they redesigned the famous logo and the bottle, and changed the taste of the syrup as part of an on-going battle with rival company Pepsi. So loud was the public outcry, however, that the company quickly reinstated all three.

Making an image and making an object have become indivisible parts of the design process. Coca-Cola owns nothing more than the recipe for a syrup and the copyright on a logo, yet it is a multimillion dollar business.

Now design is at the cutting edge of business competition. The importance of design has changed through the various phases of industrial growth, and in the years to come it will increasingly assume a high priority in corporate. Today, placing the idea of quality foremost in purchasers' minds is so important that it has spawned a new science-design technology. In today's business environment, the research and development of design ideas has become an essential part of the manufacturing and selling processes.

S1. According to the author, the term "design" can be confined to meaning the people who invented the forms which _____ _____ _____ _____ _____ _____ _____ _____ _____ _____.

S2. According to the passage, what symbolizes the power of the influences of the 20th century Western civilization on other cultures?

_____ _____ _____ _____ _____ _____ _____ _____ _____ _____.

S3. The 20th century design has had an important influence on the _____ _____ _____ _____.

S4. What has become an essential part of the manufacturing and selling processes in today's business world?

_____ _____ _____ _____ _____ _____ _____ _____ _____ _____.

S5. Coca-Cola changed the taste of the syrup as part of ＿＿＿＿＿＿ ＿＿＿＿＿ ＿＿＿＿＿ ＿＿＿＿＿ ＿＿＿＿＿ ＿＿＿＿＿ ＿＿＿＿＿ .

【答案及解析】

S1. changed our taste

【答题依据】Actually the term can also be confined to meaning the people who had the ideas and who invented the forms which changed our taste.

S2. The Coca-Cola bottle

【答题依据】The Coca-Cola bottle—the most famous bottle in the world and the classic piece of modem package design now symbolizes the power of the 20th century Western civilization to penetrate and erode other cultures.

S3. Western way of life

【答题依据】The 20th century design has had an important influence on the Western way of life.

S4. The research and development of design ideas

【答题依据】In today's business environment，the research and development of design ideas has become an essential part of the manufacturing and selling processes.

S5. an on-going battle with rival company Pepsi

【答题依据】The possibility that the Coca-Cola bottle was too familiar worried the company so much that several years ago they redesigned the famous logo and the bottle，and changed the taste of the syrup as part of an on-going battle with rival company Pepsi.

◎ **Passage 2**

Some people believe that international sport creates goodwill between the nations and that if countries play games together they will learn to live together. Others say that the opposite is true: that international contests encourage false national pride and lead to misunderstanding and hatred. There is probably some truth in both arguments，but in recent years the Olympic Games have done little to support the view that sports encourages international brotherhood. Not only was there the tragic incident involving the murder of athletes，but the Games were also ruined by lesser incidents caused principally by minor national contests.

One country received its second-place medals with visible indignation after the hockey final. There had been noisy scenes at the end of the hockey match，the losers objecting to the final decisions. They were convinced that one of their goals should not have been disallowed and that their opponents' victory was unfair. Their manager was in a rage when he said："This wasn't hockey. Hockey and the International Hockey Federation are finished." The president of the Federation said later that such behavior could result in the suspension of the team for at least three years.

The American basketball team announce that they would not yield first place to Russia, after a disputable(有争议的)end to their contest. The game had ended in disturbance. It was thought at first that the United States had won, by a single point, but it was announced that there were three seconds still to play. A Russian player then threw the ball from one end of the court to the other, and another player popped it into the basket. It was the first time the USA had ever lost an Olympic basketball match. An appeal jury debated the matter for four and a half hours before announcing that the result would stand. The American players then voted not to receive the silver medals.

Incidents of this kind will continue as long as sport is played competitively rather than for the love of the game. The suggestion that athletes should compete as individuals, or in non-national teams, might be too much to hope for. But in the present organization of the Olympics there is far too much that encourages aggressive patriotism.

S1. The Olympic Games were ruined by lesser incidents caused principally by _____ _____ _____ _____ _____ _____ _____ _____ _____.

S2. How long will the team be suspended for its player's behavior in the hockey match? _____ _____ _____ _____.

S3. The American players voted not to receive _____ _____ _____ _____ _____ _____ _____ _____ _____ _____ after the jury announcing that the result would stand.

S4. What did the American basketball team announce after the contest? _____ _____ _____ _____ _____ _____ _____ _____.

S5. According to the author, the suggestion that athletes should compete as _____ _____ _____ _____ _____ _____ might be unrealistic.

【答案及解析】

S1. minor national contests

【答题依据】Not only was there the tragic incident involving the murder of athletes, but the Games were also ruined by lesser incidents caused principally by minor national contests.

S2. At least three years

【答题依据】The president of the Federation said later that such behavior could result in the suspension of the team for at least three years.

S3. the silver medals

【答题依据】An appeal jury debated the matter for four and a half hours before announcing that the result would stand. The American players then voted not to receive the silver medals.

S4. They would not yield first place to Russia

【答题依据】The American basketball team announced that they would not yield first place to Russia, after a disputable end to their contest.

S5. individuals

【答题依据】The suggestion that athletes should compete as individuals, or in non-national teams, might be too much to hope for.

◎ **Passage 3**

To say that the child learns by imitation and that the way to teach is to set a good example oversimplifies. No child imitates every action he sees. Sometimes, the example the parent wants him to follow is ignored while he takes over contrary patterns form some other example. Therefore, we must turn to a more subtle theory than "Monkey see, monkey do."

Look at it from the child's point of view. Here he is in a new situation, lacking a ready response. He is seeking a response, which will gain certain ends. If he lacks a ready response for the situation, and cannot reason out what to do, he observes a model who can show what to do.

There is a second element at work in this situation. The child may be to attain his immediate goal only to find that his method brings criticism from people who observe him. When shouting across the house achieves his immediate end of delivering a message, he is told emphatically that such a racket is unpleasant, that he should walk into the next room and say his say quietly. Thus, the desire to solve any objective situation is overlaid with the desire to solve it properly. One of the early things the child learns is that he gets more affection and approval when his parents like his response. Then other adults reward some actions and criticize others. If one is to maintain the support of others and his own self-respect, he must adopt responses his social group approves.

In finding trial responses, the learner does not choose models at random. He imitates the person who seems a good person to be like, rather than a person whose social status he wishes to avoid. If the pupil wants to be a good violinist, he will observe and try to copy the techniques of a capable player; while some person may most influence his approach to books.

Admiration of one quality often leads us to admire a person as a whole, and he becomes an identifying figure. We use some people as model over a wide range of situations, imitating much that they do. We learn that they are dependable and rewarding models because imitating them leads to success.

S1. Sometimes the child ignored _____ _____ _____ _____ _____ _____ _____ _____ _____ _____ and takes over contrary patterns form some other example.

S2. What will a child do when he lacks a ready response for the situation?

_____ _____ _____ _____ _____ _____ _____ _____ _____ _____ _____.

S3. A child gets more affection and approval when his parents _____ _____ _____ _____ _____ _____ _____ _____ _____ .

S4. What is required if a person wants to maintain the support of others and his own self-respect?
_____ _____ _____ _____ _____ _____ _____ _____ _____ .

S5. Why do we think many people we imitate are dependable and rewarding models?
_____ _____ _____ _____ _____ _____ _____ _____ _____ .

【答案及解析】

S1. the example the parent wants him to follow

【答题依据】Sometimes, the example the parent wants him to follow is ignored while he takes over contrary patterns form some other example.

S2. He observes a model who can show what to do

【答题依据】If he lacks a ready response for the situation, and cannot reason out what to do, he observes a model who can show what to do.

S3. like his response

【答题依据】One of the early things the child learns is that he gets more affection and approval when his parents like his response.

S4. He must adopt responses his social group approves

【答题依据】If one is to maintain the support of others and his own self-respect, he must adopt responses his social group approves.

S5. Because imitating them leads to success

【答题依据】We learn that they are dependable and rewarding models because imitating them leads to success.

◎ **Passage 4**

Automation refers to the introduction of electronic control and automatic operation of productive machinery. It reduces the human factors, mental and physical, in production, and is designed to make possible the manufacture of more goods with fewer workers. The development of automation in American industry has been called the "Second Industrial Revolution".

Labor's concern over automation arises from uncertainty about the effects on employment, and fears of major changes in jobs. In the main, labor has taken the view that resistance to technical change is unfruitful. Eventually, the result of automation may well be an increase in employment, since it is expected that vast industries will grow up around manufacturing, maintaining, and repairing automation equipment. The interest of labor lies in bringing about the transition with a minimum of inconvenience and distress to the workers involved. The union spokesmen emphasize that the benefit of the increased production and lower costs made possible by automation should be shared by workers in the form of higher wages, more leisure, and improved living standards.

To protect the interests of their members in the era of automation, unions have adopted a number of new policies. One of these is the promotion of supplementary unemployment benefit plans. It is emphasized that since the employer involved in such a plan has a direct financial interest in preventing unemployment, he will have a strong drive for planning new installations so as to cause the least possible problems in jobs and job assignments. Some unions are working for dismissal pay agreements, requiring that permanently dismissed workers be paid a sum of money based on length of service. Another approach is the idea of the "improvement factor", which calls for wage increases based on increases in productivity. It is possible, however, that labor will rely mainly on reduction in working hours in order to gain a full share in the fruits of automation.

S1. What does the "Second Industrial Revolution" refer to?

_____.

S2. According to the second paragraph, the transition of the American industry will bring about

_____ _____ _____ _____ _____ _____ _____ _____ _____ _____ and distress to the workers involved.

S3. What's the labor's view on the resistance to technical change?

_____ _____ _____ _____ _____ _____ _____ _____ _____ _____ _____ _____

S4. The "improvement factor" approach calls for wage increases based on _____ _____ _____

_____ _____ _____ _____ _____ _____ _____ .

S5. Why did the unions adopt a number of new policies?

_____ _____ _____ _____ _____ _____ _____ _____ _____ _____ _____ _____ .

【答案及解析】

S1. The development of automation in American industry

【答题依据】The development of automation in American industry has been called the "Second Industrial Revolution".

S2. inconvenience

【答题依据】The interest of labor lies in bringing about the transition with a minimum of inconvenience and distress to the workers involved.

S3. It is unfruitful / Unfruitful

【答题依据】In the main, labor has taken the view that resistance to technical change is unfruitful.

S4. increases in productivity

【答题依据】Another approach is the idea of the "improvement factor", which calls for wage increases based on increases in productivity.

S5. To protect the interests of their members / Protecting the interests of their members

【答题依据】To protect the interests of their members in the era of automation, unions have adopted a number of new policies.

◎ **Passage 5**

A rapid means of long-distance transportation became a necessity for the United States as settlement(新拓居地) spread ever farther westward. The early trains were impractical curiosities, and for a long time the railroad companies met with troublesome mechanical problems. The most serious ones were the construction of rails able to bear the load, and the development of a safe, effective stopping system. Once these were solved, the railroad was established as the best means of land transportation. By 1860 there were thousands of miles of railroads crossing the eastern mountain ranges and reaching westward to the Mississippi. There were also regional southern and western lines.

The high point in railroad building came with the construction of the first transcontinental system. In 1862 Congress authorized two western railroad companies to build lines from Nebraska westward and from California eastward to a meeting point, so as to complete a transcontinental crossing linking the Atlantic seaboard with the Pacific. The Government helped the railroads generously with money and land. Actual work on this project began four years later. The Central Pacific Company, starting from California, used Chinese labor, while the Union Pacific employed crews of Irish laborers. The two groups worked at remarkable speed, each trying to cover a greater distance than the other. In 1869 they met a place called Promontory in what is now the state of Utah. Many visitors came there for the great occasion. There were joyous celebrations all over the country, with parades and the ringing of church bells to honor the great achievement.

The railroad was very important in encouraging westward movement. It also helped build up industry and farming by moving raw materials and by distributing products rapidly to distant markets. In linking towns and people to one another it helped unify the United States.

S1. What did people think of the early trains?

_____ _____ _____ _____ _____ _____ _____ _____ _____ .

S2. There were thousands of miles of railroads crossing the eastern mountain ranges and reaching westward to the Mississippi by _____ _____ _____ _____ _____ _____

_____ _____ _____ _____ .

S3. The construction of the transcontinental railroad took _____ _____ _____ _____ _____
_____ _____ _____ _____ _____ years.

S4. Which company started their work in California when building the first transcontinental
system?

_____ _____ _____ _____ _____ _____ _____ _____ _____ _____ .

S5. The building of the first transcontinental system brought about a rapid growth of _____
_____ _____ _____ _____ _____ _____ _____ _____ in the west.

【答案及解析】

S1. They were (just) impractical curiosities

【答题依据】The early trains were impractical curiosities, and for a long time the railroad
companies met with troublesome mechanical problems.

S2. 1860

【答题依据】By 1860 there were thousands of miles of railroads crossing the eastern
mountain ranges and reaching westward to the Mississippi.

S3. 3

【答题依据】(1)In 1862 Congress authorized two western railroad companies to build lines
from Nebraska westward and from California eastward to a meeting point...
(2)Actual work on this project began four years later.
(3)In 1869 they met a place called Promontory in what is now the state of Utah.

S4. The Central Pacific Company

【答题依据】The Central Pacific Company, starting from California, used Chinese labor,
while the Union Pacific employed crews of Irish laborers.

S5. industry and farming

【答题依据】It also helped build up industry and farming by moving raw materials and by
distributing products rapidly to distant markets.